P9-CRG-339

"Riley, we've gotta do better, boy," he said as he slung his arm around the dog's furry neck. "Keep reminding me that Molly won't take me seriously unless I turn over a lot of new leaves, will ya?"

Riley licked Pete's face exuberantly. The dog loved to ride in the pickup every chance he got, and he'd been excited about returning to the twins' place.

Pete sighed as he checked the road for oncoming traffic. "Should've known I wouldn't have any time alone with her, considering that she and her sister spend every waking moment together," he remarked. "After all this time, I still want to rumple Molly's short hair, you know?"

Riley woofed in agreement.

"Even though she and Marietta stick together like glue, I have to admire the way Molly's supported her sister," Pete continued as he drove toward town. "Not many Amish girls would've shaved their heads during a sister's chemo, knowing how that goes directly against the *Ordnung*! I *love* that Molly broke the rules that way!"

When his dog's eyes widened, Pete laughed.

"Uh-oh, I said that *L* word, didn't I?"

Published by Kensington Publishing Corp.

Christmas Comes To Morning Star

Charlotte Hubbard

ZEBRA BOOKS
KENSINGTON PUBLISHING CORP.
www.kensingtonbooks.com

ZEBRA BOOKS are published by

Kensington Publishing Corp.
119 West 40th Street
New York, NY 10018

Copyright © 2021 by Charlotte Hubbard

This book is a work of fiction. Names, characters, businesses, organizations, places, events, and incidents either are the product of the author's imagination or are used fictitiously. Any resemblance to actual persons, living or dead, events, or locales is entirely coincidental.

All rights reserved. No part of this book may be reproduced in any form or by any means without the prior written consent of the Publisher, excepting brief quotes used in reviews.

To the extent that the image or images on the cover of this book depict a person or persons, such person or persons are merely models, and are not intended to portray any character or characters featured in the book.

If you purchased this book without a cover you should be aware that this book is stolen property. It was reported as "unsold and destroyed" to the Publisher and neither the Author nor the Publisher has received any payment for this "stripped book."

All Kensington titles, imprints, and distributed lines are available at special quantity discounts for bulk purchases for sales promotion, premiums, fund-raising, educational, or institutional use.

Special book excerpts or customized printings can also be created to fit specific needs. For details, write or phone the office of the Kensington Sales Manager: Attn.: Sales Department. Kensington Publishing Corp., 119 West 40th Street, New York, NY 10018. Phone: 1-800-221-2647.

Zebra and the Z logo Reg. U.S. Pat. & TM Off.
BOUQUET Reg. U.S. Pat. & TM Off.

First Printing: September 2021
ISBN-13: 978-1-4201-5183-1
ISBN-10: 1-4201-5183-5

ISBN-13: 978-1-4201-5186-2 (eBook)
ISBN-10: 1-4201-5186-X (eBook)

10 9 8 7 6 5 4 3 2 1

Printed in the United States of America

Scripture:

Luke 2:8–14

8 And there were in the same country shepherds abiding in the field, keeping watch over their flock by night.

9 And, lo, the angel of the Lord came upon them, and the glory of the Lord shone round about them: and they were sore afraid.

10 And the angel said unto them, Fear not: for, behold, I bring you good tidings of great joy, which shall be to all people.

11 For unto you is born this day in the city of David a Saviour, which is Christ the Lord.

12 And this shall be a sign unto you; Ye shall find the babe wrapped in swaddling clothes, lying in a manger.

13 And suddenly there was with the angel a multitude of the heavenly host praising God, and saying,

14 Glory to God in the highest, and on earth peace, good will toward men.

In memory of my dear father-in-law, Wilber Hubbard, who was all about peace and good will.

Acknowledgments

Thank You, Lord, for helping me complete this book on time in spite of a pandemic, selling and buying a house, Neal's dad's passing, and a move to a new city. Life has been more of an adventure than usual lately!

Many thanks, as well, to my editor, Alicia Condon—who has also weathered the pandemic under challenging circumstances—and to my intrepid agent, Evan Marshall. It's such a blessing to work with both of you.

Thank you, Vicki Harding, for your continuing research support from Jamesport, Missouri!

Chapter 1

Warmed by the sunlight streaming through the window of the newly expanded noodle factory, Marietta Helfing stretched. She felt like a cat, limber and strong, soothed by the low rumble of the motors that ran the two cylindrical noodle presses. As she carefully arranged a thin length of pressed dough on her worktable, she caught her twin, Molly, gazing at her from beside the other table, where she was also preparing to cut a large rectangle of dough into long strips.

"Penny for your thoughts," Molly remarked as she picked up her sharp knife. "And you look like you have a lot of them."

Marietta smiled as she, too, began to cut her dough into long strips about four inches wide. "This time last year—the day after Thanksgiving—I was going in for my surgery, and I was frightened out of my mind," she recalled as her knife moved deftly through the dough. "It's such a blessing to be recovered and working at full steam again after all that time I was wiped out from chemo."

"And I thank the Lord every day that you're back to normal," Molly put in as they worked. "I'm looking forward to a fine, fun Christmas, not like last year, when we had to spend so much time getting you to your treatments. Another gift is being able to work side by side now that we've doubled our work space and equipment," she added with a lilt in her voice. "Mamm would be amazed at the way her little business has expanded."

"*Jah*, she would." Marietta got quiet, letting a wave of wistful nostalgia run its course. She missed their mother even more than she missed her breasts, but she was determined to forge ahead—to meet the demands of the eager customers who thronged their noodle shop each Saturday at The Marketplace, where Amish folks around Morning Star, Missouri, sold the items they'd made.

After today's noodles were cut and drying on screens, she and Molly would bag and label the noodles they'd made earlier in the week so they could load the wagon this afternoon for the drive into town tomorrow morning. They kept a demanding schedule these days, yet Marietta felt good about paying down the bills she'd accrued following her bilateral mastectomy and chemo treatments. She and Molly would soon be banking enough income to support themselves well into their later years—an important advantage, considering that Marietta would never marry.

After all, what man could possibly want a woman who was flatter than a strip of noodle dough—"damaged goods," as Marietta saw herself—and unable to bear him children?

When she glanced at her sister, who was placing the first strip of her noodle dough into the roller to flatten it again, Marietta noticed a rare frown on Molly's face.

"Penny for *your* thoughts, sister," Marietta said as she,

too, began feeding a strip of noodle dough through her roller.

Molly shrugged, focusing on her dough. "Sure is quiet without Riley and Pete around."

Marietta's eyes widened at her sister's wistful remark. For several months, Pete Shetler and his golden retriever, Riley, had rented one of their two *dawdi hauses*, where summer tourists often stayed, because Bishop Jeremiah Shetler had thought it would be an improvement over his nephew's former living arrangements. During his stay, Pete had done some much-needed maintenance around their farm, as well as remodeling their noodle factory—while his active young dog had mostly dug up Mamm's flower beds, chewed the belts on their noodle-making equipment, and found other trouble to get into.

Pete had moved into his uncle's house, however, when Bishop Jeremiah had announced his engagement to Teacher Lydianne Christner. Both men had felt it would be more convenient for Pete to live at the Shetler farm during the winter while he did extensive remodeling on the bishop's place. Although Marietta appreciated the return to a quieter routine without their renter, she sensed Molly had secretly adored the muscular blond carpenter and his rambunctious dog.

"Maybe you should pay Pete a visit," she suggested. "I bet he'd be tickled if you took over a pan of noodle pudding—"

"Why would I do that?" Molly blurted. Her tone sounded playfully defiant, but her brow furrowed. "It's not as though anything would come of a relationship—even if Pete took the hint and asked me out."

"Why not?" Marietta paused, hoping to express her

concerns carefully. "Just because I'll never marry, that doesn't mean you should forfeit a potential romance. Sure, Pete's clueless most of the time, but he seems trainable. And he's awfully cute."

"Let's not forget that Pete refuses to join the Amish church, so a *romance* would be pointless—if he even knew the meaning of the word," Molly shot back. "Truth be told, I like Riley better than Pete anyway. I intend to remain here on the farm with you, sister, as we've always agreed," she added quickly. "We're turning thirty-five next month, so why would I want to change my life—and my *attitude*—to accommodate a husband?"

Although Marietta still suspected her sister had feelings for Pete, she was greatly relieved to hear Molly's vehement insistence upon staying at the home place. The two of them had spent very little time apart, so how would she cope with life alone in their farmhouse if Molly married? She didn't even want to think about such a solitary existence.

"And besides," Molly continued as she fed another strip of her dough into the roller, "we *maidels* need to keep The Marketplace going, ain't so? With Regina married now and Lydianne engaged to the bishop, it'll soon be just us two and Jo running the place."

Marietta nodded. Jo Fussner had been the driving force behind creating The Marketplace from a dilapidated old stable nearly six months ago, and she'd planned the business venture as a project for her four *maidel* friends to share with her.

"I really miss having Regina at the shops on Saturdays, and once Lydianne's married to Bishop Jeremiah, she won't be working away from home, either," Marietta agreed. Once again she chose her words carefully, hoping Molly wouldn't realize how worried she was about being alone. "Wouldn't be fair to Jo if we married and left the management all on her shoulders. Her bakery keeps her so busy, I don't see how she'd have time to take over all of the bookkeeping, as well."

"I'm hoping Lydianne will keep doing our accounting at home after she marries," Molly remarked as they both began cutting thin strips of dough for soup noodles. "It's not even December yet and Drusilla's already clucking about Jo's extra baking for the Christmas season. Can you imagine how she'll fuss if Jo were to spend even more time doing all the organizing and accounting? Bwahk, bwahk *bwahhhhk!*"

Marietta laughed out loud. Jo's *mamm* was known for always seeing the proverbial glass as half empty rather than half full—and indeed, Drusilla Fussner often seemed to believe she had no glass at all. "We shopkeepers will *all* be busier than usual, starting this weekend when—"

The familiar rumble of a pickup truck made them look toward the window. Molly's face lit up. She quickly shut off her roller and washed her hands, laughing at the sound of a golden retriever's raucous bark. Out of habit, she opened the door just wide enough to slip outside, preventing Riley from entering the noodle factory—and spoiling their morning's work, if he plunked his huge front paws on a worktable covered with dough strips.

"Shetler, we were just talking about you!" Molly called out.

"Were you talking trash about me, or saying how much you miss Riley and me causing you trouble?" Pete fired back.

Marietta shut off her roller, bracing herself against her worktable. Molly could deny it until the cows came home, but she was sweet on Pete Shetler, and he liked Molly more than he would admit, too. Their banter continued outside for a few moments, while Marietta tried to still the apprehensive fluttering of her heart.

This is all in Your hands, Lord, but You know how lonely I'd be if Molly married and left me here by myself— even if she deserves her happiness.

As the shop door opened, however, Marietta fixed a smile on her face. After all, if she'd conquered cancer, she could face whatever changes Pete Shetler might bring into their lives.

"Riley, *sit*," the blond carpenter commanded as he stepped inside. "I'll be right back."

"Seems our bad penny has returned," Marietta teased. "You've missed the way Molly and I bossed you around, ain't so?"

Pete laughed, tucking his thumbs into the side loops of the faded jeans he wore without a belt. "Truth be told, when I left here to live at Uncle Jeremiah's place, I was paid up for two more months of rent—and I want you girls to keep that money," he replied. "I know you're still paying medical bills—and you invested a chunk of change in expanding your noodle factory, too. Besides," he added as he glanced around the room he'd recently renovated, "Riley and I caused more work for you while we were here, so you deserve that extra cash."

Marietta's eyes widened in surprise, and her sister's jaw dropped. Who could ever have imagined freewheeling, irresponsible Pete Shetler saying such a thing? It occurred to her that their former tenant was letting them keep money his *uncle* had paid ahead, but she didn't pick nits. Bishop Jeremiah had hoped Pete might become more responsible if he lived in their *dawdi haus,* so maybe the plan was working . . . a little.

"That—that's very considerate of you," Marietta stammered.

"You don't have to do any such thing!" Molly protested. "I intended to refund that money, but we've been so busy making extra noodles for—"

Pete held up his hand for silence. As he stood with one hip cocked and his clean, blond hair brushing the collar of his plaid flannel shirt, he exuded a confidence that filled the noodle shop.

He was cute and he knew it. Yet Marietta couldn't help liking Bishop Jeremiah's restless, unpredictable nephew.

"Okay, so the money was my uncle's," Pete finally admitted. "When he asked me to renovate his entire house, I went along with his suggestion about living there—even though I knew how much you girls would miss me. Uncle Jeremiah realizes what a pain Riley and I can be, so he's agreed that you should keep that rent money. I wanted you to know all the details, straight from the horse's mouth."

Outside, Riley barked as though he were adding his two cents' worth.

"Okay, so *this* part's coming straight from the dog's mouth," Pete continued with a chuckle. "Riley says he misses living here, because Mammi really lays down the law."

Marietta and Molly laughed. Bishop Jeremiah's mother, Margaret, was a stickler for clean floors and an orderly home. Marietta suspected that Riley was far more exuberant than Margaret liked—but she would benefit from the extensive renovation her grandson was doing, so as long as Riley kept his paws off the kitchen table and didn't run through the house barking, she probably wouldn't complain too loudly.

For a moment, an expectant silence filled the factory. Did Marietta detect a hint of uncertainty as Pete glanced at the two worktables covered with long, thin strips of noodle dough?

"Everything going all right here in your new space?" he asked brightly. "Did I get all your new equipment hooked up right? Do you need me to move anything to a more convenient place while I'm here?"

"Everything's great!" Molly assured him quickly. "We've doubled our noodle output—"

"And just in time, because we anticipate huge customer turnout every Saturday between now and Christmas," Marietta finished with a nod.

Pete glanced at Molly and then looked around again. "Well, you're busy, so I should let you get back to your work," he said. "See you 'round—"

"Like a donut!" Molly chimed in on their old joke. "So long—"

"Like a banana!" Marietta finished.

As Pete stepped outside, she sensed he didn't really want to leave but couldn't find a reasonable excuse for hanging around—mostly to gaze at Molly whenever he thought Marietta wouldn't notice. If her sister had found his reason for coming over a little lame, she didn't say so.

But the bright smile on Molly's face told Marietta more than words could ever say.

* * *

Pete cranked up his pickup, gunning the engine as he shot down the Helfings' lane—and then he kicked himself. He was trying to act more mature, and driving like a clueless kid—the way he had when he'd lived in the twins' *dawdi haus*—was not what he'd intended to do. But old habits died hard.

"Riley, we've gotta do better, boy," he said as he slung his arm around the dog's furry neck. "Keep reminding me that Molly won't take me seriously unless I turn over a lot of new leaves, will ya?"

Riley licked Pete's face exuberantly. The dog loved to ride in the pickup every chance he got, and he'd been excited about returning to the twins' place.

Pete sighed as he checked the road for oncoming traffic. "Should've known I wouldn't have any time alone with her, considering that she and her sister spend every waking moment together," he remarked. "After all this time, I still want to rumple Molly's short hair, you know?"

Riley woofed in agreement.

"Even though she and Marietta stick together like glue, I have to admire the way Molly's supported her sister," Pete continued as he drove toward town. "Not many Amish girls would've shaved their heads during a sister's chemo, knowing how that goes directly against the *Ordnung*! I *love* that Molly broke the rules that way!"

When his dog's eyes widened, Pete laughed.

"Uh-oh, I said that *L* word, didn't I? Gotta watch that. Gotta toughen up my attitude," he continued in a firmer voice. "It's just as well we moved away from the Helfing place, Riley. Molly's the bossiest girl I ever met—and there's no prying those twins apart anyway. So why act like I'm interested, right? Gazing into her deep green eyes can only lead me where I really don't want to go."

Riley looked forward, gazing through the windshield as though he didn't believe a word Pete had just said.

As always, the dog probably had it right.

Chapter 2

From her bakery at The Marketplace, Jo watched in amazement as Nelson Wengerd and his son, Michael, clambered up their tall stepladders carrying potted poinsettias. As they'd promised earlier, they were building a Christmas tree in the center of the commons area by strategically stacking the plants in rings that grew smaller as the "tree" got closer to the ceiling. The bright red flowers in pots covered with green foil made such a festive display that Jo and the other shopkeepers who'd been setting up watched in awe as Michael placed the final, single poinsettia on the top.

"And there you have it!" the slender young man proclaimed from high upon his ladder. "Let the Christmas season begin!"

Jo, the Helfing twins, and Gabe Flaud, who ran the furniture shop beside the bakery, broke into applause. "That looks fabulous, Michael!" Gabe called out. "Your poinsettia tower will be the star attraction at The Marketplace. You fellows outdid yourselves."

Jo caught Michael's unpretentious smile before he focused on the potted plants below him. "*Denki*, Gabe.

How's it look from down there? Everything seem balanced from one side to the other?"

"Let's adjust this third layer a bit," Nelson replied, stepping down one rung to shift the pots in that row. "We'll have a mess if any of these plants topple off and hit the floor. And if customers ask," he added, glancing at his audience, "these plants are all for sale. We'll dismantle the tower on the last Saturday before Christmas so folks who've ordered them can claim them."

"And we have dozens more they can buy before that," Michael put in.

Nelson laughed as he descended to the floor. "We have *hundreds* more, so encourage your friends to buy several! Our goal is to empty our Queen City greenhouses by the end of the shopping season."

The *ding* of Jo's oven timer warned her to take out the large pans of brownies she was baking. It was probably best that she step away from her door before Michael caught her watching the way he moved. He was such an agile man, tall and slim, with a graceful strength that caught her eye every time he was around. Jo knew her secret admiration for Michael would never come to anything, but it was fun to daydream about him while she was baking.

After she set the hot pans of brownies on the stainless steel countertop, Jo slipped two big pans of cinnamon rolls into the oven and reset the timer. The weekend after Thanksgiving was traditionally the time when English customers did much of their Christmas shopping, so she hoped she'd stocked her glass cases and shelves with enough breads and pastries to last through the day.

As Alice and Adeline Shetler bustled in, Jo smiled

brightly. "*Gut* to see you girls," she called out as she measured powdered sugar to make frosting. "Today, and for all the Saturdays in December, we'll be selling spiced cider as well as coffee out in the commons. I put the new warming pot out for you, and the first batch of cider and spices is ready to pour into it," she added, pointing toward the big jug on the floor.

"What with Rose Wagler's bayberry candles and your brownies coming from the oven, The Marketplace smells heavenly," Alice remarked as she tied her white apron behind her back.

Her twin nodded enthusiastically as she, too, donned her apron. "The aromas of the cider and coffee should sell a lot of goodies today. Plenty of husbands will be sitting at our tables while their wives finish shopping, so we'll just keep passing our trays of treats they can't resist!"

Jo laughed out loud. The redheaded Shetler twins were the perfect hostesses, and she was glad she'd hired them as her assistants. "I'm going to frost these brownies and sprinkle the tops with crushed peppermints. We'll sell the first of our cutout Christmas cookies today, too," she told them. "When you've got the cider and coffee going out front, I'd like you to arrange some of those cookies on trays for me, please."

"We'll do it!" Adeline declared.

"*Jah*, working here for you got us out of scrubbing the house to prepare for church at our place tomorrow," Alice said with a chuckle.

Jo's eyebrows rose. Their step*mamm*, Leah Shetler, who'd married their father about a year ago, had six-year-old Stevie, little adopted Betsy, and newborn Adah to tend, as well as the ducks, goats, and cattle she raised. "I hope I didn't cause a problem, leaving Leah and Lenore shorthanded with their cleaning."

"Oh, no, it's not that way at all!" Alice insisted, sharing a grin with her sister. "Leah and Mammi Lenore would rather clean than cook, so we girls have already made up a big ham-and-hashbrown casserole and a cake for supper tonight—"

"And we'll bake something for tomorrow's after-church meal when we get home," Adeline added without missing a beat. "Stevie went to the auction Dat's calling this morning, so it'll be a quiet day at home until we all get back. Just the way Leah and Mammi Lenore like it."

As the mischievous twins hurried out to the commons, Jo chuckled. The two girls had been running the roads with English boyfriends and causing their *dat*, Jude Shetler, all manner of headaches when he and Leah had married about a year ago. She was glad Alice and Adeline had made their peace with their stepmother—and they adored Leah's *mamm*, Lenore, who now lived with them. It was a blessing that they'd found special ways to be helpful in a household that bustled with three young children.

"I like that smile on your face, Jo. You're happiest when you're baking, ain't so?"

Jo's stomach fluttered when Michael stepped into her shop. The evergreen wreath in his hand suggested he had something other than flirtation in mind, and that was just as well, wasn't it? She didn't have the foggiest idea how to respond to his remark about her smile.

"That fresh wreath smells just like Christmas," she said. "I suppose you and your *dat* make those at your Queen City greenhouse, *jah*?"

"We do—and we also plan to assemble them outside our shop on these Marketplace Saturdays, where folks can watch us," Michael replied. "Meanwhile, we've brought enough of them to hang on everyone's shop entry for the holiday season."

Jo stopped stirring her frosting to gaze at him. "That's very generous—very thoughtful," she stammered. "You fellows have gone all out to decorate The Marketplace for us, and I really appreciate it. It's been wonderful-*gut* to have you and your *dat* selling your produce and all the beautiful things you grow. They've been great additions to the products we other shopkeepers carry."

The blush that tinted Michael's cheeks told Jo that he felt every bit as shy around her as she was near him. She suspected that he hadn't gone on any more dates than she had—but she'd never ask him about that, of course.

"It's been a boon to our nursery business, selling our plants here," he said with a smile that brought his dimples out. "But more than that, Dat and I, well—we've really enjoyed coming to Morning Star to spend time with you and your *mamm*, and we appreciate being able to rent your *dawdi haus* each weekend. And—and if you're interested, my invitation to come to Queen City and see our greenhouses full of poinsettias still stands."

Jo swallowed hard. How many times had she dreamed of taking Michael up on the offer he'd made a few weeks ago—even though her fussy mother had insisted she wanted nothing to do with such a visit or the two-hour buggy ride it entailed. "I—we'll see," she hedged. "Baking for the Christmas season is keeping me busier than usual this year—"

"But if you can spare a couple of weekdays in early

December, the sight of all those bright red poinsettias will take your breath away," Michael insisted. His blue eyes sparkled with enthusiasm. "We also grow Christmas cacti and amaryllis, so the nursery shop is alive with color, as well. It would be a way for you to see our home, and for us to return some of your hospitality, too, Jo."

Jo's heart was pounding so hard that Michael could probably hear it. What a joy it would be to see the Wengerds' home—not to mention those greenhouses filled with such vibrant Christmas flowers.

As she once again noticed how slim and attractive he was, however, Jo was even more aware that she probably outweighed him by thirty pounds. A guy like Michael would never look past her unbecoming height and heftiness— and even though he'd never met her deceased *dat*, there was no getting around the fact that Jo had been created in Big Joe Fussner's image.

She focused on her pans of brownies. "It sounds like a wonderful time, but I doubt if Mamm would go, so—"

"Maybe we can work around that," Michael put in quickly. "But I understand. Your *mamm* has said at various times that she doesn't like long buggy rides—nor does she like it when her routine is disrupted."

"You've got her pegged, Michael." Jo fought a sudden wave of impatient sadness, wishing her *mamm* could be more open to change and new experiences. "*Denki* for asking, though. We'll see how things go."

Michael's brow furrowed with disappointment, but he nodded. "Better hang these wreaths before we open the outer doors for our customers. Have a *gut* day, Jo."

"You as well," she called after him.

Why did she feel her hopes and dreams walking away

with Michael? She could only pray that he would, by some miracle, look beyond her appearance to give her another chance—on a day when Mamm was in a cooperative mood.

Or on a day when you follow your heart instead of letting your mother's narrow vision limit your life forever.

Glenn Detweiler dropped into one of his handmade slatted birch rocking chairs. He was exhausted from keeping up the appearance that he was caught up in the Christmas spirit, as his customers and fellow shopkeepers were. His wood shop in The Marketplace, where he sold his handmade toys and chairs, had seen a steady stream of shoppers all morning; now he craved the peace and quiet a lull in the traffic allowed him.

Peace had eluded him since he'd lost his beloved Dorcas a few months ago. The recent, unexpected passing of his *mamm* had thrown his life into even more turmoil, what with raising seven-year-old Billy Jay and baby Levi—and now keeping closer track of his aging *dat*, as well.

And *quiet* was a concept his boisterous son struggled with—not to mention the way his newborn wailed in the night because he, too, missed his mother and grand-mother something fierce.

Glenn sighed. What had he done to deserve so much heartache? During his grief counseling sessions, Bishop Jeremiah assured him that God loved him—yet Glenn wondered about that. Wouldn't a loving God have healed Dorcas's severe anemia? If God truly cared about him and his family, why had He allowed Glenn's *mamm* to pass from overexertion and the complications of her diabetes?

If all things were possible in God, why couldn't Glenn crawl out from under his heavy burden of grief? And why did his father grow more forgetful by the day?

And why did Lydianne pick the bishop to marry instead of me?

Catching sight of the pretty blond schoolteacher who assisted all the shopkeepers—and who floated on a cloud now that she was engaged to Jeremiah Shetler—took Glenn's mood down even further. Lydianne's glow announced that she was the happiest woman on earth with everything to look forward to—

"Shall I bring you some of Jo's spiced cider, Glenn? Can I help you in any way today?" The lovely blonde of his fantasies paused in the shop entry, her blue eyes alight with concern for him.

It was all he could do not to tell Lydianne Christner to get lost and never darken his doorway again. Her expression was so earnest and compassionate, Glenn wanted to spit nails. He sighed loudly to defuse his black emotions, however.

"Nah. I'm fine," he groused. "If I want cider, I'll get my own."

Her startled expression gave Glenn a little hit of satisfaction, even as he knew he'd been unreasonably rude to her. After all, Teacher Lydianne had been Billy Jay's salvation after Dorcas had died, and she was paying even more attention to him at school now that his *mammi* was gone, as well. Thanks to her, Billy Jay was showing signs of recovery and an interest in his schoolwork again.

Lydianne was a wonderful, beautiful woman. But she

would never be his. He was relieved when she turned and left his shop.

Glenn rose from the rocking chair, disgusted with himself and with life in general. Maybe a cup of that warm spiced cider would perk him up, because once again he'd neglected to bring anything for his lunch—and the thought of joining Gabe Flaud and his *dat*, Martin, for a quick meal was yet another way to torture himself: being a newlywed, Gabe radiated happiness like the sun itself. Flaud was his best friend, and he meant well, but Glenn could barely stand to be around him since he'd married Regina Miller.

As he crossed the commons to help himself to cider, Glenn knew he needed to stop blaming his friends for his black cloud of unhappiness. They were going about their everyday lives exactly as they should, being especially caring toward him and his *dat*. But their kindness only rubbed salt in his emotional wounds.

Glenn gulped a cup of the cider, grateful for its sweet, spicy warmth, and then poured himself some more. When one of the redheaded Shetler twins came up with a tray of decorated cookies and bars, he reached for his wallet.

"No need for your money," she assured him breezily. "Jo's happy to let our shopkeepers enjoy complimentary refreshments, because without our crafters, The Marketplace wouldn't be here."

Glenn wasn't sure whether he was speaking to Alice or Adeline, but he put a couple of bucks on her tray despite what she'd said. "Only fair to pay Jo for the *gut* stuff she bakes," he snapped as he chose a chocolate-frosted long john. "The Marketplace wouldn't be up and running if she hadn't gotten the original idea for it, after all."

With a wary nod, the girl took off to offer the tray to other folks seated at the square wooden tables in the commons area.

Glenn sighed loudly. He'd scared Jude's daughter with his gruff tone.

Jeremiah's right. You need to count your blessings instead of focusing on all the things that are wrong with your life right now.

Startled by the voice in his head, which had sounded very much like his beloved Dorcas, Glenn noticed that Marietta Helfing had stepped outside the noodle shop for a breather. She and her sister were enjoying nonstop traffic in their store these days—yet he caught a hint of exhaustion on Marietta's pale, pinched face. She was recovering nicely from her cancer surgery and treatments, but she was still too thin by twenty pounds. In profile, as she leaned against the entry post, she resembled a stick figure.

And she'll remain flat-chested forever, even after she's regained her full strength.

Glenn focused on his pastry before Marietta caught him staring at her from across the commons. He couldn't imagine how bereft she must feel after sacrificing part of her body to such a cruel disease. And even though she'd undergone chemo, would she always live in fear that the cancer might come back?

It was a sobering thought. And it was the kick in the rear Glenn needed—at least for the moment. As he devoured the long john in three fast bites, he reminded himself that he wasn't the only person whose life had been irrevocably altered this past year. He saw that a few customers had gone into his wood shop, so he wiped his sticky fingers on his pants and pasted a smile on his face.

The expression was fake—his cheerfulness felt a couple of sizes too small. But he had a store to tend and handmade wooden toys that folks wanted to give their kids for Christmas, so at least until closing time, Glenn had a reason for being.

Chapter 3

As Molly drove to church at Jude and Leah Shetler's place on Sunday morning, she was relieved that not many cars were on the road. "Let's hope Morning Star's plows keep this blacktop cleared today," she remarked to Marietta. "Snow seems to bring out the daredevil in our English teenage drivers."

"It's piling up pretty fast," her twin noted. "If the roads aren't passable by the time the common meal's over, Jude and some of his neighbors might hitch up their horse-drawn plows just so they won't have a bunch of folks as overnight guests!"

Molly laughed. At this same time last winter, her sister hadn't felt chipper enough to joke about the snowy weather. She was pleased that Marietta was remaining calm rather than fretting over potentially dangerous driving conditions, as she'd done when she was ill. Even so, it was a relief to pull into the Shetler place along with other church members who'd braved the weather. Molly considered herself a steady, levelheaded driver, but it only took one close call with a speeding, out-of-control car to spook a horse or cause a buggy crash on slick roads.

After she let Marietta off near the front porch, Molly parked the rig, unhitched the mare, and led her to the pasture with their friends' horses. "See you later, Opal! Play nice, now."

The white mare with gray markings nickered, trotting toward the other horses as though she was eager to exchange the latest gossip—or discuss her trip on the snowy roads—with them. When Molly entered Leah's kitchen, the folks there were doing the same thing. As she returned their greetings, she headed toward the nearest downstairs bedroom to place her black coat and bonnet on the pile of winter wraps that was accumulating on the bed.

"*Gut* morning, Reuben!" she said to Glenn's *dat*. She tugged on the sleeve of his coat, which had gotten caught on his shoulder as he was shrugging out of it. "Glad to see you out and about this morning. How're you doing?"

The elderly fellow flashed her a bright smile. "Pretty well, all things considered," he replied with a nod. He leaned closer, as though he wanted to share a secret. "If I go to the kitchen at night, after everyone else is sleeping, I can sit and visit with Elva over a cup of cocoa. She's always loved her cocoa, you know."

Molly's eyebrows rose, but she decided to go with Reuben's flow rather than remind him that his wife had passed on. "And how's she doing?"

"When she comes back to me this way, when the house is real quiet, I don't have to raise my voice for her to hear me," he said matter-of-factly. "In heaven, there's no sickness, so she's not deaf anymore. And she has brown hair again, instead of white, just like when we were young and raising the kids."

Molly noted that Reuben's eyes looked clear and bright, just as his voice and words were steady and perfectly normal. "You know, Marietta has said the same sort of thing about our mother," she remarked softly. "Mamm shows up in her dreams sometimes, and she's just like she was before she got sick."

"That's how it is, *jah*," Reuben agreed.

"I used to be jealous because Mamm showed up in Marietta's dreams and not mine," Molly confessed. "But it was such a blessing for my sister to feel that Mamm was watching over her while she was so sick with her chemo, I figured Marietta needed her more than I did."

"*Jah*, that's how I feel too—blessed by Elva's presence," Reuben said softly. "I just wish Glenn could settle himself these days, so maybe Elva—or Dorcas—would be present for him in spirit, too. He's in a bad way, my boy is."

Their quiet conversation was cut short when Gracie Wagler entered the small bedroom, followed by her mother, Rose, who carried baby Suzanna in a wicker basket. "Wow-*wee* but it's really snowin' out there!" the little girl crowed. "After church, we're gonna go out and build a snowman!"

"I'll go with you!" Ella Nissley put in as she and her mother, Julia, came into the room. "Us kids are gonna have a lotta fun, so I hope church goes really fast today."

Molly laughed. "I said the same thing when I was six," she remarked, smiling at the girls and their mothers. "My *mamm* would remind me that I should be getting myself in the proper frame of mind for hearing God's word instead of wishing my life away."

"And did you do what she told you?" Ella asked.

"Always?" Gracie quizzed further.

With their blue eyes focused so intently on her, Molly knew she should be setting a good Christian example—yet she couldn't lie to them. "Some Sundays I still wish church would go faster," she confessed, "because *jah*, it's fun to get out and play in the snow."

The girls' giggles followed her out of the small room, and for a moment she relived the memory of dropping off coats with Mamm before church, just as Ella and Gracie were doing. At their age, she'd had no idea how special such ordinary events would become after she no longer had her mother—but the sight of Glenn Detweiler entering the house with his two sons drove such fond thoughts away.

He looked haggard. His dark eyes were haunted by desperation, and he seemed as fragmented as a bag of dry noodles that had hit the floor. As Billy Jay rushed toward the bedroom, his greeting for Ella and Gracie rang out above the adult voices. Glenn barely seemed able to hold out the blanket-covered carrier that cradled fussy baby Levi.

And he stuck it out in front of Marietta. And she's taking it.

As several of the other folks welcomed Glenn inside, Molly decided that his choice of female recipients was really more a matter of timing—who was closest—than any preference as to who actually took his younger son. She wasn't sure Glenn even *realized* whom he'd extended the carrier to.

Glenn blinked, looking around the crowded kitchen. "Where's Dat? I let him off at the porch a bit ago—"

"He's fine," Molly supplied. "He was taking off his coat, and now he's chatting with everyone. Seems to be having a *gut* day."

"*Jah*, well it's nice that *someone* is," Glenn muttered under his breath. He headed toward the bedroom, oblivious to other people's concerned expressions as several of the ladies cooed over Levi.

Molly glanced at her sister, wondering how she was doing. It was a commonplace thing for babies to arrive at church after they were several months old—but neither she nor Marietta had been around newborns much.

Her twin's rapt expression made Molly pause. Marietta was studying little Levi closely as Leah Shetler removed his blanket and lifted him from the carrier.

"This wee boy's filled out a lot the past couple of weeks," Leah announced as the other women nodded their agreement.

"Must be getting the right amount of your goat's milk now," Martha Maude Hartzler speculated. "It's such a blessing that you've got those goats, and that you live close to the Detweiler place."

Molly smiled to herself. Not so long ago, before she'd married Jude, Leah had been considered odd because she was so much more adept at handling livestock than cooking or cleaning. It was nice that the neighbors' opinions of her had improved—

And it's interesting that my sister can't seem to take her eyes off of Glenn's baby.

Molly's observation sent a ping of sadness through her, however. Because Marietta's cancer treatment had been so intense, she wasn't able to bear children now—

Not that you'll have any, either, on account of how

you'll never be getting married. God's will works out differently for each one of us, after all.

In a short while, everyone filed into the Shetlers' front room. The pew benches were arranged with the men on one side facing the women, and a preachers' bench in the center, so the church leaders could see the congregation. Older members sat in the front rows and younger ones filled in behind them, so Molly and Marietta sat down in their usual spots near their *maidel* friends and Regina, who still glowed with the excitement of being the newest Mrs. Flaud. They whispered their greetings to Jo, Lydianne, and Regina until Bishop Jeremiah, Preachers Ammon Slabaugh and Clarence Miller, and Deacon Saul Hartzler greeted them. Then the church leaders went upstairs to decide who would preach the morning's sermons.

From the men's side, Gabe Flaud sang the first line of the opening hymn, establishing the key and the methodical tempo at which everyone would sing it. Folks immediately settled into the church service's routine, following the verses of the familiar hymn in their yellowed copies of the *Ausbund.* Molly wished they would sing at a livelier pace: on mornings after a busy Saturday at The Marketplace, it was easy to be lulled into a nap-like state while they sang as many as twelve or fourteen verses of the same hymns Old Order folks had sung for centuries. . . .

Next thing Molly knew, her sister's elbow was poking her from one side while Jo nudged her from the other. Her head snapped up and she blinked rapidly. Jo fought a laugh as she kept singing, tapping her finger on the current verse so Molly could find her place on the page.

As Molly resumed the hymn, she fought back another wave of drowsiness. She reminded herself that if the preachers or Bishop Jeremiah noticed her nodding off during church, they might tell her and Marietta to cut back on their noodle production—to work fewer hours in their little factory, or even to reduce the time they kept their store open at The Marketplace on Saturdays.

Now that we've expanded our work space and we're paying down Marietta's medical bills, we don't want anybody meddling with our income. Sit up! Sing louder! Look alive!

As the congregation began the twelfth verse, a motion across the crowded room caught Molly's eye. She tried not to snicker as Pete slipped onto the back bench of the men's side, obviously hoping not to attract attention. Although his *mammi* Margaret was keeping his clothes washed and pressed these days, so he appeared better dressed than when he'd lived in the Helfings' *dawdi haus*, his hair was still damp from his shower.

Had he not gotten out of bed until Margaret and Jeremiah had left the house? That seemed unlikely, considering his uncle was the bishop—and Margaret would be a stickler for Pete's helping with the livestock chores before they left for church on Sunday mornings.

Molly's musings stilled when she glanced up from her hymnal to find Pete gazing straight at her. At first she figured Pete was looking around to assess who was present. Yet as his intense brown eyes remained focused on hers, she got the idea that he was sending her a message—

"Pay attention, you slacker," Marietta whispered. "The preachers are coming downstairs."

Moments later, Bishop Jeremiah entered the room ahead of the three other leaders, all of them dressed in their black suits and white shirts. As the hymn ended, the four men removed their broad-brimmed black hats in a unified sweeping motion to signal the beginning of the worship service.

When Pete stuck his tongue out at Molly, she laughed out loud and then clapped her hand over her mouth. The women in front of them glanced back to see what had caused her outburst, but of course by then Pete was looking down at his lap as though he were deep in prayer.

Bishop Jeremiah walked a few steps forward, smiling at Molly before he began. "This is the snowy day our Lord has made," he paraphrased. "We shall rejoice and be glad in it as we open our hearts and lives to Him. Let us pray."

Molly bowed her head contritely, vowing not to allow Pete to lead her any further astray with his playful attention. Even as she apologized to God for behaving inappropriately in church, she felt an insistent gaze from the far side of the room.

Sure enough, when she peeked through the slits of her partially open eyes, Pete was watching her while his uncle invoked the holy presence of the Lord and continued the long initial prayer.

When Bishop Jeremiah's amen had folks shifting on the benches to prepare for the morning's first sermon, Jo leaned closer to Molly.

"Seems you have an admirer," she whispered.

Molly waved her off. "It's nothing," she shot back under her breath.

"Puh. Guys our age don't play peekaboo during church unless they're *interested*."

"Your imagination's running away with you, Jo."

From a couple of pew benches in front of them,

Martha Maude turned to raise a stern eyebrow. For the rest of the three-hour service, Molly refused to play Pete's little game of eye tag, even though it intrigued her enough to keep her awake. When at last Bishop Jeremiah pronounced the benediction and folks stood up to stretch, she and her sister sidled toward the aisle so they could begin setting out food and utensils for the common meal.

When Molly carried the first baskets of sliced bread from the kitchen, Pete—who had conveniently been setting up tables near the kitchen door—stepped in front of her.

"How about we eat and then skedaddle?" he murmured playfully. "You can ride around with me while I plow out the roads."

Her heart did a handspring—but then she blinked. "How can you clear the roads—"

"I put a blade on the front of my truck," he replied quickly. "Sometimes English conveniences can be used for the welfare of our Plain neighbors, you know? That's why I was late this morning—I made a few passes down the gravel lanes where our older folks would have a tough time getting home again."

Pete's dimples flickered in his clean-shaven cheeks. His blond hair had dried, and it fell in soft, clean waves that bushed his white shirt collar. He was the cutest guy Molly knew, even if he was accustomed to getting his way because of his good looks. She was impressed that he'd been performing such a useful service, but—

"C'mon, Moll, you know it'll be fun," he coaxed.

She was on the verge of saying yes when her reasonable, responsible self took over. "That would leave Marietta without anybody to drive our rig home."

Aware that other folks were watching them, Molly stepped around Pete to place her baskets of bread on the tables. "She doesn't feel comfortable driving on snowy, slick roads. If Opal should spook, Marietta probably couldn't keep her under control the way I could. Sorry."

"No, you're not! You're playing hard to get," he protested. "Surely somebody else can give Marietta a ride—"

"Nope. Not happening." Molly widened her eyes at him. "You're skating on thin ice if you think I'll shirk my responsibility to my sister, Shetler. End of conversation."

She headed for the kitchen again, sorry she'd shut him down yet feeling she'd done the right thing. After all, if Pete got carried away playing with his new snow blade, it was anybody's guess when he might decide to take her home—even though she knew one of their *maidel* friends would've gladly given Marietta a ride back to the farm.

And think of the talk that would cause. You'd never hear the end of our friends' teasing. Besides, you've told Marietta you'll stick by her. She's the last person you should leave in the lurch.

Focusing on the food that was waiting to be set out, Molly didn't make conversation with any of the other women. Something inside her jangled sadly, like a tiny, forlorn bell, but she moved purposefully toward the tables again so she wouldn't change her mind and succumb to the temptation of Pete's offer to have some fun.

Nothing would come of it anyway, right? He'll never join the church or get serious, and you're a woman of your word. Stick with your sister.

Molly knew she was doing the right thing. It was just

a shame that being right—and responsible—left her soul feeling a little emptier these days.

Glenn tossed restlessly in his bed that evening, exhausted yet unable to sleep—again. As always, he missed having Dorcas in his arms to keep him warm in their drafty bedroom. And if she were still alive, she would've helped him outside with the shoveling that had tired Dat so quickly—and she would've joined Billy Jay to build a snowman. His wife had adored wintry days, and she'd been childlike enough to engage in the snowball fights their son loved to start.

Glenn felt anything but childlike these days, however. He regretted snapping at Billy Jay after the boy's snowball had hit him square in the back while he was scooping a path between the back door, his wood shop, and the barn. But he couldn't unsay the harsh words that had sprung from his mouth. It would be a long time before he could forget the way Billy Jay's face had crumpled as he'd begun to cry.

"Mamm would've played with me," he'd whimpered.

And the truth had hurt both of them, making their loneliness and pain flare up all over again. When it came to getting past their grief, it seemed as though God just kept picking at their scabbed-over emotions to make them bleed.

With a sigh, Glenn went to the bathroom for a drink of water—but his first step out into the hall made him frown. Something was burning. Could Dat have fallen asleep while making cocoa and let the pan boil dry? Was it his imagination, or did he also smell gas?

By the time he'd reached the bottom of the stairs, he heard the crackling and saw flames dancing in the kitchen, devouring the curtains nearest the stove. He broke into a run.

"Dat! Dat, wake up!" he hollered when he saw the figure slumped over the kitchen table.

Thank God his father awoke with a start, crying out when he saw that the gas stove had caught fire.

"Dat, grab your coat and go outside!" Glenn yelled frantically. "I'll get the boys!"

As he ran back upstairs, his mind raced. Did he have time to put on any clothes? Would they be able to save any of the precious mementos Dorcas and Mamm had left behind?

"Billy Jay, grab your clothes and run downstairs— now!" he hollered as he entered his son's room. He shook the boy, rousing him from a deep sleep. "Here—take these pants and hurry outside with Dawdi. Go out the front door, because the kitchen's on fire!"

Billy Jay's terrified expression reminded Glenn of a trapped animal's, but he didn't have time to reason with the boy. Into the next bedroom he rushed, scooping his infant son from the baby bed and then grabbing a plastic basket of clothes one of the neighbor ladies had recently laundered. When he got back into the hall, he steered Billy Jay toward the stairs ahead of him.

"Let's get outside with Dawdi," he urged the frightened boy. "We'll go to the shop—and call the fire department— and whatever else we can manage. Just hurry!"

Luckily Billy Jay took more courage now that Glenn was with him. Down the stairs they sped, their bare feet slapping rapidly against the wooden stairs. As they rushed through the front room toward the door, he saw that the flames had already reached the kitchen table . . . the table their family had eaten at for generations.

But there was nothing he could do about that. It seemed there was nothing he could do about anything these days.

Out into the snow they raced. The soles of his feet felt as though a thousand needles were stabbing them as he urged Billy Jay to keep up with him. As they headed toward the safety of the wood shop, Glenn was aware that a couple more inches of snow had fallen since he'd shoveled. Fortunately, the path was still clear enough that his *dat* was able to lumber toward the white building and open the small side door.

"What happened?" his father asked in an unsteady voice. "How come the stove was—"

"I don't know, Dat," Glenn replied quickly. "Here— take Levi and keep Billy Jay out here with you. I'm going back to grab us some clothes and—"

He didn't waste any more time explaining as he thrust out the baby and the laundry basket. Despite his *dat*'s cries not to go back into the house, Glenn felt he should at least save enough of their clothing to put on over their pajamas. Flames licked like devils' tongues in the mud-room as he passed around the outside of it to reenter the house through the front door.

Propelled by sheer terror, Glenn bolted up the stairs. He grabbed his own clothes from the bedroom floor before rushing into Billy Jay's room to do the same thing. Something warned him not to linger—smoke was already filling the front room. As he shot out the door again he was coughing, and his eyes burned so badly he could barely see.

A loud explosion marked the end of the gas stove. All hell broke loose on that end of the house as flames leaped from the blown-out windows. Glenn headed for his woodworking shop again, unable to feel his numb feet as he sprinted toward its door.

Inside, Dat sat on the nearest bench, cradling a wailing Levi against his shoulder while Billy Jay clung to him, as well. Glenn dropped his armload of clothes and turned on the lights. He was thankful that because they were too far from a neighbor to share a phone shack, Bishop Jeremiah had allowed him to have a telephone in the shop so he could conduct his woodworking business. He jabbed at its keypad—nine, one, one—and tried to catch his breath as he waited for someone to answer.

"*Jah*, it's Glenn Detweiler," he gasped when a responder came on the line. He recognized the guy's voice, but he was too rattled to recall his name. "Our house is— well, the stove's just exploded and the fire's running wild, so—"

"Anybody hurt?"

"No, we all made it out, thank God—"

"We're on our way. Stay someplace safe, and we'll be there as soon as we can."

"We're out back, inside the wood shop," Glenn said before the responder hung up. As he replaced the receiver, his mind was whirling with such frantic thoughts that he didn't know what to do next. When he saw that Billy Jay was shivering, however, he refocused. He brought a space heater over so he could plug it into a car battery and warm the area where Dat had settled.

"Let's get our clothes on, son," Glenn said in the gentlest voice he could muster. "And we'll put some warm layers on Levi while we wait for the fire truck."

"But why's our house on fire? Where will we go now? What'll we do without our *stuff*?" The pitch of Billy Jay's voice rose with his fearful questions as he remained within the haven of his *dawdi*'s embrace. He seemed unaware that he was shaking with cold—

But it's terror he's dealing with, just as I am. I'm the only one here who can pull this situation together. I need to focus.

It hurt Glenn deeply when he opened his arms and Billy Jay wouldn't leave Dat's side. But he couldn't let that stop him—couldn't allow the three people in his care to get ill from exposure to the cold, on top of everything else that was going wrong.

"Let's put your clothes on," he murmured again, holding up Billy Jay's shirt. Glenn was relieved to see that Dat hadn't undressed before he'd gone to the kitchen for cocoa, and he'd put on his winter coat before he'd left the house. His father seemed anything but comfortable, however.

"Did I fall asleep and leave the stove on?" he asked in a quavering voice. "I—I was visiting with your *mamm* and I drifted off . . ."

Glenn's eyebrows shot up. It was a new wrinkle, to hear his father say he'd been talking to Mamm. Was Dat slipping even deeper into dementia than anyone had realized?

Billy Jay was still clinging to his *dawdi*, so Glenn quickly pulled his own broadfall work pants on over his pajamas and then donned his shirt. He coaxed little Levi from his father's embrace and laid him on the end of the bench to dress him. He hoped his older son would soon realize that he needed to put on clothes, as well, because Glenn wasn't sure how much longer he could maintain his relatively calm facade.

As the wail of a siren approached from the general direction of Morning Star, Dat finally reached for Billy Jay's pants and talked the boy into getting dressed. By the time the fire engine arrived, the four of them were ready for wherever they might go next, even though their immediate future was yet another topic Glenn had no idea how to handle.

When he stepped outside to greet the approaching first responder, Glenn sucked in his breath. Half of the house was engulfed in flames. As the roof over the kitchen caved in with an eerie groan, the first arcs of water from the fire truck's hoses fell onto the flames with a *hissss*.

"Everybody accounted for?" a familiar voice called out.

The snow amplified the moon's light, so Glenn immediately recognized Howard Gibbs, the new chief of Morning Star's volunteer fire department—and the fellow who'd answered his emergency call. "*Jah*, we all got out just in time," he replied with a heavy sigh. "And I'm glad my *mamm*'s not here to see her home burning down."

Howard slipped his arm around Glenn's shoulders. "I'm real sorry for all you've been through lately," he murmured. "I sent one of our fellows over to tell your bishop about the fire—Jeremiah seems to know how to handle life's emergencies. And we've shut off your propane tank. So if you're all right, I'm going to help the other guys put out that blaze."

Glenn nodded. As Howard jogged toward the fire, however, he saw that the two-story section of the house, where the bedrooms and the front room were, was filled with flames. Fire greedily consumed the curtains of the rooms where he and the boys had been in bed a short while ago. He didn't allow himself to ponder what might've happened if he'd been sleeping soundly.

A second stream of water was being aimed at the house from the front yard, but Glenn sensed that the firemen's best efforts wouldn't be enough. He and what remained of his little family were homeless. Everything except their livestock, his shop, and a couple of outbuildings would soon be reduced to rubble.

Glenn felt so hopeless and overwhelmed he couldn't even cry. He stared at the flames in morbid fascination, unaware of how much time was passing or even what hour it was. He was so engrossed in the fire's destruction that he didn't notice the man approaching from around the end of the house, which was now a pile of glowing, steaming embers.

"Glenn, I'm grateful to God to see you standing out here unharmed," Bishop Jeremiah said quietly. "Howard told me you all made a safe escape, *jah*?"

Glenn blinked, shifting his focus away from the blaze to the man beside him. "We're all here. We managed to get out with a few clothes, but otherwise everything's— it's all *gone*," he finished, exhaling harshly.

Jeremiah nodded, wrapping his arm loosely around Glenn's shoulders. "When Mamm heard what was going on, she started getting a couple of spare rooms ready for you fellows, for as long as you need to stay. The fire department got here in time to save your shop and outbuildings, at least, so let's gather everybody up, shall we? It's *cold* out here—and you don't have any shoes on."

Glenn looked down, shrugging as though he didn't recognize the pale, bare feet that protruded from his pant legs. "Shoes are the least of my worries right now. *Denki* for coming, Jeremiah. You're a true friend—once again."

Chapter 4

As Pete joined his uncle in the barn to do the livestock chores early Monday morning, he thought carefully before he spoke. Nobody had slept much after midnight, when the fireman had awakened everyone, and then Jeremiah had returned with the Detweilers in tow. Pete hoped to keep his frustration in check—and keep everyone's priorities in order, too.

"How long do you suppose Glenn's crew will be bunking at our place?" he asked as he filled a bucket with water at the barn's faucet.

Jeremiah shrugged tiredly. "I told them they had a place to stay for as long as they need one. Why do you ask?"

Pete's antennae went up. Any time his uncle said *Why do you ask?* it signaled a need for an answer with some thought behind it, rather than the first thing that popped out of his mouth. "Well, I'm concerned about all the kitchen cabinets being torn out and their contents being piled around the walls of the front room," he replied carefully. "Won't be easy for Mammi to cook for guests under these circumstances—let alone deal with a baby. And doesn't Levi require some kind of special care?"

"He needs goat's milk," Jeremiah clarified as he emptied a ration of oats into his Percheron's feeder. "One of us should head over to Jude's to get a supply of it from Leah before our little guy starts hollering for his breakfast."

"I'm on it. I'll be back in a few." As Pete took a bridle and saddle from the tack wall, he heard a chuckle behind him.

"It's very kind of you to consider your *mammi*'s kitchen situation as well as our guests' needs," Jeremiah remarked. "And *jah*, having a baby around might change your schedule, as far as how much hammering you can do and how much sawdust can be in the air."

Pete again thought about his response as he slipped the bridle over Goldie's head. The palomino was his *mammi*'s mare—much more his size than Jeremiah's tall Percheron. "Will Glenn be leaving Levi here when he goes to work in his shop each day?"

His uncle shrugged. "As lost as Glenn seems right now, I'm not sure he'll be fully aware of what's going on with his *dat* or his sons for a while," he replied. "We Shetlers should count our blessings and remember that Glenn has lost his wife, his mother, and now his home, all within the past few months."

Uncle Jeremiah straightened to his full height, looking Pete straight in the eye. "It'll be inconvenient for us to have those folks around during your remodeling work, but to the Detweiler family, it could mean the difference between lingering grief and eventual recovery."

Nodding, Pete tightened the saddle cinch and slipped saddlebags over Goldie's back. "Anything you want me to tell Jude, if he's not already left to call an auction?"

His uncle shrugged. "The news of the fire is probably enough to share with those folks—although they might've heard the sirens in the night and checked it out already," he added. "My mission today will be informing our church members about this latest Detweiler tragedy and rounding up some clothes. Then I'll recruit volunteers to clean up the remains of Glenn's home place, as well as a construction crew to build him a new house."

Pete blinked. Wasn't it just like his uncle to be spearheading such projects, mere hours after disaster had struck? Over the past few years, when Pete had felt tempted to live the English life he'd shared with other employees at the pet food factory, his colleagues' lack of caring and social connection had been a striking contrast to the Amish way he'd grown up. He couldn't imagine a single one of his English friends helping with site cleanup or home construction.

"Put me on your roster for building Glenn's new house," Pete said quietly. "I suspect Mammi—and Lydianne—won't mind waiting a little longer for their new kitchen if it means the Detweilers have their home sooner."

Uncle Jeremiah's smile erased the signs of fatigue that had been etched around his eyes and mouth. "You're on, Pete. I was already thinking you'd be the perfect foreman for that crew."

As he swung up onto Goldie's back, Pete felt ten feet tall. After he'd reached the road, he made a quick detour to the Detweiler place before heading to Jude's house, wishing he'd worn a warmer coat. With the snow had come much colder temperatures, a reminder that soon the December daylight hours would be even shorter—which would limit the time they could work on Glenn's house in the coming days.

As he approached the site of the fire, Pete felt a different kind of cold—a chill that nearly froze him, emotionally. All that remained of the Detweiler home was a blackened, roofless, water-saturated skeleton on the two-story end. The kitchen had been totally demolished, and its charred ruins were already encased in ice. It would be a major undertaking to clear and prepare the site. Working in the wintry weather would be another challenge—at least until the house's walls were up and the roof was on.

Working in the cold—cleaning up this gut-wrenching wreckage—is nothing, compared to the losses that're plaguing Glenn and his family. And what if the fire started because Reuben nodded off while the stove was going? He's old and tired, and probably doing more of the cooking these days.

"Let's go, Goldie," Pete murmured. "After we fetch Levi's milk, we've got some mountains to move."

Marietta took the teakettle from the stove burner and filled her favorite blue teapot with boiling water. As she dropped four teabags into it, she couldn't help smiling. The teapot was a cheerful reminder of Mamm, who had hand painted a bouquet of spring flowers on both of its fat sides.

When the tea was brewing, Marietta stirred the large pot of noodle remnants and then removed it from the stove, as well. As she drained the pasta pieces in a colander, the rising steam soothed her. After a very busy Saturday at the shop in The Marketplace and spending most of

Sunday at church, it felt good to putter in the kitchen and take things easier. Molly was out in the factory bagging the dried noodles they'd made on Friday, so Marietta had agreed to prepare their meals for the day.

A loud knock at the back door made her peer out the window.

"*Gut* morning, Bishop!" she said as she waved Jeremiah inside. "What brings you out on this blustery morning?"

Jeremiah wiped his feet on the mudroom rug as he removed his broad-brimmed black hat. "Didn't know if you two had heard the news," he replied. "Glenn's house burned to the ground last night. They're staying with us, and I'm letting everybody know so we can begin replacing what they've lost."

Marietta's jaw dropped. "Oh, dear Lord," she whispered. "What a shock that must've been. Is everyone all right?"

"Well, they escaped before the fire reached the stairway—and before it harmed Reuben, who'd dozed off at the kitchen table," he replied with a sigh. "As you can imagine, it'll be a while before any of the Detweilers are back to normal."

Shaking her head, Marietta gestured for the bishop to sit down. She carried the cookie tin to the kitchen table and took three mugs from the cabinet. "Those fellows are the *last* folks who need another tragedy—not that anyone should have to escape a fire in the night."

"*Jah*, Glenn's asking me what he might've done that God's heaping so much heartache on him," Jeremiah remarked as he took two oatmeal cookies from the tin. "Poor Reuben's convinced the fire must've been his fault.

He thinks he forgot to turn off the burner after he made his nightly cup of cocoa."

As Marietta returned to the sink to rinse the hot noodles before they stuck together, her mind buzzed with the bishop's news. "And what of Billy Jay? Did he go to school today?"

"*Jah*, Mamm convinced him he'd feel better if he spent the day amongst his friends and with Teacher Lydianne. Meanwhile, she's watching baby Levi while Glenn's at his place to see if anything can be salvaged after the fire." Jeremiah shook his head sadly. "I have a feeling they lost everything. The flames burned fast, and the house was half-gone before the fire truck got there."

Marietta blinked back sudden tears. What a horrible way for Glenn to spend his morning. What must be going through his mind as he picked through the wet, cold ashes, looking for anything of his former life he could save?

"Well then," she said with a renewed sense of energy. "I've just cooked these broken noodle remnants, and if you can stay long enough for me to make a pan of noodle pudding, you can take it home with you. Margaret's got her hands full cooking for four guests—in a torn-up kitchen, no less."

Bishop Jeremiah's expression brightened. "Noodle pudding! We'd love that! *Denki* for thinking of us, Marietta," he said before glancing around. "Where's your sister this morning?"

"She's bagging dried noodles. She'll be in for lunch shortly, so you might as well join us—as long as you don't mind sandwiches and chips. We *maidels* don't always cook the same big meals you're accustomed to."

"I appreciate your offer, Marietta, but I need to keep

informing folks about the fire—and I'm gathering clothes and other useful items to replace what the Detweilers lost," he replied. "I'll wait long enough for that pan of noodle pudding, though. Mamm will be glad of it."

As the bishop sipped his tea, Marietta mixed the eggs, sugar, cottage cheese, and other ingredients for the creamy pudding. After she stirred in the noodle pieces, she poured everything into a glass casserole dish. "Tell your *mamm* to bake this for about an hour at three fifty, and it'll be ready whenever she needs it."

"That's fabulous. We'll really enjoy this, Mari—"

"When you need a heavy coat to walk between the noodle factory and the house, it's officially winter!" Molly proclaimed as she stepped inside. She brightened when she saw Jeremiah at the kitchen table. "What brings you out our way, Bishop?"

"Glenn's place burned down last night," Marietta replied. "And while Jeremiah fills you in on the details, I'm going to look for those clothes of Dat's we packed away."

"We put them in Mamm's cedar chest, remember? What a great way to make Dat's shirts and pants useful again!" Molly focused on the bishop then, her eyes clouded with concern. "So where are the Detweilers now? Is everybody okay?"

"They are, thank the Lord," Jeremiah replied as Marietta headed for the bedroom their parents had occupied for their entire married life.

She lifted the lid of the chest at the foot of Mamm and Dat's double bed, pausing as a wave of wistful memories washed over her with the aroma of cedar. Their father's neatly folded clothing was underneath a faded quilt his *mamm* had made when she and Molly were born. It would be odd to see Glenn or Reuben wearing Dat's shirts and pants around town or to church . . . but what good were they doing in the chest?

Marietta picked up an armful of shirts—mostly blue and gray—and several pairs of broadfall pants. Beneath those, she spotted the two suits and the white shirts Dat had worn to church services, weddings, and funerals. As she headed toward the kitchen with the everyday clothes, her sister's voice was raised in excitement.

"Why don't you tell the Detweilers to come *here*, and they can live in our *dawdi hauses*? Now that Pete's living at your house, we're got the extra space—and your *mamm* won't have so many extra men to manage," Molly was saying. She looked at Marietta, her expression expectant. "What do you think, sister? They'd only be staying with us until their new house gets built."

Marietta swallowed hard, letting the clothing drop onto the kitchen table. Most families built a *dawdi haus* when aging parents needed a place without stairs—but because tourists often visited Morning Star during the summer, she and Molly had added a second one so they'd have more rental income. "Well, *jah*, we've got those two places for them to bunk . . . and with winter setting in, it's not as though we have any guest reservations."

She was about to remind Molly that this would mean a rambunctious little boy and a tiny baby would be moving in—not to mention two men who didn't cook much—but Bishop Jeremiah's smile stopped her.

"I can at least give them that option," he said with a nod. "And I suspect Mamm would appreciate having less cooking to do while her pots and dishes are stacked along the walls of our front room." He held up the shirt on the top of the clothing pile. "These should work fine for either Glenn or his *dat*. And if they're a little loose, so what? It's not as though we Amish chase after the latest fashions."

Marietta laughed along with her sister—but when the bishop had stepped outside to load the clothing into his buggy, she got serious. "Are you sure it's a *gut* idea to have the Detweilers staying out in the *dawdi*—"

"Margaret will be so grateful to us that she—and other neighbor gals—will be happy to help us feed them," Molly pointed out. "And besides, remember how you teased me about being sweet on Pete? This is my payback!"

Marietta frowned, confused. "How do you figure—"

"Don't even try to deny that you think Glenn's a nice fellow and that you've been gazing at his baby boy," Molly teased. "Here's your chance to see what mothering's all about and whether you want any part of it, *jah*?"

Marietta was about to protest, but Bishop Jeremiah was coming inside. "Let me fetch the rest of Dat's clothes," she said quickly.

As she left the kitchen, however, she shot her twin a look that said, *We'll talk about this later.*

Chapter 5

"Whoa, Nick," Glenn murmured. "We'll stay right here in the lane, boy."

On Tuesday, as he pulled up to the home place where he'd lived all his life, Glenn wished he hadn't come. He'd been clinging to the hope that he'd find odds and ends he could salvage from the debris—maybe a few of Billy Jay's toys or some of the pretty bone china cups and saucers he'd given Dorcas for her birthdays over the years.

But even from several yards away, he could see that there was nothing left to save. The winter wind carried away the cry that escaped him as he stepped out of the rig for a closer look. As he shaded his eyes against the intense morning sunshine, Glenn's heart sank.

The foundation was encased in a thick layer of frozen black ashes. He couldn't dig through the wreckage no matter how badly he might want to. The charred support posts that remained were bleak reminders that despite how well-built their house had been—despite how much love his family had filled it with over the generations—a fire had destroyed it in about an hour.

Before depression overwhelmed him, Glenn unhitched

Nick and led his horse to the barn so he could tend the rest of the animals. Ned, the horse that had remained here, nickered as they approached his stall—happy to see them, yet still skittish from the fire. After Glenn had fed and watered his two geldings, he filled the water tanks in the henhouse and put out more feed for Mamm's chickens.

As the weather got colder, it would be more difficult for the animals to get by without someone here on the property to look after them. Keeping the two horses in Jeremiah's barn wasn't such an imposition, but the thought of shifting dozens of chickens in snowy weather exhausted him—and he would have to build a new fence at the Shetler place to accommodate them.

Glenn sighed tiredly. He had no idea how to handle his livestock.

But then, he had no idea how he was going to make it from one hour to the next anymore, either. He was filled with such a dark heaviness, he wished he could lie down in the hay, fall asleep, and not wake up again.

The sound of an approaching engine made him stand absolutely still inside the henhouse. In this neck of the woods, Amish folks didn't operate motorized machinery— not the kind with a rumble that grew louder as it approached. For fear that someone had come to bulldoze what little remained of his life, Glenn rushed outside, waving his arms above his head.

A man in a heavy coat, sunglasses, and a stocking cap shifted the big dozer out of gear. "Glenn!" he called out as he clambered down from the cab. "I'm glad you're here!"

Well, that's more than I can say for myself. Who is this guy, anyway?

A few moments later, he realized Howard Gibbs was standing in front of him, clasping his hand. "You're just the fellow I need to talk to," the fire chief said. "How are things going for you at the Shetler place? Everybody okay?"

Glenn shrugged. "Will we ever be okay?" he demanded. "Dat and the baby are at the bishop's place and Billy Jay went to school this morning, so here I am. Trying to make sense of a senseless situation."

"You've been through a lot," Gibbs said with a sympathetic sigh. "But you should know that during our investigation after the fire, we determined that your gas line was intact. It was most likely a faulty valve or a gas leak inside the stove that caused the fire—not your *dat* falling asleep with a pan on the burner."

Gesturing at the black mess that covered the concrete block foundation, Glenn scowled. "How on earth could you tell? What with the explosion and everything being frozen solid—"

"We dug through the mess in the wee hours, once the kitchen area was cool but not frozen. We found your *dat*'s pan, and it wasn't scorched on the inside—it had flown several yards away from the house during the explosion," Howard explained patiently. "If he'd left the burner on, the pan wouldn't have been so clean inside. Reuben had an oil lamp burning on the kitchen counter, right?"

Glenn blinked. "Probably. So he could see to make his cocoa."

"We suspect a leak within the stove caused some gas to drift over, so the flame from the lamp shot up and caught the curtains on fire. From there, the blaze got going before anybody was aware of it. Doesn't take long in an older wooden structure."

Glenn shuddered. "It's a *gut* thing I couldn't sleep," he mumbled. "If I hadn't gone downstairs to get a drink—well, I don't want to think what might've happened to Dat and the rest of us."

Gibbs nodded grimly, glancing at the lumpy, black foundation. "*Jah*, the hand of God must've steered you downstairs at just the right time," he said. "I brought the dozer this morning, figuring you couldn't make any progress on a new place until this mess got cleaned up. If I work carefully, maybe you can dig through and find some pieces to keep—even if they'll most likely be burnt and waterlogged."

Glenn looked away, blinking back sudden, hot tears. "*Jah*, but the other issue will be mold, ain't so?" he reasoned aloud. "Any books or wood or other porous materials eventually stand a chance of being covered with a layer of black stuff that'll be dangerous to us, *jah*?"

"There's that."

A sigh welled up from deep in Glenn's soul. "No sense risking Dat or the boys getting sick because I was sentimental . . . clinging to the past. I'd better just let it all go."

Howard nodded. A few moments of silence passed between them while the fireman allowed Glenn to settle his emotions.

"*Denki* for thinking about us, Howard, and for coming to clear away the debris," he finally said. "Where would we Amish be if our Mennonite friends didn't share their equipment and technology?"

"We're happy to help," Gibbs insisted. "With the days

getting shorter, a local construction crew has offered to bring over big floodlights powered by generators so they—and some carpenters from your church—can work longer. They'll get your new house framed in and enclosed faster that way."

Glenn blinked. "You're already thinking about—"

"Oh, *jah*," Howard replied with a smile. "Jeremiah's nephew, Pete, has agreed to manage the building crew. Today he'll be sketching out a floor plan like the one you had before, to fit your foundation. He'll order the lumber and organize the crew, and your new home will be up in no time—or at least in a relatively *short* time," he amended.

Was Howard being honest, or just trying to cheer him up? Glenn couldn't wrap his mind around what the firefighter was saying, although he'd witnessed the rapid response of the Plain community when other folks' homes had burned down.

And don't forget how The Marketplace came together in less than a month, once Pete committed to remodeling that decrepit old stable.

Glenn let out the breath he hadn't realized he'd been holding. "Well then," he murmured, "the least I can do is help Pete with his drawings and join his crew. Meanwhile, *denki* again for coming to clear the site, Howard," he added, extending his hand. "Hope you don't mind if I leave before you start your dozing, though."

"I'd do the same thing. Take care, Glenn," he replied as they shared a firm handshake. "Might be too soon to be saying this, but I wouldn't be surprised if you and your *dat* and the boys are in your new place by Christmas."

By Christmas? How can that be, when it's already the third of December?

Glenn didn't dare believe such a pie-in-the-sky prediction. And yet, as he hitched Ned to the rig to give him some exercise, he felt the tiniest flicker of hope. Despite the fact that his soul felt as frozen over as the black wreckage covering his home's foundation, he sensed that a spark deep inside him had been rekindled.

Don't let it go out, Lord! Help me hold on—and help me believe that in You, all things are possible.

That evening before Mammi served supper, Pete sat at the kitchen table between Glenn and Reuben as they completed the sketches for the new Detweiler home. It was gratifying to see a glimmer in his friend's eyes that had been absent for a while—and he was pleased that Glenn's *dat* was following the conversation closely, too, with no sign that his mind was wandering.

"Do I remember correctly that your mudroom extended off the kitchen here?" Pete asked, pointing toward that area of the floor plan. "I'm thinking it covered the concrete slab I saw, rather than being over an excavated part of the basement."

"*Jah*, you've got it right," Reuben answered with a nod. "We added that mudroom back when we built the *dawdi haus*—which was right here, on this end."

Nodding, Pete quickly sketched the outline of the mudroom and added in the dimensions he'd jotted on his notepaper earlier in the day.

"Where's my room?" Billy Jay asked. He was seated in his *dawdi* Reuben's lap, eagerly eyeing the sketches even though he wasn't yet able to make all the connections between the paper drawings and how a three-dimensional house would result from them.

Pete smiled as he reached for the large piece of paper that showed the home's second story. "Here's the stairway up from the front room," he said patiently, following the lined rectangular section with his fingertip. "At the top of the stairs and to the left is your *dat*'s room—"

"Mamm's room, too," the boy put in softly.

Pete nodded. "*Jah*, that's right. So if this is the hallway, which of these squares is your bedroom, Billy Jay?"

Without missing a beat, Billy Jay jabbed the appropriate room with his finger. "Right here! And this is where Dawdi and Mammi were before they shifted downstairs to the *dawdi haus*."

"You got it right, son," Glenn put in, squeezing his boy's shoulder. "If you've figured that much out, it won't be long before we put a hammer in your hand and take you to the work site."

The kid's grin took Pete back to when he was a boy about that age. He recalled the sense of wonder he'd felt for carpenters who worked from drawings, as though they didn't even have to think about how to build a house from a paper sketch.

"*Jah*, and Billy Jay will soon be giving me the what's what about adding in the detail work," Pete said with a chuckle.

"But the *real* what's what will always be *my* say," Mammi teased from the stove. "Supper's ready! Let's clear away your drawings now and wash up, while the food's hot."

Nobody argued. Pete rolled up the drawings and stashed

them among the boxes of kitchen equipment that were stacked in the corner, where cabinets and a countertop used to be. When his *mammi* had set steaming bowls of green beans and crispy hash browns alongside a platter of baked chicken, he caught a secretive edge to Uncle Jeremiah's smile as they all took their places at the table.

After a few moments of silent grace, the man at the head of the table cleared his throat. "Looks like a lot of progress was made at your house site today, Glenn," he remarked as he reached for the platter in front of him.

"*Jah*, my head's spinning at how fast things are moving—thanks to Pete and Howard Gibbs," Glenn replied. "Howard was clearing the debris from around the foundation this morning. Said a local Mennonite crew would supply generator-powered floodlights so the construction team can work longer as the days get shorter."

Glenn clasped his father's arm fondly. "He also assured me that it was a leak or a faulty stove valve that caused that explosion, Dat—not a pan that boiled dry because you fell asleep," he continued. "That's great news, ain't so? You can rest easier now, knowing that none of this disaster was your fault."

Reuben's eyes widened. "You're not just saying that to make me feel better?"

"Nope!" Glenn replied.

As Pete followed the fire chief's explanation, he was relieved that Reuben hadn't caused the fire. He passed the bowl of hash browns to his uncle—and was again aware of a flickering in his grin. It wasn't until they'd finished their main meal, however, that Jeremiah revealed what was on his mind.

Mammi took the foil from a big pan of warm dessert.

"We have Marietta to thank for this noodle pudding," she remarked as she stuck a serving spoon in it. "Those twins have more ways of using noodles than anyone else I know!"

Pete's pulse revved up. He'd come to *love* noodle pudding while living in the Helfings' *dawdi haus*. Spooning the warm, creamy dessert onto his plate wasn't as satisfying as sharing it with Molly in person, but it brought her to mind—and in his mind, Pete could look beyond his memory of the way she'd shut him down on Sunday.

"We got more than dessert from Marietta and Molly today," Jeremiah put in as he focused on Glenn and Reuben. "I've also brought you several sets of their *dat*'s clothes. As soon as Mamm launders them, I bet they'll fit one—or both—of you fellows just fine."

Glenn's forkful of dessert stopped in front of his face. "Oh my," he murmured. "So much kindness that so many folks are showing us—"

"And the twins are also offering to let you Detweilers stay in their two *dawdi hauses*," the bishop continued. "What with our kitchen torn up, they thought it might be more comfortable for you—and a little easier for Mamm—"

"But you're welcome to stay here if you prefer!" Mammi Margaret quickly insisted. "We want all of you to feel at home until you move into your new place. No matter where you are, several other ladies have offered to provide extra food—and some of them are bringing clothes and supplies for the boys, too."

Pete's thoughts whirled in circles, like dry leaves caught

in a windy corner. "Whose idea was it for Glenn to move in over there? Marietta's or Molly's?" he blurted.

Uncle Jeremiah's eyebrows rose. "Molly made the offer, and her sister went along with it. Why do you ask?"

There it was again: *Why do you ask?* Pete realized that his answer would reveal more than he intended about his feelings for Molly—the hopes and dreams he secretly cherished whenever he thought about her.

"Just curious," he replied with a shrug. "Now that the twins have doubled their work space to focus on more noodle production, I'm surprised they'd want guests. But what do I know?"

"You know everything, Pete!" Billy Jay piped up from his chair across the table. "When I grow up, I wanna be just like you and build houses!"

Everyone laughed and encouraged the boy, which gave Pete a chance to retreat more gracefully from the conversation. As the evening continued, however, his doubts took root like weeds in his fertile imagination.

Did Molly really refuse my offer of a truck ride on Sunday because she's got her eye on Glenn? Maybe her noodle pudding was a farewell gift—a way to rub my nose in it because I'm no longer living at their place.

Or maybe she's thinking about the fact that Glenn will soon have a brand-new house, while I can't offer her anyplace to live. He's a family man, after all—a church member who accepted adult responsibilities long ago . . .

Chapter 6

"I hope you know what you've set us up for, sister!" Marietta blurted as she entered the noodle factory on Wednesday morning. "I was just out checking the message machine for phone orders, and Glenn has accepted your invitation to live here. Do you realize what this means?"

Molly looked up from watching the big batch of noodle dough in her mixer. "What does it mean?" she asked, trying not to laugh.

Thoroughly infuriated by her twin's attitude, Marietta measured the flour for her own batch of dough. "It means four more people to feed and clean up after!" she retorted. "It means that once Glenn takes Billy Jay to school, *we* have to deal with a tiny baby and a fellow in his eighties while we make more noodles than ever before! All things considered, life was a lot easier when Pete and Riley lived here."

"And who ever thought you'd be saying *that*?"

Frustrated, Marietta threw a cup of flour into the big mixer bowl—but missed. As fine, white particles filled the air, a sneezing fit made her dash away from her sanitized mixer. She slipped in the flour on the floor and grabbed for the supply cabinet, barely catching herself before she fell.

Molly rushed over, wrapping Marietta in her embrace. "Hey, no need to get all upset about—"

Marietta sneezed again. After feeling so strong of late, she was suddenly aware that her muscles hadn't regained as much strength as she'd believed. With her sister's help, she righted herself physically—but she was still as mad as a wet cat.

"What's up with you, Molly?" she demanded breathlessly. "Have Pete's reckless ways rubbed off on you? What possessed you to invite the Detweilers to stay with us? And without even mentioning the idea to me first?"

Her sister sighed contritely. "Okay, so I should've thought the idea through before I shot my mouth off to the bishop. I'm sorry, Marietta," she said. "I had no idea you'd get so worked up about it. I—I was just trying to help those guys, and to make things easier for Margaret."

Marietta inhaled deeply, struggling to compose herself. "I know that," she admitted. "It's just that—well, we're so used to our own routine that the thought of having two little boys and poor old Reuben around—"

"Reuben's doing better than folks give him credit for."

"—not to mention dealing with Glenn, who's like a big, black cloud ready to rain on whoever's in the room—"

"And you know all about dealing with depression and loss, ain't so?" Molly challenged gently. "Think about where you were emotionally, last year at this time. You're a *survivor*, Marietta. Your inner strength might be exactly what Glenn needs after yet another disaster has struck him down."

Marietta blinked. Had her sister changed her matchmaking tactic? Or was Marietta missing Molly's message in this situation—that she could weave her ordeal with cancer into an emotional blanket that might comfort a family who'd suffered an incredible number of losses lately?

"I thought you and I had agreed that we'll be looking after each other rather than thinking about marriage," she protested. But her words were losing steam.

Molly's eyes widened. "I never said you had to *marry* Glenn. But you could be his friend while he's rebuilding his life, *jah*?"

Marietta's shoulders relaxed. She wasn't convinced Molly was finished with her matchmaking scheme, but she listened anyway.

"As fast as Pete and our other carpenters completed The Marketplace's renovation, they'll probably have the new Detweiler house enclosed in a couple of weeks," her twin continued earnestly. "Weather permitting, the family could move in sometime after the holidays, *jah*? Glenn's happiest when he's working with wood, so putting the finishing details on his new home will surely lift his spirits—and he'll be motivated to move in as soon as possible, don't you think?"

Marietta's thoughts settled into a more orderly flow. Maybe she'd blown this situation out of proportion after all. "In the grand scheme of things, I guess having them here for a month isn't such a long time," she admitted. "But I was really looking forward to celebrating this

Christmas—and our birthday!—doing things we love to do. Promise me we won't allow Glenn's dark moods to overshadow our holiday, sister."

"I'm with you a hundred and fifty percent on that," Molly said with a nod. She stepped back over to her mixer, checking the readiness of the noodle dough. "And who knows? Maybe having a little boy here these next few weeks will make this Christmas season more fun than it would've been with just you and me. So—did we have any new orders when you checked the phone messages?"

Marietta chuckled. Wasn't it just like Molly to steer their conversation back to business when it suited her? "Just our usual amount this week for the two bulk stores we supply."

"All righty then," her twin sang out. "Let's get those orders filled so we can focus on stocking our store at The Marketplace. Sleigh bells won't be the only jingle we hear this season!"

As Molly turned on her noodle roller, Marietta fetched a broom to sweep the flour from the floor. They worked in comfortable silence, with only the whir of her big mixer and the sound of Molly's roller filling their work space. It was a blessing that the two of them had always been able to settle their minor squabbles by talking them through, and for that Marietta gave thanks.

After all, where would she be if her sister hadn't driven her to her chemo treatments? And who else would've seen to her every need when she'd felt so sick, and made her laugh when her spirits had sunk? Only Molly— spontaneous, fun-loving, spirited Molly—would've sacrificed her long, glossy hair in open defiance of the

Ordnung just to make Marietta feel better about her own appearance while she'd recovered from breast cancer.

She denies that she's sweet on Pete, too, but I know better!

Marietta smiled as she watched the large batch of dough taking shape in her mixer. Maybe it wouldn't be such an inconvenience to welcome Glenn and his family for a while. After all, it wasn't as though such an attractive man would ever give a damaged body like hers a second glance, so she could indeed simply be his friend while he rebuilt his home and his life.

And while the Detweilers were arranging their new future, she could foster a romance between her sister and the cute blond carpenter who'd been gawking at her during the entire church service on Sunday. Pete didn't have the wherewithal to build a house, so Marietta could hint that he and Molly would be welcome to live on the Helfing farm if they got hitched—and that would mean Pete would join the church, which would make Bishop Jeremiah and Margaret very happy.

And if Pete and Molly married, Marietta could surely remain in her lifelong home, as well. Then *everyone* would be happy.

Satisfied that she had a workable, worthwhile plan, Marietta smiled. The Christmas season was already shining brighter, and she couldn't wait to celebrate the way everything would surely fall into place over the next few weeks.

Jo's scarf flapped in the wind as she strode to the mailbox. Even though the snow from Sunday was still ankle-high, she relished having a few moments of fresh air and exercise—and silence. Mamm had fussed all morning about the number of cutout sugar cookies she'd been baking and decorating, claiming that she had no space to cook proper meals because Jo's Marketplace goodies were always in the oven or covering the counter-tops. When Jo had offered to bake the cookies in her shop kitchen instead, Mamm had immediately protested about being left alone for hours on end—left to do all the household chores herself.

"Lord, give me patience," Jo muttered as she approached the road. "Seems no matter what I do or say lately, it's *wrong*."

The mailbox held the usual assortment of mail-order catalogs, their festive covers advertising Christmas gift ideas. Although Jo loved the holiday season, she felt none of her usual excitement, because Mamm's negativity was wearing on her. When a white envelope addressed to her dropped out from between the catalogs, however, Jo's breath caught.

The return address was in Queen City. And the handwriting was Michael's.

Suddenly energized, Jo ducked into the phone shanty to enjoy her mail privately. She'd intended to check their messages anyway, so if Mamm was peering out the window, she wouldn't question Jo about pausing inside the little white building. Before she allowed herself to tear open the envelope, Jo listened to a message about the church ladies signing up to provide meals for Glenn and his family as they moved into the Helfings' *dawdi hauses*, as well as hot lunches for the construction crew as they began building his new home.

Jo sat down on the straight-backed wooden chair, her fingers trembling as she opened her mail. Why would Michael send her a letter? He and Nelson would be coming on Friday night—

"Oh my word, would you look at that!" Jo whispered. She gazed at a glossy, printed postcard that pictured hundreds of blooming red poinsettias. She turned it over.

Thought you'd enjoy seeing the photo a local fellow took of our greenhouse, which we use to advertise our poinsettias. The invitation for you to see them in person still stands.

Michael

Was she being a goose, reading between the lines to find a romantic motivation for Michael's sending this card? He'd surely tucked it into an envelope to keep her *mamm*'s prying eyes from seeing his message. That alone made Jo feel that she and Michael shared a delicious secret—and the potential for spending more time together during the Christmas season.

She inhaled deeply to still her runaway pulse, savoring a few moments to reread the crisp lines of black script that were as slender and angular as the young man who'd written them. Jo tucked the postcard back into its envelope, which she stuffed deep into the pocket of her apron. She hoped she could hide the excitement on her face when she entered the house, because Mamm would surely quiz her about it—and then cut her hopes and dreams to pieces with her sharp tongue.

Jo walked back to the house, planning how she'd answer any questions her mother might ask. As she hung her black coat and bonnet in the mudroom, she breathed deeply—and envisioned Michael seated across the table from her sharing a plate of fresh sugar cookies and a pot of tea.

"What was in the mail?" Mamm called out from the kitchen.

"Catalogs, mostly," Jo replied truthfully. "And there was a phone message saying the local ladies are taking food over to the Helfings while Glenn and his family stay there, as well as providing meals at the Detweiler construction site. Sounds like they'll be starting the new house within the next day or two."

Before she entered the kitchen, she smoothed the front of her apron to conceal the outline of Michael's envelope. On a sudden inspiration, Jo opened the cabinet beneath the sink, where they kept the wastebasket. "This is getting pretty full," she remarked. "I'll gather the trash from the other rooms, and then it'll be about time for lunch, ain't so?"

Mamm shrugged. "It'll be that split pea soup I made yesterday."

"Sounds *gut*." Jo pulled the half-full sack out of the plastic wastebasket, feeling downright devious as she held it in front of her until she could remove Michael's envelope in her room.

When she got upstairs, however, another surprise awaited her: as she emptied the wastebasket beside Mamm's sewing machine, several bright, shiny pieces of a postcard fluttered out.

Jo's eyes widened. As she plucked the scraps from the floor, she realized that Mamm had torn up an envelope and a poinsettia postcard just like the one she'd received—except the handwriting was different. And one of the corner pieces had Nelson's signature on it! Before her mother came to see what she was doing, Jo pieced together enough of the postcard to read what Michael's *dat* had written.

Would you like to see our greenhouses, Drusilla?
Let's talk about it Friday when we get to your place.

Nelson

A shimmer of excitement shot up Jo's spine as she stuffed the postcard pieces into the trash bag. It seemed the Wengerds were working together to coax her and Mamm to come for a visit—and her mother had ripped the invitation to shreds without saying a word about it. Jo knew better than to mention what she'd found, just as she instinctively knew to tuck Michael's postcard in her bottom drawer beneath her black stockings and the newer *kapps* she kept for special occasions.

It seemed her mother was keeping the same secret she was—but reacting differently to it.

As Jo went back downstairs, she kept a straight face as best she could. Nelson and Michael had heard Mamm's objections to a trip to Queen City weeks ago. It would be *interesting* to see what happened when the Wengerds arrived in time for supper on Friday, as they'd been doing since they'd opened their Marketplace shop and started renting Mamm's *dawdi haus*.

Who knows? Maybe if the three of us keep working on her, we'll come up with the right words—the right Christmas spirit—to change her mind. It's the season of miracles, after all.

Chapter 7

Glenn felt exhausted and rather nervous Thursday morning as he and Bishop Jeremiah stepped onto the Helfings' front porch. Dat followed a few steps behind them, hunched against the wintery wind. Levi squirmed against Glenn's shoulder, fussing about the blanket draped over his head to protect him from the cold.

Or maybe, like me, he feels the strain of all this shifting around. I'm not looking forward to bunking with the boys—and Dat—in a dawdi haus, *but it's an inconvenient time to be underfoot at the Shetler place. So here I am, coming to Marietta with my hat in my hand.*

Jeremiah knocked on the front door. "If nobody answers, we'll need to go around back to their noodle shed."

"If they peek out and see who's here, they might pretend they're not home," Dat joked as he stepped up behind them. "We Detweilers are a ragtag bunch these days."

"You're as well dressed as Alvin Helfing ever was," Jeremiah pointed out.

Glenn sighed. Showing up in clothes the twins' father had worn—possibly even garments that Molly or Marietta had sewn—was yet another thing that bothered him.

When the door swooshed open, Levi started crying so loudly that Glenn couldn't hear himself think. As Marietta peered out at them, her smile appeared as tentative as the one on his own face.

"*Gut* morning—come in, come in," she added, stepping aside.

Why had Levi chosen this moment to cut loose? The boy had amazing lung capacity for one so small—and Glenn had changed and fed him before they'd left the Shetler place so he'd be at his best.

"We brought our own siren," Dat teased as they entered the warmth of the Helfing home.

"We've also got some large jars of goat's milk in the rig, along with boxes of clothes and toys," Jeremiah said beneath the baby's squalling. "And Mamm sent along a casserole in the pan your noodle pudding was in—which was fabulous, by the way."

Marietta was nodding, straining to take in what the bishop was saying as the baby wailed. Molly appeared at the doorway to the kitchen, her eyes wide as she took in the sight of them.

Glenn suddenly couldn't subject these generous young women to the discomfort his family was already causing them. He turned and hurried back outside, muffling his son's cries against his shoulder. Why had he thought it was a good idea, disrupting the Helfing twins' quiet lives with two noisy boys, a lonely old man, and a guy who was so deep in grief that he didn't know up from down—

"Glenn, wait!"

He turned to be sure he'd heard a real voice rather than a phantom call.

Marietta's green eyes dominated her thin face as she

gazed at him. She'd dashed outside without a coat, yet she didn't seem to feel cold. "Bring Levi inside and—and get warm," she insisted. "It—it just occurred to me that our *dawdi hauses* don't have stoves, so you'll need to come to the house whenever you heat his milk. You folks could use a couple of the spare bedrooms instead of—"

"Oh, I couldn't expect you and Molly to—"

"*Jah*, you could." Marietta grasped his arm, tugging him toward the house. "Let's talk about this over cocoa. Our house has plenty of rooms to go around."

Glenn was so flummoxed, he couldn't protest. The slender hand that remained in the crook of his arm felt surprisingly strong—and he didn't want Marietta to catch a chill, so he did as she'd suggested. When he stepped inside again, the aroma of something warm and sweet welcomed him.

In the kitchen, Bishop Jeremiah was helping himself to an oatmeal raisin cookie. Dat had settled into a chair at the table before he'd even taken off his coat.

"Look at these, Glenn!" he said as he snatched two from the plate. "You *know* these girls bring the best cookies on the planet to church—and they've made some just for us! How wonderful is that?"

As Glenn headed for the table, he *almost* forgot that Levi was crying.

Lo and behold, Marietta held out her arms. "Why don't I take the baby while you relax with a snack?" she asked shyly. "And if the bishop will bring his milk inside, we'll see if we can settle him down. Warm milk makes everybody feel better, ain't so?"

Was that a knowing smile on Molly's face as she poured their cocoa? Glenn was too surprised to question it—or to refuse Marietta's offer. He loved his baby boy more than life itself, but being a single parent was a daunting job he hadn't ever expected to take on . . . just as he'd never guessed that a shy, unmarried woman would relieve him of his wailing son so he could enjoy cookies and cocoa.

As Jeremiah returned to the rig, Glenn took the seat beside his father. He crammed a cookie into his mouth, closing his eyes over the simple pleasure of sugar, raisins, and cinnamon. By the time he'd sipped some cocoa and wolfed down a second cookie, blessed silence reigned. Glenn glanced across the kitchen in awe.

Marietta was walking slowly, murmuring to Levi as she held him with his tiny head cradled in the crook of her neck. When the bishop returned with a large container of goat's milk and some baby bottles, Molly was already running water into a pot. Glenn gradually regained control of the situation and his emotions, warming milk and filling a bottle—and then handing it to Marietta as she sat at the table with Levi as though she'd fed a baby dozens of times.

Had she? Glenn noticed only a moment's hesitation before she slipped the nipple into his son's mouth.

The kitchen took a deep, peaceful breath.

After a few prayerful moments, Bishop Jeremiah leaned close to Glenn. "You folks enjoy a little quiet time while I unload the buggy. Which *dawdi haus* will you be in?"

"Bring everything into the front room, Bishop," Marietta replied, gazing at the tiny child in her arms. "We'll figure out who'll stay in which bedroom after Levi falls asleep. It's not very efficient—or comfortable—for Glenn to be warming milk here in the kitchen and then carrying it out into the cold to feed Levi in a *dawdi haus*, ain't so?"

Jeremiah's eyes widened, but he didn't argue with her logic.

Glenn blinked. He'd expected the bishop to say it wouldn't be proper for two widowers to bunk here with the unmarried twins, yet it seemed the hand that rocked the cradle—or held the bottle—ruled the world.

Even inside two pairs of gloves, Pete's hands were so cold that he could barely feel them. Several Mennonite fellows on the volunteer fire department had been helping them earlier in the day, but they'd gone home after lunch, so only Gabe Flaud and Jude Shetler remained with him at the Detweiler site.

"Once we get this last post in place, let's head home," he called out. "I'm so hungry and tired and cold, I can't see straight—much less concentrate on what we're doing."

"You don't have to tell me twice," Jude said with a short laugh.

"Maybe Howard can find us some heaters," Gabe suggested. His breath formed a white wreath of vapor around his head as he drove one final nail. "The fire department guys came up with all sorts of other equipment for us, so—"

The sound of an approaching rig made Pete look up from the tools he was gathering. His heart skipped a beat when he saw the Helfings' white mare halt at the roadside. Feeling far too excited, he watched the buggy's rosy-cheeked, well-proportioned driver step down with a foil-wrapped pan in her hand.

Don't get your hopes up. Detweiler's not here today because he's been moving into their place, remember? Who knows how much progress he's made, catching Molly's eye?

The red flags in his imagination didn't stop him from smiling as she approached, however. Molly was coming toward the site with something to eat, no doubt.

"My word," she called out with a shake of her head. "I—I had no idea what to expect when I got here, but this . . . well, it's devastating. I can't imagine how Glenn and his family must feel now that their home's been completely destroyed."

Pete refrained from asking how comfortable Detweiler was making himself at the Helfing place. "*Jah*, they're starting from scratch," he confirmed. "At least they all made it out before the stove exploded—"

"And compared to how things looked before the rubble got plowed away," Gabe put in as he went toward their visitor, "what you see now at least looks *hopeful*. Do I dare believe you've got some goodies in that pan, Molly? I'm so hungry I could eat my fingers!"

Molly's laughter rang around them, warming Pete from the inside out. "Save those fingers for holding a hammer," she teased as she removed the foil from her pan. "We made these this morning before Glenn's family arrived, but I saved some for you guys."

Pete jogged up to her and playfully slapped Gabe's hand away. "If I let you go first, Flaud, there won't be any for the rest of us."

By the time Jude joined them, Pete had crammed an entire oatmeal raisin cookie into his mouth. He stepped back to allow his friends access to the pan, assessing

Molly's mood and expression. It was too much to hope that she'd brought the cookies just for *him*—and maybe it was best that the two other men were there anyway. Kept him from asking too many questions about Glenn.

"Somebody brought you fellows your lunch, *jah*?" Molly asked with an endearing little scowl. "I don't recall who was on the list to provide your noon meal, but—"

"Rose's chili hit the spot," Jude replied with his mouth full.

"It's been hours since we ate it, though," Pete put in. "We're all cold enough that we're calling it a day. You've given us the energy to drive home."

The sparkle in Molly's green eyes rendered him momentarily speechless. "I should've brought you some coffee—"

"Oh, we'll be here again tomorrow," Jude hinted as he took another cookie. "But *denki* for thinking of us this afternoon. See you guys in the morning."

"*Jah*, I'm out of here, too," Gabe added with a shiver. "It's a *gut* thing we'll have the place enclosed by the weekend."

Pete took hold of the pan's other side and helped himself to another cookie. With his companions making their exit, he could spend a little time alone with Molly without seeming obvious about it. He allowed himself a moment to drink in her flawless complexion and evergreen eyes. Did her head get cold now that she only had a couple of inches of hair covering her scalp?

He dismissed the question before it got him into trouble. The wind had coaxed a couple of loose curls from beneath her black winter bonnet, and he suddenly wanted to remove his gloves and rumple them.

"So—how's it going?" he asked quickly. "Did Glenn get his stuff moved in okay? Probably filled up one of your *dawdi hauses*, considering all the donated clothes and toys they've already collected."

"They had a lot of boxes," she agreed, "but after Jeremiah unloaded them, we rearranged the spare bedroom downstairs and the next room, where Mamm's sewing machine is set up. The *dawdi hauses* only have hot plates, you know. Seems better for Glenn to stay in the house rather than coming inside to warm Levi's bottles and then taking them back out into the cold."

Molly might as well have sucker punched him. Apparently his uncle hadn't objected, but it sounded awfully *cozy*, having Detweiler bunk so close to the stairway that led up to the twins' bedrooms.

Pete immediately felt envious—and wished he'd found a reason to stay in the main house while *he'd* been renting there. He vaguely regretted moving in with Jeremiah, too, but at this point he had no valid reason to return to the Helfing place—even if he felt the need to chaperone.

"Sounds like you ladies are making the Detweilers very comfortable," he remarked.

Molly raised an eyebrow. "Jealous?"

Pete's mouth fell open. With one word, she'd nailed *him*.

"Why do you ask?" he shot back. But with Molly focused on him so confidently, it felt like a weak tactic.

She shrugged. "When I want to know something, that's generally the way I find out," she replied breezily, releasing the cookie pan. "Glenn says he'll be here to work tomorrow, so if you want to know more, ask him."

Before Pete could respond, she was walking toward

her rig. As he watched Molly drive down the road, his heart felt like one of the frozen black lumps of ash the dozer had removed from the Detweilers' foundation. With a heavy sigh, he opened his truck door to let Riley out for a quick run-around.

"Well, I blew *that* one," he muttered.

The big yellow dog stood up on the seat, none too eager to leave his warm napping spot.

"You don't get one of these oatmeal raisin cookies until you help me pick up my stuff," Pete said, setting them on the truck's hood.

Eyeing the pan through the windshield, Riley hopped down. As his dog loped around the construction site, sniffing and doing his business, Pete retrieved his cords and the batteries that ran his power tools. He turned in time to see his retriever leap effortlessly onto the truck's hood to devour the rest of Molly's cookies.

"Hey! Get back in the truck!" he hollered. "Those were mine!"

Riley appeared every bit as concerned—and apologetic—as Molly had been during her brief, unsettling visit. At least the dog did what he was told without giving Pete any flack, which was more than he could say for Miss Helfing.

Pete climbed into the truck and cranked its engine, gasping as cold air shot from the heater vents. Riley seemed to be laughing at him: his pink tongue dangled from his mouth, dotted with wet chunks of cookie.

"You're a mess," Pete said as he put the truck in gear. "But at least you'll ride with me—which is more than we can say for You-Know-Who."

Chapter 8

After feeling twitchy with anticipation all day, Jo was delighted to see the Wengerds coming up the lane toward the house late Friday afternoon. The wagon they were pulling was empty, so they must have stopped at The Marketplace first to unload it—which meant their evening at the house would be uninterrupted. She inhaled deeply to settle her giddiness. Because Mamm had put a large venison roast in the oven with carrots, turnips, and potatoes, the rich aroma of meat and vegetables would greet their guests when they stepped inside.

In her excitement, Jo opened the door before Michael and his *dat* reached the porch. "It's *gut* to see you!" she called out. "How was the drive? Sometimes the weather in eastern Missouri is different from what we have here in the middle."

"Went just fine," Nelson replied. "We had our Mennonite neighbors haul a big load of poinsettias to The Marketplace in their delivery truck to keep them from getting too cold. Michael rode with them to unlock the place, and by the time I got there with our wagonload of wreaths, the flowers were all unloaded."

"*Jah*, you should see the commons area," Michael put in, smiling at Jo. "We had more poinsettias than would fit in our nursery store, so we set the extras along the fronts of the shops for now."

"Oh, I bet that looks pretty!" she exclaimed, closing the door behind them. Was it her imagination, or had Michael been searching her face for a response to his postcard? Jo felt a shimmer of excitement when his fingers lingered on hers before he released his coat so she could hang it up.

"Smells like you ladies have been cooking all day," Nelson remarked as he headed into the kitchen. "Supper smells wonderful-*gut*—and look at all these cookies!"

"*Jah*, Jo doesn't know when to quit," Mamm said, grabbing her pot holders. "She's covered every square inch of my counter space, so I have no place to put this roaster—"

"Now you do," Jo countered as she picked up a large wire rack of the decorated sugar cookies. "I'll set these in the front room for now—and Michael, if you'll grab that other rack, we'll give Mamm *plenty* of space."

Michael carefully lifted the other wire rack and followed Jo. "These look *gut* enough to eat," he teased.

"Let's hope so!" Jo put in as she set her rack on the coffee table. "The frosting needs to set up before I stack them in my bins for tomorrow."

As her companion gently placed his rack beside hers, Jo glanced toward the kitchen. "I—I got your pretty postcard," she whispered.

"And?" Michael straightened to his full height, remaining between Jo and the kitchen in case anyone was watching. His beautiful gray-blue eyes were alight with the same anticipation that filled her insides with butterflies.

Jo took a deep breath so she wouldn't say the wrong thing. He probably wouldn't be surprised—but she didn't want him to be disappointed, either. "I'd love to come!" she murmured. "I'll tell you, though, that the card your *dat* sent Mamm was in the wastebasket, all torn to pieces—"

Michael briefly grasped her hand. "It's okay, Jo. We'll figure something out."

What a blessing it was to have a friend with such a positive attitude. Jo nodded shyly, glancing around his lean frame to be sure Mamm wasn't spying on them. "It's mostly a matter of *when*," she continued in a hurried whisper. "I'll need a lot of time before Christmas to do my Marketplace baking—"

"We'll figure that out, too." Michael flashed her a quick grin. "Probably better get back in there with the parents, ain't so? They'll think we're scheming something up."

Jo laughed out loud and then clapped her hand over her mouth. It was so much fun to share a secret—and to believe that someday, with Michael's help, she might get to see those beautiful poinsettias in person rather than on a postcard. As she returned to the kitchen, she knew her radiant face gave away the excitement she was feeling—

And why was that a *bad* thing? Wasn't the Christmas season supposed to be merry and bright?

When Jo and Michael came through the doorway, Nelson was placing the platter of venison roast on the table. The bread basket was already on, as were the bowls of turnip wedges, sliced carrots, and small, whole potatoes that had browned from baking in the meat's juices.

Although the Wengerds had become their good friends over the past several months, Jo suspected Nelson was trying to win her *mamm*'s favor by helping without being asked—and that wasn't a bad thing, either. Many Amish men wouldn't lend a hand with "women's work," but he'd lost his wife a few years ago, so he and Michael were accustomed to doing the household chores themselves.

A while back, Mamm had even invited Nelson to sit at the head of the table and lead them in their silent grace each Friday evening—so maybe Jo's dream about visiting the Wengerd place wasn't so far-fetched, after all. Hope thrummed in Jo's heart as she bowed her head.

After several moments of prayer, Nelson cleared his throat. He was reaching for the meat when Mamm started in.

"Before you bring the subject up, Jo and I won't be going to Queen City for a visit," she stated. "What would be the point? I'm happy right here, and I don't ever intend to remarry."

Nelson's eyebrows rose slightly. He was an attractive man whose face was distinguished by smile lines, and Mamm's sanctimonious tone didn't seem to bother him. "Who said anything about leaving your place, Drusilla? Or about getting remarried?" he asked calmly as he helped himself to venison.

"I know what you were thinking, sending me that postcard!" Mamm retorted. "And you've invited us before, remember? But we'll not be accepting your invitation."

"Who says *I* don't want to go?" Jo blurted.

Across the table from her, Michael's eyes lit up—but her mother's expression soured immediately.

"We've had this discussion, daughter," she whispered

tersely, "and it's a topic best not discussed in front of our company, ain't so?"

Something inside her snapped. Jo was treading on thin ice, because she'd never defied her mother—but wasn't it time she spoke up for herself? At thirty-one, didn't she have the right to give her own answers and to have her own opinions—not to mention hopes and dreams her mother would never understand?

Jo folded her hands in her lap, praying for words that wouldn't ruin their meal before it even began. "I got a postcard, too," she said softly. "And I would really enjoy seeing those greenhouses filled with poinsettias—"

"You're falling for it! You're thinking something serious and—and *meaningful*—is going to come of this, Josephine," Mamm warned her in a low voice.

"You make it sound as though we're hoodwinking the two of you, or luring you into a questionable situation," Nelson said as he gazed at her mother.

"It's a simple invitation," Michael put in earnestly. "We only want to—"

"There's no such thing as a simple invitation when it comes to my daughter's feelings! She has no idea about the ulterior motives men have—or about the ways they tell such pretty fairy tales at first, only to slap a woman's opinions and ideas down after they've got her where they want her!" Mamm glared at Nelson and then at Michael. "We'll not be discussing this topic any further—not if you're to continue eating supper at *my* table every weekend."

Stunned speechless by her mother's vehement response, Jo stared at her plate. Where had such remarks come from? As far as she knew, her father had treated Mamm with utmost respect—and he'd certainly tolerated her increasingly negative remarks and moods in his later years. As an uncomfortable silence filled the kitchen, her cheeks blazed with humiliation.

Nelson and Michael had done absolutely nothing to deserve such a scathing lecture. As Jo went through the motions of filling her plate with food she was no longer hungry for, she wondered what could possibly have given Mamm such an idea about men and their ulterior motives.

Jo was quite aware that she was trusting and naive because she'd had so little opportunity to spend time with young men—let alone get her heart broken or be led astray. She'd never been taken home from a singing or gone on a real date, much less received a kiss from anyone.

And isn't that the saddest thing I've ever admitted? Am I not entitled to make my own mistakes? Who knows what kind of happiness I might be passing up, simply because Mamm believes I don't know what's best for me?

Jo swallowed hard, blinking back tears she hoped Michael and his *dat* wouldn't notice. She didn't dare apologize to the Wengerds for her mother's rude remarks—and she didn't know how to relieve the unbearable silence that went on and on as they filled their plates.

At long last, Nelson cleared his throat. "Michael and I made a couple of evergreen wreaths for you ladies," he said patiently. "I suppose if you don't want them, we can sell them at—"

"What a thoughtful gift—and *denki* for thinking of us!" Jo put in before her mother could refuse Nelson's offer. "I've been so busy baking lately, I haven't had a chance to cut any greenery, so we'll really enjoy the fresh scent of your wreaths."

Michael flashed her a quick smile as he cut into his

venison. "We get a lot of our evergreen pieces from an English friend's Christmas tree farm, so we also brought you a few extra sprigs of pine to put on your mantel—if you want them," he added quickly.

Jo's heartbeat quickened. Knowing that he'd been thinking of her this past week, planning little gifts, was a whole new sensation—a rush she could get used to. "Maybe after supper—after the dishes are cleaned up," she added with a glance at Mamm, "I could get the Christmas candles and the Nativity set out of the closet. We could arrange the greenery around those, and the whole house will feel like Christmas!"

Her mother's brow furrowed. "When did you figure on wrapping all those cookies, Josephine? It's none of *my* concern if they get stale before you take them to your shop, but—"

"Now there's a job I'd like to help with!" Nelson piped up with a chuckle. "If our favorite baker spots some cookies that are less than perfect, there'll probably be a few that don't get packaged—"

"Or we can buy a plateful this evening instead of waiting until tomorrow," Michael suggested. "By afternoon on a busy day at The Marketplace, I'm ready for something sweet—"

"But Jo's cookies will be gone if we wait until then to latch onto some. *Gut* point, son." Nelson's face lit up with a smile. "You can select our goodies while I help Drusilla clean up the kitchen."

The conversation had bounced like a ball, and Mamm had been following it with a deepening scowl. "So now you're buying Jo's attention—buttering her up by paying for cookies when—"

"No, Drusilla, we're buying cookies," Nelson corrected gently. "It's *your* attention I'm trying for, and I'm having to work pretty hard at it. Why is that? What have I done to make you so suspicious of me?"

Mamm's jaw dropped. For once, someone had called her out about her negative attitude, and she had no response. Frustration simmered in the glare she shot Nelson, but she focused on her food rather than answering his questions.

Jo took a big bite of carrots to keep from laughing, which would only upset her mother further. Truth be told, she was eager to hear Mamm's answers, because Nelson and his son had been nothing but nice to her in the months they'd been staying in the *dawdi haus*.

For the remainder of the meal, Jo and the Wengerds talked about the flurry of business they anticipated at The Marketplace the next day. She was pleased that several merchants around Morning Star's business district had ordered poinsettias and wreaths and that Michael would spend part of Saturday morning delivering them.

"Sounds like it was worth your time and effort to invest in those new greenhouses," she remarked as they finished their meal. "I'm glad all that extra work is paying off for you now."

Michael's eyes twinkled as though he wanted to repeat his invitation to visit those greenhouses. "All those extra poinsettias have also given us a reason to keep coming to Morning Star through the winter," he said softly.

"*Jah*, as long as the roads stay clear, I'm looking forward to our weekly trips," Nelson agreed. "Not just because of the extra sales, but because of the special friends we've made here."

Mamm took that remark as her cue to scrape the plates.

Jo sighed, hoping their guests didn't take offense at her mother's abrupt, abrasive behavior. When Nelson went to the sink to run the dishwater, the stunned expression on Mamm's face was priceless. And when he shooed Jo and Michael out to start boxing up her cookies, Jo didn't argue.

"I'm sorry Mamm's such a prickly pear tonight," she murmured when they'd crossed the front room. "Let me get my pans and plastic bags and disposable plates. I want to package some of these cookies for individual sales, and we'll arrange the rest of them in big pans for my baking cases."

When she returned to the coffee table, Michael was studying the cookies intently. "These took a lot of time to decorate. I hope you're charging enough for your work, Jo."

She chuckled. "I'm selling the plainer frosted ones two for a dollar. The fancier outlined cookies with the colored sugar detailing go for a dollar apiece—and Mamm nearly keeled over when I told her that. She accused me of robbing my customers."

"She hasn't been to a commercial bakery for a long while, has she?" Michael smiled at her and plucked the top plate from her stack. "Dat likes lots of frosting, and I prefer less, so I'm going to choose some of each—and pay you for every one of them," he insisted. "We don't intend to eat into your profits, Jo."

"But—but you've brought us poinsettias and wreaths and greenery! And before that, it was mums and pump-kins," Jo protested, placing her hands on her hips. "Why should you forfeit the money you could be making on those items? I'd gladly barter some of my cookies for—"

"That's different."

Michael's earnest expression stilled Jo's fluttering

heart. He lowered his voice, gazing at her as he held his plate with four cookies on it. "When guys want to invest in a relationship, some *gifting* is called for, ain't so? It's our pleasure to bring you and your *mamm* some seasonal decorations, Jo. And—and I hope you really do want to go back to Queen City with us sometime."

"I'd love to!" Jo whispered earnestly. Her heart was hammering so hard she couldn't hear herself think—but then, she couldn't think when his stunning gray-blue eyes were focused on her anyway. "But I don't know when—"

"Why not come home with us Sunday morning? I can drive you back to Morning Star anytime you're ready, Jo."

She sucked in air at the thought of getting away for a couple of days, even as she anticipated the backlash from her mother. "I want to—but if Mamm decides not to—"

"That's *her* decision, *jah*? With Dat around the whole time—and our employees—everything will be perfectly proper," he pointed out. "It's not as though I'm luring you off on a wild getaway for just the two of us. Although that's a great idea."

Jo thought her knees would buckle. Her whole body thrummed at Michael's words—at an invitation she'd never dared to believe a man would extend to her.

"All right, I'm coming!"

There! She'd said it and she couldn't take it back.

Michael straightened to his full height, which was a good four inches more than hers. His slender face took on a slight flush, and he had to steady his plate of cookies with his other hand to keep from dropping it.

"I—I'll pack a bag and be ready to go at first light on Sunday morning, when you fellows usually leave," Jo continued breathlessly. "It's a visiting Sunday, after all, and that's exactly what I'll be doing, *jah*? I want to come back early on Tuesday, though."

"Oh, Jo!" Michael raked his dark hair back, appearing flustered yet overjoyed. "I—it's a *gut* thing we cleaned the house before we came—"

"Do you think I care about your *housekeeping*?" Jo teased, playfully shaking a finger at him.

He laughed out loud, catching her finger in his warm grip. "Careful there, Jo. No offense, but you're acting like your *mamm*—"

Jo laughed, too. Time stood still as Michael's hand remained around hers, and she knew a moment of unprecedented, giddy joy.

"I'll have to work on that," she murmured when she could stop giggling. Reluctantly, she slipped her hand from his. "We'd better pack these cookies, *jah*? The parents will think we're slackers if we've not made any progress by the time they've finished in the kitchen."

"Phooey on that. You know what they say about all work and no play," Michael remarked as he chose a frosted drum and a decorated gingerbread house for his plate. "And I don't want you to think I'm dull, Jo. This is new territory for me and I—well, I want to have some *fun* with you. Who can fault us for that?"

"Not a soul," Jo replied happily. "I think we're off to a fine start."

Chapter 9

On Saturday, the wind whipped and whistled as Jude and Glenn steadied the final truss of the new roof so Pete could fasten it securely in place. Their work wasn't going as quickly as it had on previous days, because Gabe was minding the Flauds' furniture store at The Marketplace, and the Mennonites had been called away to a fire on the far side of town. Even so, thanks to the many hands helping and the floodlights that made it possible to work in the evenings, the house was enclosed and they'd installed the first-story windows and doors.

In the kitchen area, sheltered from the weather, Reuben and Billy Jay were unwrapping bundles of insulation and shingles. Pete was glad to have their assistance—just as Glenn's *dat* and son were happy to be useful. Once the roof boards were in place, the crew could begin installing the shingles.

As the noon hour approached, Pete's stomach growled so loudly that Glenn laughed.

"Sounds like your inner bear just came out of hibernation," Detweiler teased. "Or did you skip breakfast because you overslept?"

"Do you think my grandmother allows me to skip meals—or to oversleep?" Pete shot back. With his battery-powered screwdriver, he drove two more long bolts into place. "I'll be glad when our lunch comes, though, so we can sit inside while we eat. Our lady of the day should be here any time now—and maybe that's her coming right now," he added as he nodded at an approaching rig. The sound of wheels on the road roused Riley from his nap, and the dog ran eagerly toward the buggy.

Glenn and Jude glanced toward the vehicle, as well—and then Detweiler groaned. "No, that's Sadie and her family," he muttered. "Now why have they driven all the way out here from Indiana, when I assured them we were doing fine?"

"They probably wanted to see that for themselves," Jude suggested. "It's a big deal when your home place burns to the ground."

"Puh! Unless my sister's turned over a new leaf, she's here to stir things up—and to insist that we need to move out to Indiana with them," Glenn retorted. "Sadie can't leave well enough alone. Please accept my apology in advance for whatever disagreeable things might fly out of her mouth. I'd better get down there before she lights into Dat."

As Detweiler started for the ladder, Pete glanced over at Jude. "It's a pretty sad state of affairs when a fellow says such things about his only sibling," he said softly.

Jude nodded. "After the words that flew between them at their *mamm*'s funeral, I'm surprised the Shank family's come back. And that's a sad thing to say, too."

Pete bent over to retrieve his tools. "Let's go on down and wait for today's lunch angel—and corral my dog. I don't feel right eavesdropping on the Detweilers' conversation from up here."

As he allowed Jude to descend the ladder first, Pete watched Sadie and her four older kids clamber down from their double rig, followed by her husband, who was carrying his newborn twins in their blanketed basket carriers. Sure enough, Sadie's face—which was the spitting image of Glenn's, except she was wearing a black bonnet tied over a *kapp*—alerted him to the urgent mission on her mind. Her scowl deepened as she pointed her finger at Riley.

"Get out of my way, dog!" she ordered. "And stop your stupid barking!"

As Pete started down the ladder, he smiled when he spotted an approaching horse-drawn vehicle. He recognized Opal immediately. It seemed one of the twins was today's lunch angel—an unexpected pleasure, because on Saturday both Molly and Marietta usually worked in their Marketplace shop.

He watched a woman emerge from the rig, noting a figure and an energy level that could only belong to Molly. After a moment Pete realized he should help her unload their meal instead of gawking at her—and that his dog's barking had grown more insistent, too.

"Riley, get over here!" he called out. "Sit, boy!"

"This dog should be tied to a tree," Sadie said sternly. "If he so much as *touches* one of my children—"

"And *gut* morning to you, too, Sadie. Nice to see you folks," Pete interrupted, nodding at all of them. When he saw Glenn talking softly to his father, he picked up a stick and offered it to the eldest Shank boy, who was around ten. "If you throw this, Riley will play fetch until the cows come home—and he'll stop barking."

The kid grinned, running across the yard so the golden retriever would chase after him. The other three children, another boy and two girls, eagerly followed him.

Pete extended his hand to Sadie's husband, Norman—a tall, lanky fellow who was looking over the construction site. "Hope you and the family are all well? Encounter any problems on the drive out?" he asked. He'd known Sadie most of his life, but Shank hailed from Indiana, so he'd only been to Morning Star for family weddings, reunions, and funerals.

Norman shook his head, baffled by what he saw. He set the baskets on the ground so he could shake Pete's hand. "No problems that compare with this one," he replied with a nod toward the unfinished house. "How'd this happen? Glenn's message only said that the stove blew up—"

"*Jah*, the fire chief made sure to tell us it was the stove at fault and not Reuben," Pete hastened to put in. "He thinks a valve might've gone bad or the gas line developed a leak. Excuse me—this gal's bringing our lunch!"

As Pete strode toward Molly's rig he reminded himself not to seem too eager—even though his noisy stomach announced his hunger before he said anything.

"Guess I got here just in time—for your lunch, and for whatever show Sadie's putting on," Molly remarked softly. She gazed past Pete to assess the conversation going on outside the house. "I should carry your lasagna inside while it's hot. We can offer the Shanks some lunch, too, of course."

Pete laughed. "I suspect we won't really want to hear—"

"Glenn, *when* will you listen to reason?" Sadie demanded. Her voice rang out as she preceded the others through the doorway. "Now that Dat's burned the house down, are you *finally* ready to move in with us so somebody can keep a closer eye on him?"

Pete scowled. "Let's get in there. I don't like this one bit."

"*Jah*, Reuben's done nothing to deserve that accusation," Molly agreed. "Grab the coffee urn, will you?"

Pete took hold of the urn's two handles and followed her toward the house. She walked fast with her box, not in the mood to tolerate Sadie's bad-mouthing.

"And when will *you* ever listen?" Glenn retorted. "The fire wasn't Dat's fault—"

"And I don't appreciate you talking about me as though I'm deaf—or not standing right in front of you—either, daughter."

Pete's eyes widened as Molly entered the house ahead of him. Reuben and Billy Jay rose from the stools they'd been sitting on while they unwrapped the shingles piled where the studs defined the front room. Ordinarily, Glenn's *dat* didn't buck the current of a conversation— but hadn't he just nailed what Sadie had done?

Sadie bristled, planting her hand on her hip. "We're making this offer for your own *gut*, Dat," she insisted stiffly. "Families should be together, ain't so? We have room for you at our house—"

"We're staying with the Helfings for now," Glenn put in. He gestured at the walls, windows, and the ceiling around them. "And you can see it won't be long before we settle into our new home."

"We're pleased to have them with us, too," Molly put in. She placed her foil-wrapped casserole on the card table Pete had set up and removed a stack of disposable plates from her box. "Yesterday your *dat* glued the labels on more than two hundred bags of noodles for us—and Billy Jay helped him, didn't you, sweetie?"

The little boy's eyes had grown wide with trepidation as he witnessed the conflict around him. He came over to stand by Molly. "Whadaya got in that pan?" he asked shyly. "It smells really *gut*."

Molly's gentle smile brought the sun out from behind the clouds that had darkened the adults' conversation. "Didn't you tell me lasagna was your favorite?"

The boy's eyes lit up and he nodded eagerly.

"How about if you pass everyone a plate from this stack?" Molly suggested as she pointed at them. "Our lasagna's cut and ready to eat. And isn't it better if everyone eats together?"

Sadie let out an unladylike snort. "We didn't come all the way from Indiana to eat your *noodles*, Marietta. I'm trying to—"

"You're talking to Molly," Pete interrupted. "We carpenters have been raising the roof all morning, and it's time to warm up with some hot food and coffee. You folks are welcome to join us."

"Hear, hear," Jude said as he stepped forward. "Quibble if you want, but I need to sit down with some lunch."

"I'm with you, Jude," Reuben said as he accepted a plate from his grandson. "Billy Jay and I have been working all morning, too—because to *these* folks, we still matter and we're still *gut* for something. I don't want to move in with you, Sadie. And that's that."

Sadie's dark eyes shot sparks. "You have no say about— now that you don't have Mamm looking after you—"

"I have Glenn and two Helfings and an entire church district looking after me," Reuben countered. He kept his tone low and steady as he focused on his daughter. "And I *do* have a say, because I'm still the head of the Detweiler family. I didn't put up with your sass when you lived at home, Sadie, and I don't intend to start now."

Pete wanted to applaud. He winked gratefully at Molly as she placed a generous square of lasagna on his plate. "This looks fabulous. *Denki* for your food and your kindness today, Moll."

"*Jah*, this lasagna's great," Jude put in with his mouth full. He'd perched on a wooden stool across the room so he could concentrate on his food rather than the confrontation.

Glenn accepted his plate from Molly, too, before he looked at his sister again. "See how they look after us here? You and Norm better round up the kids and have some lunch. Then we're going to put on the plywood for the roof—"

"So we can install the shingles on Monday," Pete chimed in. "Ordinarily, we have more helpers. But even though we made less progress today, I predict this house'll be ready to move into by Christmas."

Sadie's face had grown pinker with each remark the men around her made, so Pete wasn't surprised when she threw out her arms in exasperation. "Doesn't my opinion count for anything?" she demanded. "I drove all the way out here from Indiana to—"

"Actually, I did the driving," Norman murmured as he gazed longingly at the casserole pan.

"—give my *dat* and brother the help they need, and *this* is the thanks I get?" she continued angrily. "You're eating and going on with your day as though nothing horrible has happened here. And you don't care one *whit* that my childhood home has burned to the ground, along with all my memories and treasures."

Reuben shrugged as he accepted the generous piece of lasagna Molly served him. "Your mother and I told you several times over the years that you should claim your stuff from the attic," he reminded her. "Your brother and the boys and I lost everything, too, you know. But we're moving forward, thankful that Pete and other friends have jumped in to put a new roof over our heads. We'll be *fine*, Sadie. Right where we are. Right where we belong."

"*Jah*, we like it at Molly and Marietta's house," Billy Jay said proudly. "Marietta's helpin' me with my schoolwork—and she lets me work in the noodle factory, too! And Levi stops cryin' when she picks him up, just like she was his *mamm*."

Glenn's face registered an emotion Pete couldn't quite interpret—and Sadie wasn't about to let it pass.

"So that's the way of it, Glenn? You've taken up with the Helfing sisters?" she blurted. "Your wife—and our *mamm*—are hardly cold in the ground and you're cavorting with—"

"Stop right there, Sadie Shank." Molly stood stockstill, pointing her sauce-smeared metal spatula. "We'll have no such talk in front of Billy Jay—"

"And I won't tolerate what you're suggesting about Glenn *or* about the twins," Pete interrupted sternly. "If you can't control your tongue, you should leave right now."

The words had rushed from Pete's mouth before he realized he'd jumped into the Detweilers' fray. For several moments, the only sound was the whistle of the wind outside.

Jude gripped his plate, nodding in support of what the others had said. Billy Jay reached for Molly, and she immediately stooped to wrap her arm around him. Reuben pressed his mouth into a thin, tight line, as though he might never speak to his daughter again.

And poor Norman looked mortified. He gingerly placed his hand on his wife's arm. "It's like I tried to tell you, Sadie," he murmured. "Your family doesn't need your help—"

"When Dat needs more help than you can give him, don't you *dare* come running to me, Glenn!" Sadie blurted, jerking away from her husband's grasp. "Fine. We'll go home. My work here is finished."

With a scalding glare, Sadie stalked out of the house. Her older children had gathered outside the doorway, and with a few cross words, she steered them toward the double buggy at the road.

The babies in the baskets were starting to fuss, so Norman picked them up with a sigh. "I'm sorry, folks," he said beneath their crying. "Sadie's been spinning like a top ever since she heard about the fire. I'm glad you've picked up the pieces so you can move forward."

"*Denki* for checking on us, Norm," Glenn said quietly. "Sorry about the shouting match. I'm as much to blame as my sister, and you got caught in the middle again."

With a resigned shrug, Sadie's husband stepped outside

as his little twins began to cry in earnest. In the kitchen area, Pete and everyone around him relaxed, visibly releasing the tension created by the Detweilers' confrontation.

Reuben, however, put his plate on the card table. He sat down on a pallet of shingles in the far corner, his elbows on his knees. His head dropped forward.

"That whole scene was just *wrong*," he said in a broken voice. "I've prayed for years—and Elva did, too—that God would help us resolve the differences that have separated us from Sadie. But He hasn't answered us yet."

Glenn sat down beside his *dat*, slinging his arm around his stooped, shaking shoulders. "She really did want to help us," he said quietly. "But maybe God's showing us once again that Sadie's way and our way will never be the same."

Reuben's sad sigh filled the room. "At least your *mamm* wasn't here to go through this again."

"But *I'm* here, Dawdi," Billy Jay put in as he, too, sat down beside Reuben. He wrapped his two little hands around his grandfather's weathered, gnarled one. "And we got all these friends watchin' out for us—like angels, ain't so?"

The boy's face lit up with a wonderful idea. "They're just like the angels that came outta the sky when Jesus was born, sayin' '*Fear not!*' to the shepherds!" he continued in a rush. "Coz God doesn't want us to be afraid—or lonely. Coz He's with us all the time, *jah*?"

Pete's throat got so tight he couldn't speak—not that he could top what Billy Jay had just said. In all his years of sliding onto a back pew bench on Sunday mornings because he'd been out too late on Saturday night, he couldn't recall a sermon that had affected him as deeply as this child's simple statement of faith.

"You got that exactly right, Billy Jay," Molly replied quietly. "When we take care of each other the way Jesus intended, He and God are with us. Right here in your new house."

The little boy gazed around the tops of the bare wooden studs as though hoping to see a flicker of movement or a telltale shadow that belonged to God. As the clouds outside shifted and the sun shone through a window, the kitchen area glimmered with a burst of light.

"Wow," the little guy whispered. "He really is here. I can *feel* Him!"

Once again Pete stood in awe of the childlike faith that had totally changed the atmosphere for everyone gathered around. He still felt bad about the Detweilers' family dynamics, yet he sensed that Glenn, Reuben, and Billy Jay were already healing after their unfortunate encounter with Sadie.

He took another bite of his forgotten lasagna. It had almost grown cold, but it was still *so* good, he found himself wishing he lived at the Helfing place again.

It struck him then: during the fracas with Sadie, he'd forgotten to be envious of Glenn—or suspicious of his friend's feelings for Molly. Moments ago, however, Molly had been the first to jump in and put Sadie in her place. Was it because she liked Glenn best?

If she does, maybe I need to change that. I went to Molly's defense, too, after all—and it was a perfectly natural thing to do. If Glenn is winning Molly over, it's because I'm allowing him to.

Noting that Jude had finished his lunch and Glenn was

nearly ready to return to work, Pete jammed another forkful of lasagna into his mouth. He hated to rush through such a wonderful meal, but now that they weren't moving around he was starting to feel cold in the un-heated house—and Molly had to be getting chilly, as well.

"I—I was surprised to see you delivering lunch today, Molly, since these December Saturdays must be really busy at your Marketplace store," he remarked, scraping the last bite from his plate. As another realization dawned on him, Pete glanced at Glenn, too. "And who's keeping your wood shop open? This is a prime time to be selling your wooden toys, ain't so?"

Glenn licked the last trace of tomato sauce from his fork. "Bishop Jeremiah stepped in for me, because I really wanted to be working on our new house. And his *mamm* was kind enough to watch baby Levi today so the twins could be at The Marketplace. Gotta love those Shetlers," he added with a smile for Jude.

"And when Lydianne said she'd rather help Marietta in our shop than cover her lunch shift for you fellows today, I took her up on her offer," Molly explained. "I'll be going over to The Marketplace from here, so—"

"Can I go, too?" Billy Jay pleaded, hopping up from the pallet. "I could help ya sell noodles!"

Molly nodded. "It would probably be a *gut* idea for you to get in out of the cold—and how about you, Reuben? I bet Martin and Gabe would welcome your help today."

"Or they'll at least have a comfortable place for you to sit—and maybe take a nap," Glenn teased gently. "It's no secret that Martin sneaks a few winks back in the corner. You two guys have been a great help to us today, so you deserve a break."

"Yay! Me and you, Dawdi," Billy Jay said, hopping from one foot to the other. "We can see all those folks at The Marketplace and drink some of Jo's spiced cider, *jah*?"

Reuben rose slowly from the stack of shingles, wincing because his legs had stiffened. "You talked me into it."

A short while later, Pete followed Jude and Glenn up the ladder to start closing in the roof. It felt good to see such progress—especially considering Sadie's unanticipated interruption. Even more interesting, however, was the way Molly, Reuben, and little Billy Jay walked toward her rig, nodding and talking among themselves.

They look like a family.

Pete blinked. If he was to win Molly's affection, Glenn wasn't his only competition, was he? A bright, eager little boy and a needy widower seemed to be capturing her heart without any effort at all . . .

Chapter 10

Jo stepped out of her bakery to tape a sign to the entry post. She was amazed at the noise level in the commons area as shoppers passed from store to store with their bulging sacks and wide smiles. Never in her wildest dreams had she envisioned such a crowd at The Marketplace—and it was only December seventh, the first Saturday of the month.

"Sold out?" an English woman read from behind her. "But I wanted to buy some of those adorable decorated cookies I've seen other folks carrying around."

Jo smiled apologetically. "I baked all week to prepare for today's crowd, but I had no idea how many folks would be here," she said. "I'm really sorry to disappoint you—"

"Would you take an order? I'm hosting a Christmas party next Saturday evening," the lady said eagerly. "A big tray of your cookies and one of those Christmas trees I saw—made of pineapple cream cheese rolls—would be perfect! I'll even pay you for it right now!"

Jo blinked. Knowing she'd be gone for a day and a half this week made her hesitate, but the customer's pleading expression won out. "Okay, let's write up an order, and

I'll have those items wrapped and ready for you when you get here next Saturday."

"Oh, thank you! Thank you!"

A few minutes—and more than a hundred dollars—later, Jo was staring at the list of specific decorated cookies the lady had rattled off, as well as the filled sweet rolls baked in the shape of a Christmas tree, and an entire sheet cake pan of brownies topped with crushed peppermints. Jo would have to ask Michael to start back from Queen City at the crack of dawn on Tuesday so she'd have all afternoon to start baking for next Saturday's crush of customers—

"That's a mighty sparkly smile on your face, Miss Jo, considering that you've run out of goodies to sell. What's *really* on your mind?"

Jo chuckled at Lydianne Christner, who was gazing at the empty shelves of her bakery cases. These days, as Lydianne anticipated her marriage to Bishop Jeremiah— and moving into a completely remodeled home—the pretty blonde sported a very sparkly smile, too. "Well, truth be told—"

"Hold up! I want to hear *this*!" Molly peered through the slatted divider that separated the bakery from the noodle shop. "Marietta and I have seen that grin on your face, too, Jo. There's something you're not telling us, ain't so?"

"A secret? I can't miss out on *this*!" Regina Flaud chimed in from the furniture shop on the other side of the bakery.

Before she could decide whether to respond or to keep her news to herself for fear of jinxing her trip to Queen City, Jo found herself surrounded by three of her closest friends. And Marietta was watching eagerly from between the slats of the noodle shop's divider, as well.

Jo shrugged, feigning ignorance. "I don't know what you think you've seen—"

"Hey, this is *us* you're talking to, Miss Fussner!" Molly teased. "Stall all you want, but we know something's going on—right, girls?"

"Oh, *jah*," redheaded Regina replied, playfully tugging at Jo's sleeve. "I've been embroidering my linens here for the past few Saturdays, sitting where I have a direct view into Jo's bakery. She's got something a lot more fun than *baking* on her mind, if you ask me."

Jo's cheeks blazed. Was she really so easy to read? "All right, so Michael—"

"Aha!"

"He's coming out of his shell?"

"High time he did something besides gawk at you!"

Jo's mouth dropped open. Apparently her friends had seen this coming—and wasn't it nice to hear their excitement? Her mother had nothing but discouraging words about Jo's desire to go to Queen City.

The glow on her face felt fragile yet so appropriate. Wouldn't any woman be happy to catch Michael's eye? "The Wengerds have invited Mamm and me to their nursery—to see the thousands of poinsettias blooming in their greenhouses," she added quickly. "And I—I said I'd do it, even though Mamm refuses to make the trip."

"You *go*, girl!" Molly blurted, clapping her hand on Jo's back.

"Michael's such a nice guy," Regina put in. "Oh, but this is *gut* news, Jo."

"When are you going?" Lydianne asked eagerly. "I bet that'll be quite a sight, seeing all those poinsettias—"

"As though she'll be looking at the flowers," Marietta teased from the noodle shop.

As her circle of friends laughed, Jo felt so light and happy, she wasn't sure her feet were still on the floor. "We'll leave first thing tomorrow," she replied in a rush. "This evening I'll have to pack—I just wish I had some newer dresses—and I'm sure Mamm'll lecture me again about how I shouldn't fall for Michael's attention—"

"Why not?" Lydianne broke in. "The Wengerds are two of the nicest men I know."

"Just because your *mamm*'s a stay-at-home doesn't mean you have to be!" Regina assured her. "If Nelson's in on the invitation, he's trying to get your mother out for some fun, as well, right?"

Jo sighed. "*Fun?* Do you suppose Mamm even knows the meaning of that word?" she asked softly. "She believes the Wengerds—men in general—say whatever it takes to get a gal to hitch up with them, and after the wedding it's all downhill. And it's a cruel joke from the beginning, the way she tells it."

Her friends' eyebrows rose. Each of their dear faces took on a puzzled expression.

"Any idea where that attitude came from?" Lydianne asked. "I didn't know your *dat* very well, but I never got the idea that he'd trapped your *mamm*."

"Me, neither," Molly put in with a shake of her head.

Embarrassed to have her friends dissecting her parents' marriage, Jo shrugged. "I don't know," she whispered. "But when Mamm insinuated that the Wengerds were up to no *gut*—while they were sitting right there at the dinner table with us—I wanted to disappear through a crack in the floor."

Her friends sighed sympathetically.

"Well, I'm glad you spoke up for yourself," Regina murmured. "And I hope you have a wonderful-*gut* time!"

"*Jah*, that's the important thing," Molly agreed. "Maybe—if you and Michael hit it off during your visit—you'll prove your *mamm*'s got it all wrong."

"We're with you a hundred and ten percent, Jo!" Marietta said from the divider. "If nothing else, it'll be nice to visit another town and enjoy the pretty drive between here and Queen City."

"It'll give you two some time to really talk," Lydianne put in. "You're both so busy here on Saturdays—and your parents are always within earshot at your house. Maybe this'll be the chance to break out of that pattern, just you and Michael."

Jo hoped they were right. And wasn't it better to believe the positive things her friends were saying than to assume her *mamm*'s dire predictions would come true?

"*Denki* for your thoughts," Jo said. "I'll need all the prayers I can get if this visit's to work any Christmas magic for Michael and me."

"*Christmas magic*," Regina echoed with a grin. "Hold that thought, Jo!"

By the time Glenn drove into the stable at the Helfing place, it was nearly six thirty. He'd worked past dark, because the huge lights their Mennonite friends had provided had lit up the house site like daylight, and he hadn't felt right about stopping work before Pete and

Jude. As they'd hoped, they'd gotten the roof completely covered with boards. While his friends had picked up their tools, Glenn had loaded a few bales of hay and a bag of feed into his rig so he wouldn't deplete the twins' winter supply for their horses.

He was cold and bone-tired and hungry. Everything took longer than he wanted it to, so he hurried—not wanting to make supper any later than he already had. When Glenn stumbled over a stone that stuck up in the Helfings' uneven, unfamiliar walkway, he cried out in frustration as he hit the ground.

For a few moments he lay there in the darkness, catching his breath. He felt stupid for falling, and his palm stung where he'd scraped it on a rough stone—and he was lucky he hadn't banged his face on the walkway and knocked out a tooth.

But Glenn didn't feel lucky. He was exhausted. His thumb throbbed because his hands had gotten too cold up on the roof and he'd banged it with his hammer. He wanted to curl up in a ball and let the world leave him behind—at least until morning.

But he had two sons and a father to look after. He couldn't burden Marietta and Molly with caring for his family, because he was already too deeply indebted to them.

So he got up. He took a deep breath. And somehow he convinced himself he could make it through the evening until it was time to collapse in bed, hopefully to sleep. As Glenn approached the back door, he prepared himself for the tongue-lashing he deserved because he'd arrived so late and—

When he stepped into the mudroom, however, a savory

aroma wafted around him. The light from the kitchen soothed him, and the furnace's warmth eased the tension he'd been holding in his shoulders. As Glenn removed his coat, he saw that the table was set for five—shiny white plates on a blue gingham tablecloth, with the silverware neatly arranged at each setting.

Such simple things, yet they'd been missing from his life, because with their women gone, he and Dat hadn't bothered with such niceties.

"Hey there, Glenn!" Molly said as she entered the kitchen. "Bet you fellows got a lot done on your—oh, what happened to your hand?"

Glenn looked at his stinging palm as though it belonged on someone else's body. He'd scraped it worse than he'd thought—but he wasn't about to admit that he'd fallen on the walkway. Before he had to conjure up a story, however, Molly joined him in the mudroom and pointed at the big sink.

"You'll want to scrub that wound," she suggested, holding up a bar of soap. "And a splash of this peroxide will sting like the dickens, but it'll flush out the grit—and keep the cut from getting infected. Take your time. Marietta's coaching Billy Jay on his part in the school's Christmas Eve program."

Glenn blinked. Molly was being so patient with him. Marietta was working with his son—something he'd had precious little time to do since Dorcas and Mamm had passed. And supper smelled so heavenly, his mouth was watering.

He swallowed hard. "*Denki*, Molly. You girls are *angels*."

Molly chuckled. "No, Billy Jay is the angel—at least in the school program. My sister and I are just ordinary, everyday women getting from one day to the next, doing what needs to be done."

As he turned on the faucet, Glenn nearly wept with the gratitude that welled up inside him. He knew such an emotional upheaval came from being exhausted and overwhelmed, yet it also occurred to him that he hadn't felt so thankful in a very long time.

Maybe that's part of my problem. Maybe I've been so focused on my losses, I haven't noticed the gifts that God—and my friends—have given me every single day. In sunshine or shadow.

When he'd dried his hands, he poured some peroxide directly onto his scraped palm. It *did* sting, but as the white foam appeared in the tiny lines of his irritated skin, Glenn felt a cleansing—a sense that impurities were indeed being released.

He blotted his palm with the towel and passed through the twins' kitchen, zeroing in on the little-boy voice in the front room. Glenn stopped in the doorway, mesmerized.

Marietta sat on the sofa, cradling Levi in the crook of her arm as she held a bottle of goat milk to his lips. Beside her, Billy Jay lay stretched out on the rest of the couch with his head on its arm and his sock-covered feet on her leg. His eyes were closed in concentration as he spoke in a halting voice.

"'And there were in the same country . . . shepherds abiding in the field, keeping watch over their flock by night.'"

"*Jah*, you've got the words right," Marietta remarked with a nod. "Now say them again, and make *shepherds* the most important word. And then tell me who showed up and scared them."

Billy Jay clapped his hands to his head, straining with the effort of memorization. Glenn knew his boy's pain: he vividly recalled having to learn passages of Scripture for the Christmas Eve program, and he'd never been good at it.

"'And there were in the same country *shepherds* abiding in the field, keeping watch over their flock by night,'" Billy Jay repeated. "'And lo, the angel of the Lord came upon them, and' . . . um—"

"'The glory of the Lord,'" Marietta prompted softly.

"Oh, *jah*—'the glory of the Lord shone round about them: and they were so afraid!'"

"'They were *sore* afraid,'" she corrected gently. "That's Bible talk, saying the shepherds were scared to death, because an angel showed up and the sky got bright, and the shepherds had no idea what was going on!"

"This is makin' my brains wanna spill out of my head," the boy said with a loud sigh.

"Put that whole section together for me, and we'll quit for today. You're doing a really fine job, Billy Jay. You've got this, sweetie."

Glenn felt a whole new sense of admiration for Marietta Helfing. He'd always known her to be patient and kind, yet he'd never figured her for a woman who'd spend countless hours helping a child learn Christmas Scripture—and then recite it as though it told the world's most important story, rather than just blurting out the words to get them said.

Glenn noticed that Dat was tilted back in the recliner, snoozing. And wasn't that a fine sign, that he felt so comfortable in this home? Before Billy Jay caught sight of him, Glenn stepped back into the kitchen.

Molly was pulling a blue enamel roaster out of the oven. When she opened it, a big meat loaf gave off a puff of beef-scented steam. Carrots, potatoes, and onions were arranged around it, baked to simple perfection.

"I hope I didn't poke my nose where it didn't belong today, shutting down your sister," she remarked. "What she was hinting at was so—so ridiculous—"

"Why *wouldn't* you shut her up?" he interrupted wearily. "Sadie was way out of line, and you and Pete were just calling it like you saw it. I—I'm sorry you got sucked into our ongoing drama."

"I'm sorry you folks even *have* that drama," Molly replied without missing a beat. "That scene with Sadie really wore your *dat* down. At The Marketplace this afternoon, he mostly sat at one of the tables in the commons and stared at all the customers. Didn't say two words—not even after Martin joined him."

"Well, at least he's relaxed now," Glenn remarked. "*Denki* for taking him and Billy Jay over there, out of the cold."

"Oh, we put your boy to work," Molly said with a laugh. "He carried bags of noodles from the storeroom to replenish the shelves when they got low—and that happened a lot today! He got pretty excited when we sold out."

"I should say so." Glenn could picture the scene as she described it. "I don't suppose you had a chance to see how things were going at my wood shop."

"We sent Billy Jay over for a report," she said matter-of-factly. Glancing around the countertop, cluttered with pot holders and cooking utensils, she snatched up a piece of paper. "The bishop and Lydianne sent this tally back with him."

Glenn skimmed Jeremiah's precise printing, his eyes widening. "They had a great day," he murmured. "If they sold six birch rocking chairs and all these toys, I need to get cracking to restock my store before next Saturday," he said in a rising voice.

Then he sighed. "But I ought to be helping at the house, because Pete and the other guys shouldn't do all the work when it's not even their—"

"They'll understand if you take time to work for your living, Glenn." Molly held his gaze with her sincere green eyes. "If Jude had an auction to call, he'd be in the sale barn rather than working on your house. And Pete, well— you're doing everyone a favor, keeping him busy building your new place. From what I've heard, Margaret's probably enjoying a break from hearing noisy power tools in the house."

Glenn wasn't sure he believed that, but he accepted it as Molly's way of reassuring him. Wasn't it wonderful that she wanted him to feel better about how he spent his time, now that he was homeless and wifeless and motherless?

He sat down at the table, careful not to mess up the place setting in front of him or the clean, crisp tablecloth. As he reread the bishop's account of all the items they'd sold today, Glenn felt his tension easing away.

His sister had expressed her opinion, but she hadn't *won*. Dat had stood up to Sadie—sounding perfectly focused and rational—and his friends had supported his wish to remain in Morning Star.

Maybe it hadn't been such a horrible day after all.

"Dat! You're home!"

When Billy Jay scrambled across the room and into

his lap, Glenn held him close, inhaling his boy smell and feeling rejuvenated by his restless energy.

At that moment, Glenn *did* feel at home. He didn't want to analyze the emotions behind those words. He just accepted the way Billy Jay had said them so naturally, as though his son knew they were true.

Chapter 11

Pete rose from the breakfast table, suppressing a sigh: visiting Sundays drove him nuts. Now that he was living with the bishop, he couldn't slip out in his truck to do things—or drive around with Riley for the fun of it—as he had when he'd bunked in the Helfings' *dawdi haus*. He and his uncle and grandmother had eaten in a kitchen that still resembled the aftermath of a tornado, because he'd spent his week at the Detweiler place. Even though the premade cabinets Lydianne had chosen awaited him in the barn, there would be no fudging on the no-work rule. Uncle Jeremiah took the Sabbath seriously.

Trying not to appear bored out of his mind, Pete went to the picture window in the front room. As he absently scratched Riley's head, he gazed out over the snow-covered fields. He prayed for a snowstorm so he'd have an excuse to go out and plow roads—even if his uncle made him hitch the V blade to the horse rather than use the new blade on his truck.

At the sight of a rig coming up the lane, he brightened. "Company's coming," he called out.

"*Jah*, that would be Glenn," Uncle Jeremiah remarked

as he joined Pete at the window. "I suggested he come over for a counseling session here, where the rest of his family and the Helfing twins couldn't listen in. He's got a lot on his mind these days."

"He does," Pete agreed. "Ask him about Sadie's visit yesterday. It wasn't pretty when she showed up at the construction site and insisted—again—that he pack up his family and move out to Indiana."

"Oh, my. I hadn't heard about that."

"I probably should've mentioned it last night," Pete murmured as Detweiler's rig stopped in front of the house. "I'll head upstairs so you and Glenn can talk in private. Come on, Riley—let's go, boy."

As he and his golden retriever climbed the steps, Pete fought a grin. The spare bedroom next to his, where Mammi did her sewing, was directly above his uncle's office. If he situated himself near the heat grate in the floor, he'd be able to hear most of what his uncle and Detweiler talked about—and as long as he sat absolutely still and quiet, no one would be the wiser.

It wasn't an honorable way to pass the time, but it was better than pacing like a caged tiger—or pretending to read his Bible. And it was a way to catch any hints that Detweiler was developing a serious crush on Molly.

"You've got to be totally quiet, Riley," Pete warned as he entered the sewing room. He winced when a floorboard creaked beneath his weight. The *click-click-click* of his dog's claws was amplified by his somewhat guilty conscience.

As Pete stooped low to sit against the bedroom's back wall, under the extended lid of Mammi's sewing machine cabinet, he told himself that he should leave before his uncle and Glenn began their session. Most folks swore Bishop Jeremiah had an extra set of ears and eyes, because during church, he could hear the rattle of a candy wrapper from across a large room or spot somebody's head drifting down before they jerked awake. Pete's chances of getting caught ran pretty high.

But he sat on the slick floor anyway, next to the black metal floor grate with openings that allowed heat to rise from downstairs. It wasn't the most comfortable place to sit, because the exterior wall felt slightly cold against his back and the floor was hard—and the lid of Mammi's sewing machine cabinet extended over the top of his head, forcing him to sit hunched over.

His grandmother was making shirts for him and Jeremiah from the same bolt of purple fabric she'd bought to make herself a new dress—and some of the cutout pieces hung over the edge of the lid. Pete had been careful not to bump them with his head, because if Mammi found them in disarray she would immediately suspect someone had been snooping where he didn't belong.

When he heard voices in his uncle's office, Pete gestured for Riley to lie down. He placed a finger over his lips, looking his dog directly in the eye.

"How's it going for your family at the Helfing place, Glenn?" Jeremiah inquired.

During a slight pause, Pete imagined Detweiler taking the armchair in front of his uncle's desk while the bishop lowered himself into his wooden swivel chair—and a familiar *creak* confirmed his supposition.

"What a blessing it is to be there," Glenn replied. "Molly and Marietta have taken us in like family—"

Pete's eyebrows rose. Hadn't he noticed that Molly, Reuben, and Billy Jay seemed emotionally connected as they'd left the construction site yesterday?

"—and talk about food!" Detweiler continued with a lilt in his voice. "Molly made a big meat loaf with potatoes and vegetables last night. And when I got home, Marietta was feeding Levi on the couch while she helped Billy Jay learn his passage for the Christmas Eve program."

When you got home? Pete counted on his fingers to determine that Glenn had been at the twins' place only four days, yet already he considered himself a member of the household. And the picture of domestic bliss Glenn had painted of Molly's dinner, along with Marietta taking up where Dorcas had left off with the boys, sent a bolt of envy through him. When Pete had lived at the Helfing place, Molly's cooking had been hit-or-miss, and Marietta had hardly noticed his presence.

That's because I stayed in the dawdi haus. *The Detweiler tribe is getting special attention because the twins feel sorry for Reuben and the boys.*

"The Helfings are kindhearted souls," Jeremiah agreed. "They were hesitant to have Pete and Riley around at first, but it came to the point that they spoiled him, too. Truth be told, I think they'd have kept Riley after Pete came here to live."

Pete's brow furrowed—and when the dog perked up at the sound of his name, he quickly wrapped his hand around Riley's muzzle.

So his uncle thought the twins had *spoiled* him? Jeremiah was obviously unaware of Molly's merciless teasing—and he'd forgotten about all the repair work Pete had done around the Helfing farm, too, not to mention the way he'd expanded their noodle factory.

Glenn laughed out loud. He thought it was *funny* that Molly and Marietta had liked his rambunctious dog more than they'd enjoyed Pete's company.

"*Jah,* Riley's a handful," Glenn remarked. "He really gave my sister the what-for when she showed up at the house yesterday. Not that she didn't deserve it."

"Sadie came to Morning Star?"

"*Jah*, and I told her straight-out she'd made the trip for nothing." Detweiler's voice was rising with his irritation. "Because we've lost the house—and she immediately blamed Dat for the fire—she again insisted that it's time we joined her out in Indiana.

"Dat stood up to her, too," Glenn continued proudly. "Told Sadie he was still the head of the family, and he wasn't taking any of her guff. But Molly! *She* was having no part of my sister's foolishness, either."

Pete stiffened. Even through the floor grate, Glenn's admiration for Molly rang like a church bell.

"Molly? Why was she involved in your conversation?" Jeremiah's careful tone suggested the concern of a bishop for a member of his congregation, but Pete sensed he was fishing for deeper information. And Pete was *very* interested in Glenn's response.

Detweiler let out an exasperated sigh. "Sadie suggested that because I'm staying at the twins' place, I surely must be engaging in *hanky-panky*—with both of them," he added disgustedly. "I thought Molly was going to whack my sister with her spatula—and I would've cheered her on. What a woman!"

Glenn's enthusiastic remark made Pete jerk to attention—and as his head struck the lid of the sewing machine, he cussed loudly. Purple fabric pieces flew into the air, and Riley sprang from the floor. Breaking free of Pete's grip, the dog barked with gleeful abandon, spinning in excited circles until he dashed out of the sewing room and down the steps.

Pete closed his eyes as guilt dropped like a bomb. Even if Glenn hadn't been aware of the grate in the office ceiling, he and Uncle Jeremiah had caught Pete red-handed. The bishop would insist that his errant nephew apologize, too.

Way to go, Shetler. What are you, about ten? That was a stunt like Billy Jay would've pulled. So now when Detweiler tells Molly what I've done, she'll be even more impressed with my maturity and sense of responsibility.

With a sigh and a throbbing head, Pete rose from the floor. After he placed Mammi's fabric pieces back on her sewing machine, he started for the stairway. No matter how contritely he apologized to Glenn and Uncle Jeremiah, words weren't going to adequately express his regret.

There's no explaining stupidity. Anything I say will only dig me into a deeper hole.

When he got downstairs, Pete drew in a deep breath. Mammi peered out the kitchen door, ready to quiz him about the ruckus—but his taut expression silenced her. She was well aware of his tendency to act first and think later, so she stood with one eyebrow raised as Pete approached his uncle's office.

Seated behind his desk, Uncle Jeremiah met Pete's gaze with dark brown eyes that had always pinpointed people's wayward tendencies. He didn't say a word.

Glenn appeared startled—and wary—when he looked over his shoulder at Pete, who'd paused in the doorway.

"I'm sorry I disrupted your session," Pete blurted. "Eavesdropping on your conversation was a thoughtless, juvenile thing to do. Please forgive me."

Detweiler's dark eyebrows rose, as though he'd never expected to hear a plea for forgiveness coming from the likes of Pete. Or maybe he still didn't know about the heat grate.

Uncle Jeremiah, however, seemed well aware that Pete had been hovering above his office the whole time. "If you're trying to keep tabs on Molly now that you don't live at the Helfing place," he said with a perfectly straight face, "why not go visit her? You could do that right now, for instance, while Glenn's speaking with me."

The bishop might as well have scorched Pete's cheeks with a welding torch.

Pete pivoted, rushing toward the mudroom to grab his coat. Riley shot out the door with him, racing in circles through the snow as Pete fumbled his keys from his pocket. As soon as the truck door was open, Riley hopped up to take his place on the passenger side, leaving the driver's seat wet with paw prints. He gazed at Pete with his usual goofy grin, ready to ride.

Pete cranked the ignition. He envied his dog's ability to enjoy relationships without getting entangled in the social niceties—or the second-guessing that went with getting closer to the first woman he'd taken an interest in for a while.

Am I keeping tabs on Molly because I'm afraid Glenn will win her away from me? If he wasn't in the picture— or staying in her home—would I be as interested in her?

Pete let out a mirthless laugh. *She's exactly like Detweiler described her: What a woman!*

He pounded the steering wheel. It had been truly stupid—not to mention insensitive—to eavesdrop on a confidential counseling session. It was no way to treat a longtime friend, either. And when Molly found out what he'd done, she'd know beyond the shadow of a doubt that Pete Shetler was a loser.

As he grabbed the gearshift, another reality smacked him like the cold air that shot from the vents: if he was trying to prove himself to Molly—to show her that he'd become worthy of her notice—driving his pickup was the *last* thing he should do. Amish men didn't ride in English motorized vehicles on Sunday . . . much less own them.

Detweiler's horse-drawn rig was hitched to the railing on the side of Uncle Jeremiah's house. Detweiler wore broadfall trousers, dark shirts, and a black felt hat—and his face was framed in a beard that matched his raven-black hair, befitting a married man who'd long ago taken his vows to the church. Detweiler might be grieving his many recent losses, but he still came out way ahead on the eligibility scale with which Molly would measure potential mates.

For several seconds Pete stared out the windshield, now fogged by Riley's breath. He switched off the engine.

"Riley, we're in deep doo-doo," he muttered. "How are we gonna dig ourselves out?"

The dog yipped, wondering why they weren't getting anywhere.

And didn't that paint an accurate picture of his current situation? Pete saw himself in the wrong place, doing the wrong thing, when he was old enough to know better— whether that meant the stunt he'd just pulled in Mammi's sewing room or automatically heading to his truck to drive away from the mess he'd made instead of facing it head-on.

Pete's sigh fogged the windshield even more. "If Molly's going to take me seriously, I'll have to join the church," he said quietly.

Riley barked impatiently, as though Pete's admission hadn't gone far enough.

"And I'll have to ditch these jeans and my plaid flannel shirts."

The dog woofed more insistently, pawing the dashboard.

Pete smiled glumly at the golden, rubbing the dog's neck. "Yeah, you're right. I'll have to sell this truck, too. I'll have to invest in a buggy so I'll look like a responsible family man—like Detweiler, except blond."

Riley let out a bark that morphed into a howl.

"Okay, you're right. I'll have to be *better* than Glenn," Pete amended. "But how can I pull *that* off? He's got two cute little boys and a *dat* who needs some extra love. Who ever thought that having a family would make him such a chick magnet? How can I possibly compete with—"

Exasperated, the dog pawed Pete's elbow, growling in that playful way that seemed to imitate speech. Riley was eager to hightail it down the highway, but the answer to Pete's predicament suddenly came to him, plain as day.

"I've got *you*, Riley!" he crowed. "Molly likes you better than me, so we've got to work that to our advantage. You've been trying to tell me that all along, and I've finally caught on."

Riley, ever the optimist, cocked his head expectantly at Pete's brighter tone of voice.

Rather than falling for his dog's plea for a truck ride, however, Pete pocketed his keys and opened the door. "Yep, that's it. You're going to be my front man, Riley. Because we all know—especially Molly—that you're way smarter than I am about these things."

Pete slid to the ground and held the door open, not surprised that his dog remained in the cab for a few moments before hopping down into the snow with a reluctant sigh.

"We also have to remember that Glenn's working on his house—feathering his nest," Pete remarked as he started toward the back door of his uncle's home. "That's quite a nice Christmas gift he can entice Molly with, so we have to come up with something she'll think is even more wonderful. I should be working on it—should've started on it weeks ago."

Riley sat down in the snowy yard, gazing directly at Pete. It was a stalling tactic; the dog was hoping for a change of mind that would lead to the ride he wanted.

"You're right again, boy," Pete said as he continued toward the mudroom. "I need to sit my butt down—just like you!—and get on with this gift planning. And—and I know just what I should do! Why didn't I think of this before?"

With a resigned *woof*, Riley followed him inside.

When Mammi sent him a questioning glance from her seat on the sofa, Pete waved at her. He took the stairs two at a time—heading for his own room—and grabbed a pencil and the large tablet of paper he used for sketching his building projects. Leaning against the headboard of his bed, Pete drew the Helfings' kitchen from memory.

"How many times have the twins mentioned things that needed fixing?" he murmured as his pencil danced across the page. "That room needs a total renovation—like I'm giving Lydianne and Mammi. I could spruce up a few other rooms, too, and build some shelves in their storage areas, and make their whole house a lot more efficient, because—"

Pete grinned at Riley, who'd curled up on the floor for a nap. "Because the twins *love* that place, and they hate to be apart, so I'll be giving them exactly what they want! It's a better offer than Glenn's, because the Helfing sisters will still be together after Molly and I get hitched."

Molly's name made Riley raise his head in the hope that they'd go over to see her. But Pete focused again on his sketches.

"This is working on the Sabbath, you know," he confessed under his breath. "But under the circumstances, it's the lesser of several evils, ain't so? Since I haven't yet taken my vows to join the church—but I've come to see the wisdom of doing that—we'll hope God considers this as an improvement in my attitude."

Chapter 12

As Jo stepped out of the café ahead of Michael and his *dat* on Sunday morning, the sun made the snow-covered hills around them glisten like a million tiny diamonds. After a hearty breakfast in the family-owned restaurant where the Wengerds often stopped on their way back to Queen City, she inhaled the crisp winter air. She would never forget her mother's words as she'd carried her suitcase to the Wengerds' rig, but pancakes, sausages, and fried apples had settled some of the tension of her departure.

So that's the way of it? You're taking up with the Wengerds and leaving me behind? You'll face some serious consequences for this, daughter.

The men had been waiting for her at their buggy, so Jo hadn't lingered to make amends with her mother—because short of staying home, there was no possibility of that. She'd clambered into the buggy ahead of Michael and Nelson, grateful that she could gaze out over the dark countryside for several miles without her tears being so obvious.

Had her companions overheard Mamm's remarks? Jo

was too mortified—too upset—to ask them. She was grateful that they'd kept the conversation light and hadn't tried to console her or delve into the reasons behind her mother's veiled threat.

Once again Jo entered the rig ahead of the men and settled into her spot against its far side. She felt strange riding with someone other than her mother or her *maidel* friends, and she hoped that long-legged Michael didn't feel cramped sitting between her and his *dat*. She was more aware than ever that he was a string bean of a fellow, while she was built wide, with more padding than was fashionable.

As the light of early morning filled the rig, however, Michael's shy smile reassured her. He seemed as nervous as she was, yet didn't it feel wonderful to be sitting so close to him? His gray-blue eyes were wider than usual, as though he enjoyed the way the rig's rocking brought them into constant contact—more than was socially acceptable for a couple that wasn't courting yet.

"Not a lot farther now," Nelson remarked as he urged the horse up to speed. "From here, the countryside gets hillier, so on this narrow two-lane road we have to be more careful about cars popping up behind us too quickly."

Michael sighed. "That's how Mamm died. I think about it every time we get to this leg of the trip."

As Jo's heart shot up into her throat, she grasped his hand. "I'm so sorry," she whispered.

"Unfortunately, English traffic is a part of Plain life," Nelson put in softly. "The way we understand it, the truck that crashed into Verna's rig came over the hill so fast that neither driver had time to react. At least we have the small comfort of knowing that she died immediately, without suffering."

Ah, but the living always suffer longer than the dead.

Nodding, Jo kept her remarks about death and suffering to herself. It was enough that Michael was still clasping her hand and didn't seem inclined to let it go.

Jo swallowed hard. After so many months of daydreaming about handsome, gentle Michael, it was a thrill to be holding his hand—and even better, he wasn't hiding the connection from his *dat*. Would Nelson set rules for their behavior during her visit? Would he watch them every moment so he could report back to Mamm that they hadn't spent any time unchaperoned?

"Over the top of this next hill—where the warning sign about horse-drawn vehicles is—was where Verna left us," Nelson remarked quietly. "Michael and I always observe a few moments of silence in her memory when we reach that spot, and we pray to be spared the same fate. We don't talk again until we're far enough beyond the hill to be relatively safe."

The men's sentiment brought tears to Jo's eyes. The atmosphere inside the rig grew still as the horse pulled them through the zone where the Wengerds' wife and mother had passed, and she bowed her head in respect. What a horrible way to leave this earthly life—without getting to say any sort of goodbye. After several more seconds of the *clip-clop, clip-clop* of the horse's hooves on the blacktop being the only sound breaking the silence, the Wengerds relaxed.

"Just another couple of miles," Michael remarked, pointing ahead of them. "Once we're around the next curve, you'll see the back part of our property and some of the greenhouses."

Hundreds of times Jo had ridden through the Missouri countryside, now covered with snow, yet the moment she caught sight of the semicylindrical structures with their metal framework and translucent, rounded sides, her heart quickened. A large white road sign with deep green lettering caught her eye.

WELCOME TO WENGERD NURSERY
MAIN ENTRANCE ¼ MILE

"This looks much larger than the garden centers out our way," she remarked. "I bet you keep a lot of local folks employed during the spring and summer."

"And fall, right through December," Michael added proudly. "Our mums and pumpkins are a big draw—"

"And we kept most of our employees on longer this year, tending the expanded crop of poinsettias," Nelson put in. "Come January, they'll get some time off."

"But we anticipate so much more business at The Marketplace this spring, we'll start more seedlings in February," Michael finished with a smile. "And we have you to thank for that, Jo. Renovating that old stable was your idea, ain't so?"

Jo's cheeks flushed with his compliment. Her whole being felt light and alive when he squeezed her hand. "My four *maidel* friends had a hand in that, too," she pointed out. "And if Bishop Jeremiah hadn't taken up the reins and driven the idea home with our church leaders, The Marketplace wouldn't exist."

"The way Jeremiah tells it, *you* were the woman who envisioned possibilities where everyone else saw a dilapidated stable," Nelson said. "It's highly unusual for a woman to talk up such an enterprise and then do the grunt work required to bring it to fruition."

Jo shrugged. "Maybe I'm just odd—and too outspoken by half," she blurted out.

Michael's blue-eyed gaze intensified as the rig turned off the county highway and onto the snow-packed lane that led to the nursery showroom.

"Phooey on that," he said under his breath. "You have every reason to claim your accomplishments, Jo. It's a real balancing act to spearhead such a successful business venture while keeping your humility intact. Don't let anyone—especially not your *mamm*—tell you any different."

Jo was speechless. The intensity of Michael's words, coupled with the way his clear gray-blue eyes focused on her, left her unable to think—much less voice any sort of reply for several moments.

"You fellows are very nice to say such things," she finally murmured. "But you're also businessmen who saw an opportunity, and you took it up and ran with it. I can't think you'd still be making the weekly trip to Morning Star—much less expanding your nursery to such an extent—if your profits didn't justify it."

Michael and his *dat* exchanged a smile that suggested they'd discussed this topic many times . . . and it also held a private meaning she couldn't interpret.

"Once again you're proving your own wisdom when it comes to managing The Marketplace, Jo," Nelson remarked as he brought the horse to a halt between the nursery showroom and a modest white house. "How about if I unload the luggage while you two look at the poinsettias? Always feels *gut* to stretch your legs after the morning's ride."

Michael's *dat* stepped down from the rig and went around to the back of it. Michael slid out next and then reached up as though he might grasp Jo around the waist to lift her down.

Startled—and concerned that he might crumple beneath her weight—Jo quickly grabbed one of his hands, allowing him to steady her as she stepped down. The *last* thing she wanted was to begin her visit by having Michael figure out just how much heavier she was than he—a fact that would occur to him soon enough. She wanted to enjoy as much time with him as possible before he backed away from a potential romantic relationship with a woman of her height and size.

Michael's shy smile reassured her. Jo suspected he wasn't any more accomplished at impressing potential partners than she was. It was comforting to believe he hadn't left a string of broken hearts in his wake as he'd matured into his late twenties. Her mother's accusation that he was stringing her along simply didn't fit the Michael Wengerd who was gesturing toward the lane that led to their greenhouses.

"These units are where we grow our hothouse tomatoes," he remarked as they walked between the first two buildings. "We supply the local supermarkets with them throughout the winter."

Jo's eyes widened as she peered in through the glass sides. Long green tomato vines were growing side by side, winding up ropes that hung from the ceiling! "I never imagined tomatoes could grow that way," she murmured in amazement.

"And here's where we raise the Christmas cacti and amaryllis," he continued. "Let's look at the rest of this stuff later. Far as I'm concerned, these buildings up ahead are the star attractions."

The excitement thrumming in Michael's voice made Jo's pulse accelerate with anticipation as she followed him to a few greenhouses with heavy-duty plastic sides.

Michael paused in front of the first building's door. His eyes blazed a clear blue, as though they'd gotten lighter and more sparkly because he was ready to share a wonderful secret. "We have to shut the door immediately behind us to maintain our climate control," he explained patiently. "To keep the plants in optimal condition, we can't let the temperature dip below fifty-eight degrees."

Jo nodded eagerly. When he gestured for her to precede him inside, she stepped quickly over the threshold and immediately stopped. Her mouth dropped open. The enormous roomful of deep red blooms shifted subtly in the current from the ventilation system, surpassing her wildest imaginings of how glorious hundreds of poinsettias would look all together. The postcard he'd sent her paled in comparison to the rich splendor of the thousands of crimson leaves filling the huge room.

She was so enthralled, she didn't realize she'd stopped right in front of the doorway. Michael pressed against her back as he shut the door behind them.

"Oh! I'm sorry—"

"I'm not," he whispered. "The poinsettias are even more fabulous when I'm looking at them over your shoulder, Jo."

She wanted to laugh and cry and sing all at once as he gently grasped her shoulders and remained standing close to her. He could have nudged her out of his way or reminded her to keep moving, but Michael had chosen to remain in close contact. Even with the thick layers of their winter coats between them, Jo reeled from the nearness of him.

Then his words sank in: *Michael was looking over her shoulder.* And if she dared, she could lean back and rest her head on *his* shoulder.

She'd always considered herself too tall and ungainly, certain no man would ever feel comfortable with her height and width, yet Michael was taller than she. And as Jo thought back, she couldn't recall a time when he'd ever seemed uncomfortable with her height—or implied that he found anything wrong with her size, either.

Jo fanned the air with her hand. "Compared to how cold it is outside, it does feel toasty in here—even if it's only fifty-eight," she added with a nervous laugh.

Did she sound like a complete idiot? Michael remained quiet for a long time—or maybe time had stopped when he'd grasped her shoulders.

"Our special heaters burn the wood chips from a couple of nearby sawmills, where they convert all their scraps into fuel for us," he murmured. "This might sound really odd, but sometimes I come into this greenhouse just to breathe . . . and pray. The air quality—and the roomful of beautiful crimson plants—makes me feel as though I'm standing on the shore of my own private Red Sea."

Jo blinked. She'd always figured Michael for a man who was more sensitive to color and natural beauty than most, but she'd had no idea he could express himself so eloquently. Inspired by his thoughts, she inhaled deeply. When she focused solely on the brilliant red blooms, breathing in again, a sense of deep peace seeped into her soul.

"You've got it exactly right, Michael," she whispered. "It's so hushed and still here. The peacefulness settles right into your bones, if you let it."

He wrapped an arm around her shoulders, gently holding her against him. "This is my special place. It's one of the reasons I look forward to the Christmas season every year," he murmured. "I—I'm so glad you feel it, too, Jo."

Jo closed her eyes to savor a moment she'd never believed she would experience. She tried not to read too much into it, however, for fear she'd jinx the miracle of Michael's tender words.

After a few more moments, Michael eased away from her. "I should probably be a *gut* host and show you the house—carry your suitcase to your room and give you time to catch your breath after the drive."

Jo chuckled. "*Jah*, your *dat*'s probably wondering what we're up to," she said before she thought about it. "I mean—that sounded so—it was rude of me to imply—"

Michael stilled her nervous outburst by gently placing a finger across her lips. "Dat knows exactly what's going on with us, Jo. And he's fine with it."

Chapter 13

As Pete drove Mammi's horse-drawn rig up the Helfings' lane late Monday afternoon, a folded envelope burned a hole in his back pocket. All Sunday evening he'd sketched and rethought and sketched some more, devising ways to update the home that hadn't changed since the twins' parents had married years ago.

Because Detweiler had mentioned spending all afternoon in his workshop building chairs and toys to sell on Saturday, Pete figured it was a great time to visit Molly—and at the least suggestion, he'd show her his remodeling plans. He did his best thinking with a pencil in his hand, and while he'd drawn out a kitchen with an enlarged pantry, roll-out shelves, and a more efficient sink arrangement, he'd also convinced himself to state his case. *Soon.*

Pete wanted to court Molly in the worst way—but in the *best* way. She was one of the few people who really understood him, and she tolerated his missteps even when he said or did something totally inappropriate. Molly had joined the church years ago, so she deserved his most mature effort as a potential mate.

Beside him on the buggy seat, Riley wiggled in anticipation. Pete chuckled as he pulled up alongside the house, where—in his freewheeling, almost-English days—he'd parked his pickup.

But that foolishness was behind him now. At breakfast, he'd told Uncle Jeremiah he wanted to begin his church membership instruction—which had made his *mammi* cry, grateful to God that he'd finally seen the light. First thing after that, he'd put down a deposit on a courting buggy, which had widened Saul Hartzler's eyes enough that the deacon and master carriage maker had placed Pete's order ahead of everyone else's.

So I've got to go through with this. No more horsing around, letting Detweiler turn her head.

With an impatient *woof*, Riley climbed over Pete's lap, demanding to be let out. Pete had barely opened the buggy's door before the golden pushed his way through the opening to land on the snow-covered ground. He announced their arrival with several boisterous barks, whirling in circles on his way toward the noodle factory and the *dawdi hauses*.

When the factory door popped open, Billy Jay dashed out into the snowy yard. "We're *workin'* in there!" When the golden retriever licked his face, his laughter rang through the crisp, wintry air. "Molly don't let us sit around watchin' her. Dawdi's baggin' dry noodles and I'm stickin' on the labels!"

Pete smiled as he imagined the familiar scene. "And what're Molly and Marietta doing? Sitting around watching *you* work?"

Billy Jay laughed again. It was wonderful to hear the kid sounding happy after all that had happened to him, even as Pete suspected the little boy was becoming very attached to Molly.

"Molly's cuttin' noodles. Marietta's in the house cookin'," he replied. He glanced back at the noodle factory and lowered his voice to a mysterious whisper. "She's really bakin' a cake for their birthday on Sunday, but that's a big secret."

"We won't tell a soul," Pete whispered back. "I'm going inside to say hi. When you come in from romping with Riley, don't let him into the twins' workroom with you. We'll both be in big trouble."

Stepping up to the factory entrance, Pete let himself in and quickly closed the door. The floury, vaguely sweet aroma of wet noodles wafted around him. The sight of Molly running her knife through a long section of rolled-out dough made him want to rush over and hug her. He missed being around her every day, more than he wanted to admit.

Reuben glanced up, smiling. "Look what the dog dragged in! *Gut* to see you, Pete," he remarked as he shook the noodles he'd measured down into a clear sack.

Molly's immediate grin made Pete's heart race. "Glenn said he'd be working in his shop this afternoon. So you've taken some time off from building the house, too?"

He tried not to sigh because she'd mentioned Detweiler first. "*Jah*, we ran short on roofing nails, so we called it a day. Just as well, considering how cold it is—and the fact that all of us fellows have other business to tend to."

He wanted to tell Molly exactly what he'd done this

morning with his uncle and Saul Hartzler—but not with Reuben looking on.

"Awfully windy today, too," Glenn's *dat* put in. "I'd think your hands would get numb working outside on such a day—and *denki* from the bottom of my heart that you're willing to rebuild our place right now, considering the weather and the remodeling project you already had going at your uncle's place."

Pete smiled patiently, aware that he wouldn't be holding a meaningful—or private—conversation with Molly anytime soon. He heard the doorknob turn as Billy Jay came inside. "Happy to do it for you, Reuben. If my house had burned down, you and Glenn would be right there doing the same thing for me."

Billy Jay, pink-cheeked from playing out in the snow without a coat, jumped feetfirst into the conversation. "But, Pete, you don't have a house!"

Pete stifled a groan. Leave it to a little kid to point out the obvious—even though Molly was well aware that he lacked a home to offer her.

"Pete's talking about the way neighbors help each other in a pinch," Reuben pointed out with a purposeful gaze at his grandson. "And there's nobody nicer or more helpful than Pete, ain't so, Billy Jay?"

It was a valiant attempt to save the conversation, but Molly's expression told Pete she was amused by the little boy's remark. She turned back to her work, deftly pulling her sharp knife through the large rectangle of dough on her worktable.

"Pete is a *gut* and helpful friend," she said, focusing on her cut. "And if he goes to the house to say hello to

Marietta, I bet she'll share some of what she's been baking today."

Just that fast, Molly had dismissed him.

Biting back a wounded retort—because they had an audience of Detweilers—Pete headed for the door. "*Gut* to see everyone. Stay warm," he remarked. The old Pete Shetler would've blown off the lot of them and raced down the lane in his pickup to go joyriding with Riley—

But that Pete's not me. Not anymore.

When he stepped outside, he inhaled deeply to settle himself. The cold air filled his lungs, but it did nothing to ease the void in his heart. Once upon a time he'd been the one to fire off words that had probably wounded others—he'd teased the Helfing twins mercilessly while he'd lived here—and he'd been too clueless to think about the damage he might've done. Now that Molly was setting him aside, not taking him seriously, Pete felt like a seventh wheel: the two Helfings and the four Detweilers seemed to have quickly rolled into a family unit. He was on the outside looking in.

Even so, he decided to peek in on Marietta—mostly so Molly wouldn't think he was slinking away with his tail between his legs.

"Hey there—what smells so wonderful-*gut*?" Pete called out as he entered the house through the mudroom. It had been his usual greeting as he'd joined them for meals when he'd lived here. He hoped he sounded as carefree as he had back in the days before Molly had wadded up his hopes like pieces of scrap paper and tossed them away.

"The bad penny's returned!" Marietta teased from the kitchen. "Pete! Come in and take a load off."

It was the most exuberant invitation he'd received all day. As Billy Jay had said, Marietta was making a birthday cake, and she kept on frosting it, as though she intended to whisk it out of sight in a few minutes.

"Aha! A little bird told me you were surprising your sister with a cake," he said lightly.

"A little Jay-bird," Marietta said fondly. "You can't keep anything secret from that little guy, so it's best to let him in on the surprise from the start. I'm stashing this in the deep freeze to take to the common meal after church on Sunday."

With a flourish of her slender metal spatula, she smoothed the top of the chocolate frosting and then tossed the utensil in the sink. "You'll no doubt see another birthday cake there, too, because Molly always finds a way to make one for me," Marietta remarked as she placed her surprise inside a cake keeper. "It's one of our sister traditions, now that Mamm's not around to bake us a birthday cake."

Pete blinked. As the too-slender woman placed her creation in the deep freeze and concealed it beneath several packages of meat from the butcher shop, he envied the twins' close-knit relationship. His *dat* had died years ago, from an infection stemming from Lyme disease, and when his *mamm* had remarried, Pete had disliked her new husband so much that he'd refused to go to Indiana to live with them. Uncle Jeremiah and Aunt Priscilla had given him a loving home, but he had no siblings . . . no one with whom to share traditions and rituals that Molly and Marietta took for granted.

He suddenly had an even more compelling reason to want Molly for his wife. Living in the Helfings' *dawdi haus* had given him a taste of how it would feel to be included in their family—and he yearned for the ordinary, everyday happiness they'd shared with him for those wonderful weeks.

But Molly obviously didn't care enough about him these days to even talk to him. She was too wrapped up in her noodle making, and the Detweiler clan had already fit themselves into her routine—and into the space he'd once occupied in her life.

"Hey there! Why such a glum expression? Where's that grin that makes your butt-ugly face worth looking at?"

Marietta's lighthearted joke caught Pete off guard. He was fumbling for a smart-aleck response when she beat him to the punch.

"You know, if you hitched up with my sister, you could live here again, Pete," she said, cocking an eyebrow at him. "It would serve you both right, goofy as you are."

Pete's mouth fell open. Had Marietta read his mind? Or was she making fun of him, knowing that Molly preferred Glenn's company these days? She'd taken him totally by surprise—made him feel so vulnerable, so overwhelmed by his inability to win Molly's affection, that he turned and hurried out the door.

"Riley!" he hollered hoarsely. "Let's go!"

The dog bounded toward him. Luckily, no one was outside to quiz him about why he was in such a hurry to leave. Even so, after Pete had quickly untied the horse and urged the retriever into the rig before him, Riley gazed at him with a quizzical expression.

"Don't ask!" Pete muttered.

All he could think about as he drove down the lane was how badly he wanted to race out onto the road in his pickup and floor the gas pedal—and how many hours he'd lavished on sketches that would transform the Helfings' house into an even cozier home . . . a home he would never share with Molly. Bitterness and self-pity welled up inside him, to the point that when Riley placed a sympathetic paw on his arm, Pete hastily brushed it off.

You know, if you hitched up with my sister, you could live here again, Pete.

The horse clip-clopped past several snow-covered farms before his vision cleared. He couldn't recall the last time he'd wanted to cry, and the inclination upset him even more than Molly had. He'd poured way too much hope and earnest effort into winning her, and now it seemed he'd wasted his time—

It would serve you both right, goofy as you are.

Pete stared at the horse's muscular haunches as they rolled a little farther down the road. With a sigh, he slung his arm around his dog. "We *are* goofy together," he murmured.

Riley licked his face and settled against him, happy to be his confidant again.

"Do you suppose I took Marietta all wrong?" he wondered aloud. "What if she was giving me a big *hint* and I missed it?"

Encouragement rumbled in Riley's throat.

"What if Molly's only *pretending* to be sweet on Glenn—maybe to wake me up?" Pete continued hopefully. "And what if I've been totally clueless about it? Marietta's not the type to make jokes about me marrying her sister, because then they'd have to be separated— *unless I came to live at their house!* That's it, Riley! That's what she was telling me!"

The dog let out a bark that turned into an excited howl. As he kept vocalizing in that doggy way he had, his warm breath fogged the rig's windshield, but Pete didn't care.

"We're on the right track!" he crowed. "I've got the house plans ready—now I just have to find a way to state my case to Molly. Even though girls always seem to know how you feel about them, they make you say it to their face, a million different ways, before they act like they believe you."

"Woof!"

"You're absolutely right, Riley—as always," Pete added with a laugh. "We've got this. You and me, boy—and Molly. We'll make it happen!"

Chapter 14

Come Tuesday morning, Jo was floating around the Wengerds' kitchen on a cloud of euphoria. What a wonderful time she'd had during her visit! It had been sheer joy to spend the hours with Michael as he'd shown her around the nursery and explained the various aspects of their burgeoning business. Both he and his *dat* had spoken to her about such matters as though she was an equal, discussing everything from supply and demand to bookkeeping and expanding their inventory.

"*Denki* for making us such a tasty breakfast, Jo," Nelson said as he drained his coffee cup. "We're not used to having somebody cook for us—"

"But we could adjust!" Michael put in quickly.

His gentle smile made Jo feel as warm and bubbly as the butter she'd fried their eggs in. Still unaccustomed to so much praise, Jo quickly gathered up their plates. "Won't take but a minute to wash these dishes, and then I'll be ready to go. I'm all packed and—well, I can't thank you enough for showing me such a fine time these past couple of days."

"We're glad you decided to come, dear." Nelson smiled at her, too, although his happiness didn't run as deep as his son's. "Hopefully we can convince your *mamm* to join you next time."

The mention of her mother was a sudden reminder that she was going home . . . that she would have to face whatever mood Mamm was in when she arrived. She feared it wouldn't be pleasant.

For the rest of the morning, however, Jo was determined to enjoy the Wengerds' calm, comforting company. She was glad Nelson was returning to Morning Star with them. As much as she'd come to crave being with Michael—as much as she would've loved to sit near him in the rig, just the two of them—his *dat* had made a *gut* point the previous evening: it was best for her mother to see that Nelson's presence had kept everything proper.

Jo also suspected that Michael's *dat* was hoping for some time with her mother after they made the three-hour drive. She'd assured Nelson that he and his son would be welcome to stay for a bite of lunch before they hit the road again.

As they rolled along the road in the early light of dawn, Jo was delighted that Michael was grasping her hand. Jo was again seated against the side of the buggy, and when she gazed at Michael's slender, handsome face, she lost track of everything else. They gently jostled each other as the rig rocked from side to side with the rhythm of the horse's hooves.

Jo felt warm and alive, happier than she had been in years. She and Michael had talked late into the evenings, so whenever the buggy conversation ebbed into a comfortable lull, she almost dozed. About halfway to Morning Star, however, Michael's whispered words startled her wide awake.

"Jo, I—I'm hoping it'll be okay to take you out now—to court you. You want that, too, *jah*?"

She sucked in her breath. She must've heard him wrong, yet she didn't dare ask Michael to repeat what he'd said. It was true that they'd discovered many things they had in common during her visit, but he surely didn't want to take this to the next level.

"Oh, Michael! I—*jah*, I'd love that!" Jo blurted. "But you can't be serious! We're *gut* friends, but—well a fine-looking fellow like you could court any pretty girl he wanted, so—"

"So I'm asking *you*, Jo."

She couldn't believe what she'd heard. Slender, eloquent Michael Wengerd had just said he wanted to enter into a serious relationship with Joseph Fussner's big, bulky daughter. Jo sensed no teasing behind his words; she saw no quirk of a smile to indicate that he was leading her down this path as a colossal joke. Michael just kept looking at her, patiently waiting for her to grasp what he'd said.

His gray-blue eyes drew her in until she lost herself and all ability to think. His *dat*'s kindly chuckle reminded her that Nelson had heard their conversation—and that was all right, wasn't it? Once she and Michael were going out alone together, they would have plenty of opportunities to share sweet secret words.

"Let me be the first to congratulate you," Nelson said, leaning forward so he could smile directly at Jo. "I think you two are well suited. After years of wondering if

Michael would ever find a young woman who'd draw him out of his shell, I'm delighted that we'll be spending more time with *you*, Jo."

She thought her heart might explode, it was beating so fast. She and Michael had his father's blessing to court and to marry when they were ready! It was a blessing she'd never dared to hope for, a future she'd never believed she would find. A thousand questions whirled in her mind: Would she be moving to Queen City next year? Would the wedding need to be held between the Wengerds' busy seasons at the nursery?

How could I keep managing my bakery and The Marketplace?

Jo stared out the rig's windshield, hoping Michael wouldn't see the change in her expression and suppose she was having second thoughts about their budding romance before it had a chance to bloom. When Regina Miller had married Gabe, she'd started doing her special embroidery at home. After school let out next May, when Teacher Lydianne Christner married Bishop Jeremiah, she wouldn't have as much time to keep The Marketplace's books, either—if indeed the bishop allowed his wife to be associated with the business at all.

And when Jo and Michael married, it would leave the Helfing twins as the last *maidels* to oversee all the many aspects of running The Marketplace. Their noodle business was extremely successful, but they'd never shown any inclination toward taking on any of the managerial responsibilities.

So if your dream of marrying comes true, does that mean your dream for The Marketplace falls by the wayside? Who will carry on, now that so many shop owners have invested in their inventories—and now that so many groups are scheduling reunions and other gatherings in the commons area, too?

The gentle pressure of Michael's hand brought Jo out of her woolgathering.

"If it's your *mamm*'s reaction you're worried about, we'll figure out a way to bring her into the picture, too," he said softly. "We won't leave her all alone. Dat and I suspect that's what she's worried about, deep down."

Jo blinked, willing herself not to cry. Of *course* Michael had read her expression and anticipated her concerns— even if he hadn't addressed the issue she'd actually been stewing about.

"Michael and I have talked about this, and we've considered several options," Nelson put in. "Hopefully Drusilla will find at least one of them acceptable."

When has Mamm ever found anyone else's ideas acceptable?

Jo swallowed that thought before she blurted it out, not wanting to ruin the Wengerds' fine mood. Their handsome smiles told her they were ready to move beyond the grief of losing Verna, to try a new life despite the many times Mamm had snipped and snapped at them—and despite the ominous remarks her mother had made the last time they'd all eaten supper together and then again when Jo had left on Sunday morning.

By the time the buggy rolled up the lane toward the house, Jo's happiness was overshadowed by a huge cloud of doubt. Her stomach was in a knot. She frowned when she saw dresses flapping on the clothesline—her mother was a stickler for doing all the laundry on Monday. Did this mean Mamm had taken ill? Or were the garments flapping like flags of warning, an omen of her mother's attitude?

Drusilla Fussner never did anything without a reason. Perhaps she considered the neglected laundry just one of the many chores Jo hadn't helped her with because she'd become a willful, disrespectful daughter who'd abandoned her *mamm*. As Nelson pulled up alongside the rail at the side of the house, Jo steeled herself for whatever might happen next.

Lord, we need Your love and Your presence with us— and so does Mamm. Guide me in the way You'd have me go, because right now I'm being ripped apart at the emotional seams.

While Nelson tied the horse, Jo and Michael went to the front door. He followed a few feet behind her, knowing that any show of their affection might upset her mother. Through the glass, she saw Mamm's shadowy silhouette—as though her mother had been watching and waiting, ready to pounce at the moment of their arrival.

The door swung open. Mamm stepped out onto the porch, blocking the doorway as though to prevent their entry. Her lined face, stern and unsmiling, looked twenty years older than when Jo had left on Sunday.

"You Wengerds can go right back where you came from," she announced loudly. "Don't come back, and don't think you'll be staying in my *dawdi haus* anymore. You're not welcome here."

Chapter 15

On Wednesday evening, Glenn slumped wearily at the workbench in his home wood shop. As he chose the various sizes of nails to complete the willow chair he was making, his vision was bleary from another restless night. His head and sinuses felt dry because he and Pete and Gabe had sanded and installed the new kitchen cabinets this morning. Ordinarily, the finishing details were what he did best—and it was a blessing that the house was totally enclosed now, because a drastic drop in the temperature had confined them to working indoors.

He felt anything but blessed, however.

All morning as he'd worked with his faithful friends, Glenn had tried hard to feel grateful and excited about the new house that was quickly taking shape. But the unpainted drywall and wooden studs were nothing like the rooms where he and his family had once lived such a wonderful, ordinary life together—and where he'd taken refuge after Dorcas and Mamm had passed. The sharp tang of new wood was far from comforting as he struggled to recall how his wife's cooking had filled their home with such heavenly aromas. He missed the front room's cozy, careworn chairs and sofa. He longed for the bed, with its familiar dips and creaks, where his sons had been conceived.

This new place will never be home.

As he'd hammered and sanded the cabinets, Glenn had been going through the motions of rebuilding his life, but there'd been no love in it. The Scripture from First Corinthians had it right: even if a man had the gift of prophecy and could understand all mysteries and had all faith—but didn't have love—he was nothing. At this point, Glenn had no idea about the future, and he didn't understand anything. Worse still, he'd all but lost his faith. Instead of love, he was feeling a whole lot of loss and spiritual emptiness.

Had God forsaken him?

Rather than descending into the hell of that particular question, he'd kept his mouth shut and kept working all morning. It was better than doing nothing, adrift in his lonely little boat without a paddle as one storm after another tossed him around.

It also rankled Glenn to be such a burden to his friends—and to be so dependent upon them for every little thing. He was pretty sure the dark blue shirt he was wearing had once belonged to the twins' *dat*. He regretted dumping baby Levi on Marietta and Molly, too, so that he could work—and he felt bad that his father preferred to remain underfoot in the Helfings' warm home rather than at the unheated work site. And Billy Jay was such a chatterbox when he came in from school, he was surely driving the twins crazy. Glenn sensed their noodle making was falling way behind during this Christmas season, when their sales could be spectacular—all because his family required so much of their attention.

With a sigh he slipped off his high wooden stool. Out of habit, he tucked nails between his lips in the order, by size, that he'd need them. The thickness of the branch and the tension caused by curving it to the shape he wanted determined the size he'd need—longer nails, or nails with more threads—to keep the willow from splitting.

The chair's slatted seat, legs, arms, and back were complete, so Glenn told himself he could quit for the day after he'd attached the supple branches that formed rustic, decorative arches around the back and the arms. The slender, flexible lengths of willow transformed an ordinary piece into the one-of-a-kind custom chair a longtime English buyer had come to expect of Glenn— and he'd paid top dollar for it, because it was to be a special Christmas gift for his wife. He was to pick it up on Saturday, only three days away.

Glenn slipped one end of a willow branch through the arm slot on his right and nailed it to the chair's front leg with three deft whacks of his hammer. Working his way upward at intervals of about four inches, he held the slender branch against the chair, tacking and carefully bending the wood around the curve of the back until he went down the other side and ended at the bottom of the other front leg.

First branch attached. Hallelujah.

Once again he placed nails of the various sizes he needed between his lips. He picked up the second willow branch, which he would attach to the first one at the bottom of the chair's leg, as before. Then he would gradually arch it a few inches away from that original branch as it looped around the chair's back to allow a curved space about three inches wide before rejoining it on the opposite side. Glenn had worked with willow so many times, he could almost put a chair together in his sleep. It was a matter of following the pattern his client had chosen, creating the graceful curves around the chair's back and arms.

Tap-tap-whack. He attached the second branch to the leg and deftly continued with it, his hands acting as an extension of his mind. The willow felt dryer than he preferred because it had been stacked in his shop for the past couple of weeks while he'd worked on the new house. *Tap-tap-whack . . . tap-tap-whack.*

Second rung done. One more on the back, three on each arm, and I'm outta here.

Sighing tiredly, Glenn repeated his procedure of choosing nails—longer ones this time, and the nails where the curve at the back became wider had more threads to anchor the branch securely. He picked up the remaining willow branch, which was the longest of the three.

Tap-tap-whack . . . tap-tap-whack. Up the chair's leg he went. This third and final branch curved around the top at the same distance from the second one, but it required more patience and reinforcement because the willow was following a much more pronounced reshaping than the previous two branches had.

Pressing the branch firmly in place where the willow went into the curve, he slipped a nail from between his lips. He positioned it between his thumb and index finger, and hammered it.

Tap-tap-CRACK.

With a sickening sound, the branch split open. Frustrated beyond belief, Glenn cried out, spewing nails. The willow had felt dry—he should've soaked it, but he hadn't taken the time—and then he noticed that he'd accidentally chosen a larger nail than he'd intended to use.

"I can't believe you—what a stupid thing to—" Glenn's self-accusations morphed into a cry that filled the shop with his pent-up frustration and anger. He threw his hammer against the wall. The willow branch was ruined, and he didn't have another one long enough to take its place. He'd have to go to the river where the willows grew and see if he could find a replacement, which meant the chair couldn't possibly be ready by Saturday.

Too angry to see straight, he shut off his shop lights and stalked outside. Dusk was falling, so it was too late to hunt up more willow branches. All he could do was hitch up his rig and go home—

But no, I don't have a home, I'll go back to the Helfing place, and everyone there will see how upset I am—and I'll drag them right down into the pit of my despair. And that's just too bad, isn't it?

Sensing his foul mood, Nick sidestepped and hesitated before Glenn ordered him to head down the road. As the rig lurched forward, Glenn's thoughts circled like angry crows, black and noisy, jeering at him for ruining that chair. All he wanted was to walk through the twins' house without anyone stopping him to ask questions, straight up the stairs, where he could slam the door to his bedroom and stew for the rest of the evening. He was hoping his scowl would discourage Dat or Billy Jay from trying to engage him in conversation—and heaven help them all if Levi was crying again.

When he'd pulled into the Helfings' stable, Glenn quickly unhitched the horse and tossed some oats into his feed trough. Up the snowy path he strode, wondering why his lazy seven-year-old son hadn't shoveled it. His boots thunked noisily across the wooden porch—and when he yanked the front door open, the baby's wailing immediately set him off.

Glenn stalked toward the kitchen, determined to stop the fracas before he exploded into a million pieces—

But the desperation on Marietta's tear-streaked face stopped him cold.

He couldn't bear to witness the same naked terror in her eyes that he was feeling in his own soul, so he turned and stormed out the front door again. Grabbing the porch post, Glenn sucked in cold, wintry air. He had to get a grip—had to take charge of himself and this situation before he did something unthinkable or irrevocable.

That woman in there is at the end of her rope—because my baby is bawling again and she has no idea how to stop him. Because I've dumped my son on her and ruined her day—and she doesn't know how to get me out of her home and out of her life.

Glenn gasped for more air. "How long, oh Lord?" he whispered hoarsely. "What am I supposed to do? I don't have any more idea than Marietta does about how to stop Levi's crying, and it drives me up the wall, and—"

A flashback hit him, a recollection of when Billy Jay had been a colicky infant and Dorcas, as a new mother, had worn the same shell-shocked expression he'd just seen on Marietta's face. As the scene in his mind continued, his mother spooned some sugar into the center of Dat's bandanna, tied it off with string, and stuck the little bulb under the faucet.

Glenn's body relaxed—just as his firstborn son had, once he'd started sucking on the homemade pacifier.

This time when he entered the house, Glenn went upstairs and fetched a clean handkerchief. As the baby's wailing escalated, he tamped down the urge to cry along with him. Instead, Glenn headed for the sugar bowl on the kitchen table and repeated the solution his deceased *mamm* had provided for him, direct from heaven.

Marietta, bless her, continued to walk and rock and coo even though she was clearly at her wit's end. After he doused the bulb with water, Glenn walked up behind the slender woman and gently grasped her shoulder to stop her pacing. He popped the pacifier into Levi's red, open mouth and prayed.

Within seconds, the baby was suckling. The kitchen went quiet.

"*Denki*," Marietta whispered as she blinked back tears. "I've tried feeding him and burping him and—and I didn't know what else to—"

"Shhh." Glenn gently held her against him, resting his head on hers. Levi's baby-powder scent soothed him— and so did Marietta's elemental fragrance, enhanced by the aroma of bacon. When he glanced toward the stove and saw that she'd started supper—a meal interrupted by his son's neediness—he knew he owed her more of a debt than he could possibly pay.

For several long moments Glenn let the tension melt from his body, praying that Dat and Molly and Billy Jay remained in the noodle factory until he and Marietta could simply breathe again. He became aware of the fact that it had been way too long since he'd held a woman in his arms. When he could trust himself to remain calm rather than dumping all of his day's frustrations on her, he eased away.

"I'm sorry," he whispered. "When I came here to stay with you and your sister, I never intended—"

"I'm sorry, too, Glenn," Marietta said with a shake of her head. "You must feel so fragmented and scattered right now, while you work in your shop and rebuild your home, trying to hold your family—and yourself—together."

Fragmented and scattered.

With three words, she'd described his life—the state of his soul. And without a thought for herself or how he'd inconvenienced her, Marietta had consoled him. As she shifted contented little Levi higher onto her shoulder, her smile returned.

Glenn was suddenly struck by her beauty. He'd known Marietta for years, yet her face had taken on a glow he'd never noticed before. She was angular—bony to the point of appearing frail, without the alluring feminine curves he'd always adored on Dorcas. And because her *kapp* was slightly askew from frantically tending his son, uneven tufts of her brown hair reminded him of the ordeal she'd undergone during her cancer treatment. Because her face had lost all of its excess flesh, her lips looked too large—

Yet he suddenly wanted to kiss them.

"It's been a rough day," he murmured before he followed up on that momentary urge. "For both of us."

"It has," she agreed. She smiled again at the baby resting in her arms, and then she handed Levi over to Glenn. "But we got past this bump in the road, and on we go.

Everything will get better once supper's underway, *jah*? I'm making pancakes tonight."

Just that quickly, Marietta set his world back on its axis.

Glenn settled into a chair at the kitchen table, cradling Levi in the crook of his elbow. As his baby boy drifted off to sleep, a return to a happy, purposeful life didn't seem so impossible anymore.

Chapter 16

Very early on Saturday morning, Jo unlocked the back entry to The Marketplace and flipped the light switches. Ever since her return home on Tuesday, she'd been desperate to get away from Mamm's probing, disapproving gaze—as though her mother suspected Jo had engaged in something horribly immoral during her time with the Wengerds. All hope of defending Michael's and Nelson's honorable motives had vanished, along with her wish to share the lush, colorful tranquility she'd found amid the poinsettias in their greenhouses. Jo knew better than to even *hint* at Michael's wish to court her . . . to marry her someday.

"You deserted me," Mamm had repeatedly accused over the past few days. "You openly defied my authority—and you don't even have the decency to act remorseful or repentant about it!"

How was she supposed to answer that? In all her years of tolerating Mamm's negativity, Jo had never dreamed there would come a time when she wanted to pack up and leave home—forever. Baking and decorating Christmas cookies for her shop had been her salvation, yet even that activity had inspired her mother's disdain. It seemed she couldn't do or say anything right and that she might live under this dark cloud of Mamm's condemnation for the rest of her life.

As she slid large pans of cookies into her glass bakery cases, Jo took comfort in the soft hum of her refrigerator and the stillness of the remodeled stable that housed The Marketplace. In a few hours, the high-ceilinged commons area would be teeming with shoppers and the noise would escalate to an amazing level, but for now the empty building provided a much-needed sanctuary—a solitude that would help her pull herself together.

It was December fourteenth. Today and next Saturday were the final remaining shopping days at The Marketplace, so Jo had to radiate the joy and Christmas cheer her customers had come to expect of her. This was not the time to provoke their pity with red-rimmed eyes or a faltering smile.

The click of the stable's back door made her straighten to her full height, her stomach tightening. It was only six thirty—still dark and too early for the other shopkeepers to show up. Although she'd never had cause to worry about intruders, Jo wished she'd locked the employees' entry.

Moments later, Michael's tentative smile made her heart dance even as she gripped the countertop to support herself.

"Hey there, Jo. Are you okay?" he asked softly. "I wanted to stay longer on Tuesday—I had hoped to reassure your *mamm* about my intentions—"

"She would've had none of that," Jo said with a shake of her head.

"—but I didn't want to get you in hotter water than you already seemed to be in," he continued. "I'm so sorry you're going through this on my account."

Nelson stepped up beside his son, his handsome smile dimmed by concern. "I hope Drusilla's settled down by now. I—I'm sorry she reacted so harshly when we took you home, Jo," he said. "And frankly, I'm puzzled—and very disappointed—that after all the time she's known us, she doesn't trust us or believe that as a parent I would provide the proper environment for your visit."

Jo sighed. The Wengerds' words soothed her, yet there was no undoing the emotional damage Mamm had inflicted this past week. "I'm not sure what put such a brutal bee under her bonnet. I still had a *gut* time seeing your place and your poinsettias, though, and I'm not sorry I did!"

There were a lot of unsettled emotions she didn't feel like sharing with Michael and his *dat*, because what good would it do? Why should she make them feel even guiltier about showing her such a wonderful time?

There was no point in telling them her future appeared bleak and pointless, either. If she stayed home and did what Mamm considered right, she'd be miserable. And if she left home to marry Michael without her mother's blessing, was that any way to begin a marriage? She and her mother would be on difficult terms—perhaps not speaking to each other—for the rest of their lives if she defied Mamm's wishes again.

Nelson nodded. "We decided to get an early start today,

to be sure all of our loose ends here at The Marketplace get tied up by next week," he began, glancing at Michael. "Considering Drusilla's mood—and the probability of fewer customers after Christmas—it seems best to stay in Queen City for the rest of the winter and return to our store here in the spring. If you'd like an advance on our shop rent—"

"Absolutely not!" Jo blurted before he could finish. It cut her like a knife to think she wouldn't see Michael and his *dat* each Saturday—which would've been the one bright spot of each week. But if she expressed such a sentiment, there would be no stopping her tears before the other shopkeepers arrived. "Your space will be available for you whenever you want to sell your greenhouse items again. You're a huge draw, and the customers around here love you."

I love you, too. But I can't say that now, can I?

Jo's heart thudded dully as she gazed at Michael's dear face. She saw all her hopes and dreams reflected in his beautiful eyes, even though she suspected that he, too, had known some soul-wrenching moments since Tuesday.

He nodded sadly. "We've begun notifying the folks who've ordered poinsettias that they can claim their plants—even the ones in the commons Christmas tree display—any time. You and the other shopkeepers can keep the ones in front of your stores, though—along with your wreaths. Those were intended as gifts."

"That's very generous," Jo murmured. She looked away so the Wengerds wouldn't see the tears filling her eyes.

After an awkward silence, Michael cleared his throat.

"Guess we'll let you get back to your work. I'll peek in whenever I can today—will that be all right?"

Jo nodded, closing her eyes against the lonely pain that welled up inside her. Which would be more difficult—not seeing Michael again after Christmas, or visiting with him for a few moments here and there today and next Saturday, knowing nothing would come of it?

When the Wengerds had gone, she resumed displaying her baked goods. Were her decorated cookies less cheerful because she'd been rushed while preparing enough of them to fill her pre-order from last Saturday? Or was her dismal mood affecting the way she saw the treats she'd arranged in her glass cases? Jo's breads and desserts were a labor of love, yet Mamm's recent behavior had robbed her of the pleasure she usually took in each squeeze of her pastry bag, each dollop of frosting she spread over a pan of brownies.

"Lord, You've got to help me through this," Jo rasped. She bent forward, hugging herself with the effort it required to keep body and soul together. "Have You led me to Michael—to the possibility of a marriage I never dreamed I could have—only to dash all my hopes into pieces because Mamm's determined to keep us apart?"

Self-pity wasn't something Jo often indulged in, but for a few moments she allowed herself to acknowledge that her life had hit rock bottom. The future looked bleak. She couldn't imagine how lonely and painful the rest of the Christmas season would feel—not to mention the rest of her life—knowing that the only man in the world who adored her was now out of reach.

To whom did she owe her allegiance? Her mother—or Michael and herself?

"Uh-oh. You're not coming down with the flu are you, Jo?"

The familiar feminine voice behind her made Jo straighten, blinking rapidly. "Lydianne! I was only—what brings you to the shops so early this morning?"

One look and her friend would realize she was an emotional train wreck, but Jo turned anyway. The pretty blond schoolteacher, wearing a dress of deep cranberry red that set off her dewy complexion, stood in the doorway with a look of great concern on her face.

"I was going to work on the bookkeeping, but if you need me to mind your shop today—oh, Jo, what's wrong, sweetheart?" Lydianne asked, entering the shop to take Jo in her embrace. "You look like you've lost your last friend. Did your time at the Wengerd place go wrong? We *maidels* were all hoping you and Michael would get along so well that you'd be dating when you came home."

Unable to repress her sorrow any longer, Jo began to sob against Lydianne's shoulder. She felt awkward having to lean down to return her shorter friend's hug, but it felt so good to have someone sympathetic to confide in. "Oh, we did get on together—so well that Michael wants to court me. His *dat* has given us his blessing—"

"So what could possibly be making you cry this way?" Lydianne murmured, rocking Jo gently from side to side. "In all the years I've known you, I don't recall you ever getting so upset."

Jo exhaled harshly, scowling as she eased away from her friend's embrace. "Mamm," she muttered. "She's told Nelson and Michael not to come back to the house ever again. The way she's acting, you'd think I'd committed the world's worst sin by visiting the Wengerd place."

Lydianne's brow puckered. "She doesn't want Michael to court you? He's a wonderful fellow—"

"But he'll be taking me away from *her*," Jo pointed out bitterly. "The way my mother sees it, I defied her wishes by going to Queen City. I had such a wonderful time, Lydianne, and—and the way Michael and I talked and laughed together, you'd think we'd known each other forever."

Jo paused to draw in a breath. Now that the schoolteacher had heard the awful truth, it wouldn't be long before their friends and Bishop Jeremiah knew about her predicament. Jo wasn't sure she wanted to delve into such emotional turmoil when customers would soon be coming into her store.

But she couldn't unsay what she'd just admitted, could she?

"I don't know what to do," Jo confessed with a hitch in her voice. "Nelson feels bad, Michael and I feel we've been torn apart, and Mamm's accusations and criticism haven't let up since I came back. It's been the worst few days of my life, and—and frankly, I don't even want to go home today!"

Lydianne's clear blue eyes widened. "Oh my. You're in a real fix," she whispered. "If you want to bunk over at my place—"

"That would only make it worse. Even though right now I can't comprehend anything feeling worse."

Jo sighed, blotting her face with her apron. "Well, I don't have time for this pity party," she remarked as she glanced at her clock. "It's nearly seven, and I have dough and batter that need to be baked. *Denki* for hearing me out, Lydianne. It means a lot that you're on my side, wishing things were different now that I've finally met someone who—who makes me so happy."

Lydianne squeezed Jo's arm. "Let's don't give up on your happiness before it's even gotten off the ground," she said earnestly. "I filled the teaching position with every intention of being in our new schoolhouse for years to come, but God—and Jeremiah—had a different idea. It might work that way for you, now that Michael's set his sights on you, Jo. I choose to believe the best, and you should, too!"

Jo didn't think Lydianne could realistically predict a happily-ever-after for her and Michael, but she nodded anyway.

"I'll work upstairs until the doors open, and then I'll be down here to help with customers," Lydianne said. "You're not in this alone, Jo. All of us *maidels*—and Regina, and everyone else you know—are pulling for you. The power of our positive thinking might move heaven and earth in ways none of us can imagine. After all—who ever thought I'd be marrying Jeremiah Shetler in the spring? And before that, we never could have predicted that Regina would hitch up with Gabe, either."

As the pretty blonde left her shop, Jo sighed yet again. Not long ago, Lydianne was being pursued by *two* men, because Glenn Detweiler had been determined that she should be his new wife even as the bishop was falling for her. However, that sort of fairy tale only happened for young women with trim figures and flawless features—and whose *mamms* didn't interfere.

Jo yearned to continue seeing Michael and planning to someday be his bride. But at this moment, such pie-in-the-sky hopes seemed as ridiculous as the English belief that a man in a red suit delivered Christmas gifts to all the children of the world in a sleigh pulled by reindeer.

In times of trouble, work had always been her salvation. Jo took a batch of sweet dough from her refrigerator and rolled it into a large rectangle. As she spread on the pineapple cream cheese filling, the repetitive motions soothed her frazzled emotions. After shaping the dough into a long log and slicing it, she arranged the individual rolls into Christmas trees on three baking pans. Customers were excited about these pineapple sweet rolls, so she hoped she had enough of them.

Jo didn't allow herself time to think. After she made three big batches of cinnamon rolls, she poured brownie batter into four large pans. Keeping track of each item's baking time, checking and removing the pans from her oven, and mixing the powdered sugar glaze kept her focused on the day's business. By the time the redheaded Shetler twins came in to work, Jo had composed her emotions again.

"It smells so *gut* in here!" Adeline exclaimed as she entered the bakery.

"Customers are going to snap up all these goodies early today," Alice predicted as the two of them tied on their white aprons. "It's sunny and clear and cold—perfect weather for Christmas shopping!"

"We'd better get the big coffee makers going out in the commons," Adeline said, smiling at the pineapple cream cheese trees Jo was drizzling with glaze. "Anything else we need to do for you first thing?"

Jo found a smile—because who wouldn't feel better just being in the presence of her freckle-faced, cheerful assistants? "I really appreciate the way you jump in each

Saturday without my having to tell you what needs doing. Why, I think you could run this shop yourselves!"

The twins laughed, squeezing Jo's shoulders. "You'd have to teach us all your baking tricks," Alice pointed out.

"We're no strangers to making pies and cakes at home," Adeline put in, "but you *amaze* me, the way you plan out so much of your Saturday baking ahead of time to serve fresh goodies."

"You just revealed my biggest baking secret," Jo remarked, gesturing toward the coolers she'd emptied while she'd baked this morning. "Planning ahead is the key. Making the dough and having the fillings already mixed is the only way to have these treats soft and warm when shoppers arrive. I bake the other items all week long and freeze some of them so they don't get dry."

"And you do those things really well," Alice said with a big smile. "We'll get the commons area set up. I can't wait to see the shoppers today, carrying around all the stuff they've purchased."

For a fleeting moment, Jo realized that if she married Michael, the Fussner Bakery might cease to exist. If she was a wife, how could she possibly bake so many items at home during the week, or transport her dough and batters from Queen City?

No need to worry about that, is there?

Before her doubts ambushed her again, Jo glanced out into the commons area, where she heard the voices of incoming shopkeepers. She waved at Martha Maude, who was wheeling a cartload of quilted items into her shop in the corner. Glenn came inside, as well, and the beautiful willow chair on his dolly was ornamented by the fanciest bentwood back and arms she'd ever seen. Jo also watched the Wengerds display some fresh greenery wreaths on the big pegboard outside their shop. The folks who ran Koenig's Krafts were placing craft kits, jigsaw puzzles, and fabric bolts on their sale tables, too.

When Regina came around the corner, her smile lifted Jo's spirits immediately. "Want to see something pretty?" she asked. "I embroidered a Christmas tablecloth and napkins for a gal who's picking them up today. Had to stay up awfully late to finish them in time."

Jo's eyes widened when her friend tossed her the end of the white tablecloth so they could open it out. "Oh my stars, Regina! Evergreen branches with cardinals—and look at these holly sprigs with those pretty red berries. This is surely your finest piece yet."

"*Denki*, Jo. Martin says I spend way too much time on each of my specialty pieces—and that I don't charge enough for them," Regina murmured. "But I can't take shortcuts when this customer expects the same depth of detail she's seen on my other pieces."

"*Jah*, you've built up your embroidery business based on the shading and bright colors you blend so well," Jo agreed. "If your customers are willing to wait—and pay— for your best work, that's what you have to give them."

Nodding, Regina carefully folded the tablecloth again. "I knew you'd understand. And Gabe realizes I'll always be an artist at heart, even if I'm no longer painting. He says that's the reason I was such a *gut* stainer when I was working at the furniture factory."

Jo nodded. It was a delight to watch Regina's love for her husband color her cheeks with a soft glow—and to know that her friend had found a man who was truly her soul mate.

I could have the same sort of relationship with Michael someday—if I keep believing we're meant to be together. Lydianne and Regina have made that dream come true, after all.

"And this is for your *mamm*, because she loves cardinals."

Jo blinked. Regina was handing her a small gift bag, smiling gently.

"Something tells me Drusilla might need a special gift this Christmas, Jo," the redhead continued. "And you're just the sort of daughter who'd give it to her, ain't so?"

Blinking back the surge of conflicting emotions Regina's suggestion caused, Jo removed the bag's bright green tissue paper. "Oh, this is so—let me get my wallet right now and—"

"No need." Regina squeezed her arm. "I started this piece a while back, just for the fun of it."

Jo gazed at the kitchen towel's unique design: baby Jesus in His bed of hay, smiling at a bright red cardinal perched on the foot of His manger. "This—this is priceless, Regina," she whispered.

"*Jah*, it is," her friend agreed, "because I couldn't possibly put a price on our friendship, Jo. Merry Christmas."

"Ohhh, and Merry Christmas to you and Gabe, as well," Jo said as she wrapped her arms around Regina. "I wish you two every happiness as you celebrate your first Christmas together."

A loud *ding!* came from the bakery, and Jo eased away from their hug. "My last batch of brownies is calling me. I'll bring you some as soon as they're frosted. Have a great sales day, Regina!"

"I'm sure we all will," the redhead said as she turned to enter the Flaud Furniture shop adjacent to the bakery.

Jo carefully draped the embroidered towel over her countertop, away from the area where she cut and frosted the goodies she was making. After she removed the last pans of brownies and turned off her ovens, she allowed herself a moment to contemplate the unexpected gift Regina had given her.

Something tells me Drusilla might need a special gift this Christmas.

It touched Jo deeply that her friend was perceptive enough to pick up on the emotional turmoil that had sprung from her visit to the Wengerd place. On the one hand, Jo didn't feel inclined to give her mother anything special for Christmas this year, because her negative attitude had become so unbearable—and had put Jo's future in such a pinch. But didn't Regina have it right? Didn't Mamm feel pinched and displaced, as well, now that Michael was paying such close attention to Jo?

With a hopeful smile, Jo folded the towel and put it back in the gift bag. Truth be told, she'd been so busy baking this Christmas season, she hadn't given much thought to her mother's gift. Regina might've provided her a way back into Mamm's good graces—or at least a way to start a conversation that would restore some peace between them.

Peace on earth begins with peace at home. Show me how to make that Christmas wish come true, Lord.

Chapter 17

Molly felt a special glow as she sat next to her sister on the pew bench Sunday morning. She especially enjoyed church services when the congregation gathered in the Hartzlers' large, comfortable home: Deacon Saul, proprietor of the local carriage company, was by far the wealthiest member of their district. Although his home reflected traditional Amish simplicity, he had provided his mother, Martha Maude, and his wife, Anne, with higher-end kitchen appliances and furnishings than most Plain families could afford. The exquisite woodwork glowed with polish. The mantel and window frames, decked with greenery and red candles, looked especially festive on this fifteenth day of December. The Hartzler home radiated a sense of comfort and joy that always made Molly feel *welcome*.

Molly loved the humbler home she and Marietta had lived in for all of their thirty-five years—wouldn't trade it for anyone else's—but it always felt like a special occasion when they gathered in the deacon's home. God had blessed Saul's family, and in turn, he and his wife and mother shared those blessings with everyone in their Plain community.

She blinked, catching a movement across the room, on the men's side. Billy Jay sat taller, gazing expectantly at Marietta from his perch on his *dat*'s lap—and Glenn was focused on her twin, as well.

Probably checking to see how Levi's doing after spending the entire service with her. But we all know it's more than that, don't we?

Molly smiled. The connection between Marietta and Glenn had strengthened these past few days, even if they were acting as though nothing had changed.

"May the *Gut* Lord bless and keep you, and make His face to shine upon you, and grant you His peace," Bishop Jeremiah intoned as he pronounced his benediction. "May we all feel the Savior's precious presence as He comes to us again as a helpless, humble baby in a manger."

The roomful of worshippers sighed in communal contentment, awash in the glow of the Christmas message the bishop had delivered earlier in the morning. Molly never tired of hearing about Mary and Joseph on their journey to Bethlehem and about the holy boy who'd inspired choirs of angels, shepherds, and wise men to follow His star.

The tale seemed more personal this season, with Levi in the house—and Marietta's expression as she beamed at the baby in her arms gave Molly a whole new perspective on the Christmas story. She once would've found it odd for her twin to be holding a wee one during church, yet in the two short weeks since Glenn's family had joined them, Marietta's role as a surrogate mother had become an everyday relationship—and probably a deeper emotional connection than her sister was admitting.

When Billy Jay waved, Molly returned his greeting— and then her breath caught. On the pew bench beside Glenn, Pete was gazing intently at her, apparently with something urgent on his mind. Then he shot her a goofy look, wiggling his fingers alongside his ears as he stuck out his tongue.

Molly laughed out loud. As she clapped her hand over her mouth, Marietta elbowed her playfully and their *maidel* friends leaned forward to see what was so funny.

Bishop Jeremiah smiled indulgently at Molly before continuing with the announcements. "Our scholars have been practicing and preparing for the annual Christmas Eve program—the first to be held in our new school-house," he said as he gazed out over the crowd. "Also, Teacher Lydianne and her friends have asked me to remind everyone of our Second Christmas gathering in the commons area of The Marketplace on the twenty-sixth. We'll mark this joyous occasion with a potluck lunch, a sing-along with our men's chorus, and games for kids of all ages."

Molly couldn't help grinning when Jeremiah flashed her and Marietta a big smile.

"And speaking of joyous occasions," the bishop continued, "today we help the Helfing twins celebrate their birthday—with not one but *two* big cakes they've brought to share with us. Be sure to give them your best wishes, no matter how *old* they're getting!"

Folks around them laughed good-naturedly. The ladies were rising to head toward the kitchen when a strident voice near the front of the women's side made everyone stop chatting.

"Bishop, before we start in on all this *happiness*, we need to call for a confession—right here and now!"

Molly groaned inwardly. Drusilla Fussner had risen from her pew bench, fist planted on her hip. Her scowl could've curdled milk.

"My errant daughter hasn't seen fit to speak up, so I'll say what needs to be said," Jo's *mamm* continued in an escalating voice. "I expressly warned Josephine not to fall in with the Wengerds, but she disobeyed me and went to Queen City with them anyway! I'm quite sure things went on there that our Lord doesn't approve of—and *I* certainly don't condone them, either."

Molly's heart went out to poor Jo, who sat on the other side of Marietta and Lydianne. With her head in her hands, slumping as her mother spoke, Jo was the picture of humiliated dejection. It was highly irregular for a member to call for someone's confession at church. The proper procedure was to speak with the bishop or one of the preachers *before* the day of worship.

Bishop Jeremiah's face clouded over. "You and Jo and I need to talk about this privately, Drusilla," he suggested. "Shall we step into Saul's office?"

Folks remained quiet as Jo and her mother sidled out of their pew rows.

"How embarrassing for Jo," Marietta whispered. "This explains why she wasn't her usual cheerful self at The Marketplace yesterday."

"Who could believe Nelson would allow anything improper to happen while Jo visited their place?" Molly asked with a frown. "He and Michael are two of the finest men I know—and I was really hoping something more serious would come of Jo's and Michael's friendship."

"It isn't as though Drusilla hasn't had time to get to know the Wengerds, either," Lydianne put in as they all rose from the pew bench. "If I recall, it was *her* idea for them to join her and Jo for supper on Friday nights while they stayed in a *dawdi haus*. What a shame that she's putting Jo through this—calling her out in front of everyone."

"It puts a damper on Christmas, too," Regina remarked with a shake of her head. "Let's not allow this issue to spoil your birthday, girls. Everyone brought *gut* food, and you two have a whole raft of candles to light on your cakes—"

"And we need to sing the birthday song!" Anne Hartzler exclaimed from the row in front of them. "I suspect the bishop will be talking with the Fussners for a while, so I'll get Gabe to lead the singing. This is supposed to be a party!"

Once again Molly was glad they'd had church in the Hartzler home today, because Anne and her mother-in-law allowed nothing to stand in the way of celebrations. As the women gathered in the big, sunny kitchen to handle the common meal preparations, they whispered among themselves about the flare-up that had erupted between the Fussners.

But as the men set up tables in the front room, Gabe spoke above the chatter and the *clicks* of table legs locking into place. "This is one of those birthdays that ends in a five for Molly and Marietta," he called out. "We need to sing loud and proud to the twins—while they can still hear us!"

Laughter filled the kitchen and front room, and everyone around Molly and Marietta burst into the familiar song. Several of the men were singing in harmony. As the final line stretched out and got louder, Molly hugged her sister.

"Doesn't get any better than this—celebrating amongst our friends," she said as applause erupted around them.

"*Jah*, you've got that—oh, what's this, Billy Jay?" Marietta eased out of their embrace, smiling at the dark-haired boy who'd suddenly rushed in from the front room. He handed her an envelope that looked a little lopsided, as though he'd folded the edges and glued them together himself.

"I made you a birthday card, Marietta! And happy birthday to you, too, Molly!" The boy shot back into the crowd of men as though he was too shy to watch Marietta open his card.

As Marietta popped the envelope's seal, some of the women smiled knowingly. Molly wasn't surprised that Glenn's son had made a card for her sister but not for her. After all, Billy Jay spent every afternoon working very hard on his recitation for the Christmas Eve school program with Marietta before joining his *dawdi* and Molly in the noodle factory.

Molly was astounded, however, when Marietta burst into tears.

"Oh my word, what a sweet—" She turned to compose herself, thrusting the homemade card toward Molly.

The card was made from a piece of plain paper folded

in half. In his best second-grade penmanship, Billy Jay had written *Happy Birthday, Marietta* with a purple crayon—but he'd run out of room, so the *tta* was underneath the first part of her name. On the lower half of the front, a brown birthday cake sprouted several red candles with yellow flames. It was so cute, in its little-kid way, that Molly couldn't help smiling as she opened the card.

Her heart lurched when she saw the message inside: stick figures of two men—one with a long gray beard—a little boy, and a baby's face in a basket carrier were clearly meant to represent the Detweiler family. *WE LOVE YOU!*, printed in bold red letters, spanned the bottom of the card. Billy Jay, Glenn, and Reuben had all signed it.

A lump rose in her throat. Molly was struck by the utter sincerity of such a birthday greeting—and by the intensity of the emotion behind it. Glenn had surely coached his son so he'd spell the words correctly . . . but had he suggested the text to Billy Jay, as well, to win Marietta's affection in a way a grown man could not? And had Glenn sent his adorable, rumple-haired son to deliver the card, figuring Marietta might turn away from him but would never reject his child?

What difference does it make? He got the job done— got the message across—didn't he? This is your sister's business, not yours.

Molly slipped the heartfelt card back into its envelope and handed it back to Marietta with a smile. "That's quite a birthday present," she murmured.

Blinking rapidly, Marietta slipped the card into her apron pocket. "I—I didn't see that one coming," she stammered, although the flush of her thin cheeks and her tremulous smile announced that she was pleased rather than put out. "Guess we're never too old for a birthday surprise, *jah*?"

"I'm not really surprised, sister," Molly remarked gently. When she glanced at the other women in the kitchen, they resumed their preparations for the noon meal as though they hadn't been observing the twins' conversation. "This gives you plenty to think about, ain't so? And meanwhile, we need to set our cakes out on the dessert table—"

"I'll follow you out there and stick these on them," Martha Maude declared as she picked up two packages of cake candles. "A birthday's not official until you've made your wishes, after all!"

Molly smiled gratefully at their hostess as she and Marietta picked up their cakes. Moments later, they were the center of attention again in the large front room.

"We're going to have the twins blow out their candles now," Martha Maude announced as the crowd got quiet. "That way, you can help yourselves to birthday cake whenever you're ready for it."

Although their *mamm* had always made a fuss over the two of them blowing out the candles on the oversized cake she baked for them, Molly felt vaguely nervous about standing behind the dessert table with her twin while Martha Maude lit a smattering of candles on top of each cake. When she caught Pete's eye, however—saw the hint of yearning in his gaze—she realized why the ritual felt edgy this morning. Just as the women had been quietly speculating about Marietta's reaction to Billy Jay's birthday card, folks were probably aware that the casual friendship she and Pete had shared for so many years might be developing into something more.

"All right, girls," Regina called out. "Make your wishes!"

"And wish *big*!" Lydianne chimed in.

Molly slipped her hand around her sister's as she leaned toward the beautiful chocolate cake Marietta had made for her—and her twin smiled delightedly at the cream cheese–frosted hummingbird cake in front of her. She closed her eyes and inhaled deeply, wondering what to wish for—

I wish Pete would tell me how he feels about us!

Molly's eyes flew open and she blew out all her candles, with air to spare. Exuberant applause filled the room. Thin wisps of smoke rose from Marietta's candles, as well, and she squeezed Molly's hand.

"It's going to be a big Christmas—a big year—for us, Molly," she predicted beneath the noise of everyone's clapping. "Just you wait and see!"

As conversations resumed around them, the men finished setting up the tables while the women began carrying out trays of desserts, baskets of bread, and the platters and bowls of food folks had brought to share. Molly felt grateful for the birthday wishes everyone extended to them. Now that Mamm and Dat had passed, it was much happier to celebrate with all of these friends rather than at home with just the two of them.

Someone came up behind Molly and slipped a large, warm hand over her eyes. "If you sit with me at lunch, I promise I won't bite," a familiar voice whispered near her ear.

Laughing, Molly turned to look at Pete. "Well, *that* would be something new and different, wouldn't it?" she teased. "Have your table manners improved since you moved in with your *mammi* Margaret?"

Pete's brown eyes sparkled. "Riley and I have agreed to let him do all the biting," he shot back. "So keep your teeth to yourself when you look at this present I've got in mind for you. See you in a few."

He was off like a shot, apparently inspired to help Gabe and Glenn and Reuben shift the last few pew benches into place beside the tables.

Molly blinked, wondering why Pete's long white envelope felt awfully fat to be a birthday card. She sensed she shouldn't open it with other folks close enough to look over her shoulder, so she slipped into the bathroom and shut the door.

Her fingers trembled as she pulled several sheets of folded paper from the envelope. Molly sucked in her breath.

Pete had made sketches of a kitchen, a mudroom, a front room—nearly every area in a home. His bold, precise printing, along with the dimensions he'd jotted beside the kitchen and bathroom cabinets, made Molly squint as she turned the sketches this way and that. Was Pete trying to tell her he was building a new house? Her heart hammered in her chest, wondering what message she should be reading between the meticulous lines he'd drawn.

Quickly folding the papers back into the envelope, Molly left the bathroom just in time to hear Bishop Jeremiah calling for everyone to bow their heads before they ate.

"Oh—and earlier, I forgot to announce another important happening in the life of our congregation," the bishop put in with a big smile. "My nephew Pete has begun his instruction to join the church; if anyone else feels compelled to do the same, you're welcome to join our sessions. Now—let's join together in a silent word of thanks for our meal."

Molly's jaw dropped. When she found Pete in the crowd, he resembled a deer frozen by the glare of headlights. After he'd waited so much longer than most folks to join the church, what did it mean that he was taking his instruction *now*? Most fellows admittedly joined when they had marriage on their minds rather than because of a burning commitment to religion . . .

Pete looks like a man whose secret's been revealed before he was ready. In fact, he seems downright terrified. You could tease him mercilessly—

Molly slipped the envelope into her apron pocket, her mind racing. As Bishop Jeremiah returned to the room in the hallway where the Fussners awaited him, Gabe and Glenn and the other fellows near Pete clapped him on the back and gave him a hard time about taking his instruction.

—but maybe it's best to cut him some slack. Pete could use a little compassion about now. He's taken a big step, after all.

Something in her soul settled, similar to when Riley turned a couple of circles before finding just the right position in his dog bed. She didn't really have to know whether Pete's sketches were of a new home, did she? Molly instinctively realized that he was a man with a new plan—and his plan included her, even if he hadn't yet found the nerve or the words to tell her that.

When she saw Glenn picking up Levi's carrier basket, imploring Marietta to join him with a hopeful gaze, Molly carried the last two bread baskets from the kitchen to place on the tables. Pete needed his space. He would either dash out the door, too embarrassed to sit with her now, or he would recover and resume his usual jokester attitude.

As Molly sliced their cakes to make them easier to serve, Rose Wagler and little Gracie wished her a happy birthday—and so did Esther and Naomi Slabaugh, the other *maidel* sisters of Morning Star. They were Preacher Ammon's kin, rather sanctimonious and spinsterish at times, but Molly decided not to let their personalities rub her wrong on this special day.

"So how old does this make you and Marietta now?" Naomi asked. Her furtive tone and narrowed gaze suggested that she was about to welcome Molly and her sister to the Old Crones' Club, where aging ladies had nothing better to do than gossip and criticize other women's husbands.

"*Jah*, there were too many candles on those cakes to count!" her sister put in a little too cheerfully.

Knowing that she and Marietta were no longer destined to live out their lives alone together, as the Slabaughs were, gave Molly a whole new reason to smile. "The more candles on your cake, the lighter your life," she replied happily. "We're thirty-five now—and our future's so bright, we've got to wear shades!"

With that, Molly turned to find Pete in the crowd. When she spotted him near a back table, his happy-go-lucky grin in place again, she made her way through the other folks who were taking their seats.

Today's the first day of the rest of your life. Make it count!

As her *mamm*'s favorite words rang in her mind, Molly knew they'd never been truer.

Chapter 18

As the bishop's approaching footsteps echoed in the Hartzlers' hallway, Jo prayed as hard as she ever had in her life.

God, You've got to help me—and help Mamm, as well. We can't go on this way any longer—because I have nothing to confess!

Her mother was seated a few feet away from her, glaring incessantly—as though this would prompt Jo to admit her guilt and return their lives to the comfortable, everyday companionship they'd known before they'd ever met the Wengerds.

But Jo couldn't turn back the clock. And she refused to act as though her feelings for Michael didn't matter.

Bishop Jeremiah entered the office and closed the door behind him. He rolled Saul's wooden chair from behind the big desk so he could sit closer to Jo and her *mamm*, without a massive piece of furniture between them. "Have either of you come to any new conclusions?" he asked softly. "Before I went out to lead the table grace, we prayed on this situation. And I reminded you of the proper steps leading to a member's confession—"

"Well, you were wrong, Bishop!" Mamm blurted out. "As a parent watching out for the welfare of my daughter's soul, I have every right to call her to confess. Especially because she's too blind—or too stubborn—to come clean on her own."

Jo sighed. Not only was her mother repeating her earlier misguided logic, she was also speaking loudly enough that folks out in the front room could probably hear her. And she'd defied the bishop to his face!

Jeremiah was gracious enough not to point this out. He settled back in the creaking chair, watching Mamm more closely now, as though reconsidering how to approach the difficult topic they were dealing with. "And what is it you believe Jo needs to confess, Drusilla?"

Mamm sat taller, determined to make her point—and to get her way. "Not only did she go—unchaperoned— to the Wengerd place for three days, she did it after I'd told her not to!"

The bishop smoothed his beard on either side of his mouth, perhaps to wipe a smile from his face. "Children have been acting against their parents' wishes since Adam and Eve raised their two sons," he reminded her. "And let's not forget that Jo's an adult, with the firm sense of right and wrong you and Joe instilled in her as a child—"

"But she's been hoodwinked! Blinded by love—or what she *thinks* is love—because Michael's been sweet-talking her!" Mamm countered. "She's not thinking straight these days."

Jo's cheeks blazed with humiliation. Was there anything more embarrassing than hearing her mother dismiss her tender feelings for Michael with the leader of the church present—and as though Jo weren't sitting right there?

"Falling in love can do that to the most levelheaded amongst us," Bishop Jeremiah pointed out kindly. "It's God's way of opening our hearts and souls to let another person into our lives on a level that allows for two to become one."

"She's not going to marry him!"

Jeremiah's expression became more wary and more concerned as he gazed at Jo's mother. "But, Drusilla, it's the natural order of things for men and women to marry—and it's one of the most important pillars of our Amish faith," he insisted. "The loving, stable relationship you and her father shared served as an excellent example to Jo, showing her how two people learn to live with each other and—"

"Let's leave Joe out of this." Mamm smoothed her apron over her lap, focusing on hands that were getting knobby with arthritis. "I've tried to warn my daughter about the pitfalls of—tried to protect her, because she's led a very sheltered life, Bishop. But despite my efforts on her behalf, she betrayed me by taking up with Michael and Nelson. She's leaving me behind as though all my years of devotion and care mean *nothing* to her."

Tears sprang to Jo's eyes. "That's not true," she protested, turning away in her pain. Even to her own ears, however, her emotion-choked voice sounded less than convincing.

After Bishop Jeremiah gave her a few moments to compose herself, he asked, "And what's your side of this story, Jo? While you were visiting the Wengerd place, did you do anything you need to confess—"

"Absolutely not!" Jo blurted. She hesitated to discuss the soulful hopes and dreams she and Michael had shared as they'd walked together and basked in the beauty of thousands of red poinsettias. But unless the bishop heard the truth, as only she could tell it, her mother's accusations would stand, wouldn't they?

"Matter of fact, Nelson is very aware that Mamm's afraid she'll be left alone if Michael and I—even though they invited her to come along on the visit and she refused to join us," Jo insisted. "Truth be told, I think she's afraid of her feelings for Nelson—who is a very nice man—"

"What a bunch of baloney!" Mamm broke in. "This is just one more example of how the Wengerds have warped your thought process, Josephine."

Only the spark of mirth in Bishop Jeremiah's eyes kept Jo from walking out of the room in total exasperation. Was he reading between the lines, drawing his own conclusions despite the way her mother railed at her?

His expression softened as he held Jo's gaze. "Has Michael made his intentions known to you, Jo?" he asked gently.

She swallowed hard. This still seemed like such a private subject, too tender and new to jeopardize by allowing other folks to analyze it. But she sensed the bishop was taking her side—and for that, she was very grateful.

"*Jah*, he wants to court me, and Nelson has given us his blessing," she whispered. "Michael and I—well, we understand each other. He and his *dat* have expanded their nursery into an *amazing* business, and they appreciate the way I've been able to develop The Marketplace, and—and we speak the same language about such business concerns.

"I have *not* been hoodwinked, Bishop," Jo continued in an urgent rush. "I have been welcomed and included and *valued* for the talents God has given me—more than just cooking and sewing and running a household. I—I already know I'll be expected to give up my bakery and my role as The Marketplace's manager if I marry—"

"How can you even be thinking about marriage?" Mamm demanded incredulously. "You hardly know these people!"

"I've heard enough." Bishop Jeremiah sat forward, his gaze lingering on Jo before he focused on her mother. "I sense nothing sinful or secretive about what Jo has told us, Drusilla. I know you don't agree with me, but I believe your fears for your daughter's welfare are unfounded and—well, they're *your fears*."

He paused until he was sure Mamm wasn't going to interrupt him again. "Every parent wonders if her child's on the right life path, but I feel Jo is living out the aspirations God has had for her all along," Bishop Jeremiah continued. "I see no need for a public confession—or a private one, for that matter."

The bishop allowed a few moments for his decision to sink in. "I know better than to tell you it's time to remarry, Drusilla," he continued carefully, "but I sincerely believe you'd be better off if you had someone to share your life with again—and Nelson Wengerd is a compassionate, upstanding man who would support you well. So's Michael, and I believe he'll take *gut* care of your daughter. Because both of them are somewhat older than a lot of young folks who marry, they stand a better chance of finding true happiness together."

The emotions at war on Mamm's face made her

expression change with every word the bishop was saying, but she held her tongue.

Bishop Jeremiah rose from his chair, smiling at Jo. "I wish you all the best, dear. I hope that—despite your *mamm*'s objections—you and Michael will find a deeply satisfying and lasting love for each other as time goes by."

Mamm stood up, bristling like a cat that had been splashed with water. "All my years of guidance and devotion, tossed aside just like *that*," she said, snapping her fingers for emphasis. "I hope we don't all come to regret your decision, Bishop."

Holding the office door open, he gestured for Mamm and Jo to precede him into the hallway. "God's in charge—and God is *gut*."

"All the time," Jo chimed in. She waited for her mother to head down the hallway before speaking to Jeremiah. "*Denki* so much for your support, Bishop."

"You're welcome, Jo." He sighed as they watched her mother find a place at a table with some of the other ladies. "I'm concerned about your *mamm*'s anxiety. It reminds me a lot of my own mother's difficult disposition a while back, until she got a handle on her um, time of life."

He cleared his throat as he ventured into a topic Jo sensed he didn't speak of often. "I hope this is just Drusilla's hormones we hear talking, and I'm going to encourage my *mamm* and some of the other ladies to speak with her. There are some issues a man should just stay out of."

Hormones? Jo hadn't thought about her mother possibly going through the change of life, which made a lot of women cranky and a little crazy. Jo admired Jeremiah's willingness to mention such a private matter to her—even as she couldn't help chuckling at his tone of voice.

"I don't think I'm the one to be counseling her on such things, either, because no matter what I say, she'll disagree with it," Jo said with a shake of her head. "It's another matter we should pray over and leave to God. Hopefully she'll listen when He and your mother speak to her."

Pete watched Molly approaching him, her gaze so intense that he gripped the top of the table to keep from collapsing unceremoniously onto the bench. What was she thinking? She'd heard his uncle's announcement about his taking church instruction, and she'd surely figured out what his sketches meant by now—

At least she's not running the other way. Whatever she dishes out, I'd better just suck it up.

"Pete! It's *gut* to see you—to finally have a chance to catch up with you today," Molly said breezily. "How've you been?"

Her green eyes seemed catlike and elusive, and after Pete got lost in them he had to remind himself that she was waiting for his response. "Uh—busy!" he blurted. "Really busy."

He gestured toward the bench, wishing his uncle wasn't heading for a spot on the other side of their table—and wishing he didn't sound like a tongue-tied adolescent in Molly's presence. "Well? What'd you think?"

"*Well,*" Molly echoed as she gracefully stepped over the bench and sat down. "That's a deep subject, Shetler."

Pete groaned at their longtime joke. Would he have to

ask her for every specific detail about her thoughts on the drawings—or about his joining the church? He sat down beside her, as close as he dared, considering Uncle Jeremiah's proximity. The bishop had been waylaid by Reuben Detweiler, however, so Pete blundered ahead.

"Do you think those drawings will work—that they'll be something you'd like me to start on?" he whispered nervously. "I'll have to finish Glenn's place first, of course, and then the big remodeling project at my uncle's house, but after that I can—"

When Molly rested her warm hand on his forearm, Pete's mind blanked out.

"I'm not sure I understand," she said hesitantly. "Those sketches are the neatest, most precise renderings I've ever seen, but why are you designing a new house, Pete? Are you tired of living with your unc—"

"That's *your* place, Moll! When Marietta told me we'd be welcome to live there after we got hitched, I— oh, phooey!"

Pete's face flared so hot and red that it would take a fire engine to put out the blaze in his cheeks. Oh, but he'd messed up now! Molly's green eyes suddenly took up her entire face—a face that was turning as pink as his was.

"My—my sister never told *me* about this idea," she rasped. "Does she know you plan to marry her? Do you know that she and Glenn are—"

"I must've left my brains at home today," Pete muttered. "You make me crazy, Molly."

"No, no—don't blame *me* for the condition you were in long before you bunked at our place," she retorted. But at least she was making her usual jokes rather than grilling him—or flat-out rejecting him.

"Let me get this straight," Molly went on in a low voice. "The sketches you gave me are suggestions for remodeling the house where Marietta and I live—"

"Because it's the best birthday present I could think of," Pete put in earnestly. "Because, what with Detweiler building a new house—and he's obviously been trying to win you over ever since he moved in with you—I wanted to offer you *my* alternative. It's tough to compete against a guy with a new house, a cute little boy, and a cuddly baby, not to mention a sweet older *dat* who's been helping you with—"

Once again the warm pressure of Molly's hand on his arm sent Pete's mind into a tailspin. It didn't help that Uncle Jeremiah was taking his place across the table from them—and obviously enjoying the spectacle his blabbering, blundering nephew was making of himself.

Molly's eyes were glowing like an evergreen forest alight with sunshine. "Pete," she whispered. Then she said his name again, as though she, too, needed to regain control of her thoughts. "Pete, you've got it wrong."

His heart stopped beating. What did he have wrong? Did Molly care so much for Glenn that he was too late offering her his remodeling plans—offering her his heart? If she was giving him a kiss-off, why did she have to look so pretty? And why did her mouth, mere inches from his own as she leaned toward him, look so very kissable?

"H-how do you mean, *wrong*?" he stammered.

She smiled sweetly. "Before we twins lit the candles on our cakes a while ago, Billy Jay gave my sister a homemade card that knocked her socks off," she explained patiently. "If you'd noticed the way Marietta has taken to little Levi and Billy Jay—and if you'd seen this card picturing all four of the Detweilers, saying they *love* her—you'd realize that Glenn's falling hard for my sister, Pete. Not for me."

Across the table, Uncle Jeremiah was choking on his laughter, as though Molly had just stated the world's most obvious truth. Apparently the bishop—and everyone else—already knew that Detweiler was pursuing the other Helfing twin, and Pete was the last person to figure it out.

He swallowed hard, digesting what he'd just heard. "So Detweiler hasn't been using his cute little kid and his *dat* to make you want to—to become a part of his family?"

Molly shook her head, holding his gaze. It was one of the most sincere, straightforward answers she'd ever given him. No punching his arm. No teasing or spinning his words in a different direction. No fingers crossed behind her back.

A weight lifted from his soul. Pete's mind and body relaxed as he realized what this meant. "So you're telling me I didn't need to sketch remodeling plans for your house to convince you—"

"Oh, I'm not letting you wiggle out of your offer, Shetler," Molly challenged. "Our house *does* need some updating. And if a top-shelf carpenter like you wants to take on such a project, who am I to say no?

"But we're just talking about the remodeling, understand," she continued, raising one eyebrow. "Before you go thinking new kitchen cabinets will be your ticket to living at our place again, you have some *talking* to do! A man who's finally decided to take his church instruction has a lot on his mind—and I'm not going to *read* your mind, Shetler. I'm not making any assumptions, either. You'll have to spell it all out for me."

"*Gut* for you, Molly! You go, girl!" Uncle Jeremiah said, slapping the table in his excitement.

Pete let out an exasperated sigh. "We'll talk later," he muttered, although he felt as lighthearted as he'd ever been in his life. Molly knew exactly what his intentions were—and she'd cleared the slate for him. Glenn was no longer a rival. It was all good, and he intended to do a lot more than spelling things out when he and Molly could be alone, without his uncle and the other folks who were passing platters in the Hartzlers' crowded front room.

Before anyone could further distract them, Pete grasped Molly's hand and held her gaze. "After lunch we're going for that truck ride you refused a while back, all right? Just you and me and Riley—"

"Oh, I'd love to see Riley!"

Pete looked helplessly toward the ceiling, hoping God might eventually rescue him from all these little rabbit trails Molly was leading him along. "I should've stuck with my original plan and had Riley be my front man—should've had him deliver those drawings to you," he remarked under his breath.

Molly considered this statement. "*Jah*, that would've been a fun touch, but his slobber would've smeared your sketches, ain't so? You spent a lot of time and thought on your drawings, Shetler."

Hope glimmered within him at her compliment.

She smiled demurely, including his uncle in her gaze. "But getting back to your invitation—you realize that as a member of the Old Order, I'm not supposed to ride in anyone's car on a Sunday. And the bishop's wondering if I'll respond properly or if I'll break that rule right under his nose."

Pete blinked. Leave it to Molly to bring up one of those obscure Amish regulations that he'd never understood the need for. He kept his mouth shut, however, awaiting Uncle Jeremiah's reaction.

The man across the table pretended to weigh the pros and cons of the situation. "Under the circumstances, Molly, I believe I can trust you to steer my nephew onto the straight and narrow if I say you can take that ride with him," he said lightly. "*Denki* for reminding him that a steadfast church member knows and follows our *Ordnung* as a part of everyday life in the faith."

"And *denki* for your understanding and your permission, Bishop Jeremiah," Molly said sweetly. She gazed at Pete full on, a hint of victory shining in her deep green eyes. "It won't be long before you get rid of your pickup, Shetler, so I'd better ride in it this afternoon, *jah*? With my buddy Riley."

Pete reminded himself that Molly would always have the upper hand when it came to getting in the first—and last—joke. And that was fine, as long as she was joking only with him.

"That's the plan—and we'll be riding in my new courting buggy, once Saul gets it built," he confirmed as he reached for the platter of sandwiches to his left. "Let's eat and have some birthday cake—and then we'll start the *real* celebrating."

Chapter 19

Molly laughed out loud. As soon as Pete—who was being exceptionally polite—opened the passenger-side door for her, Riley leaped into the truck and planted himself in the center of the front seat.

"Riley, *move!*" Pete muttered. "I'm sitting by Molly—"

"But Riley wants to be next to both of us," she pointed out as she took her place between the dog and the door. "And that way I don't have to sit between those two seat belt fasteners."

Frowning, Pete got in on the driver's side. "But I got a truck with a bench seat and the gearshift on the column so somebody could sit in the middle—"

"Your girlfriends?" Molly teased. She leaned forward to look around Riley so she could nail Pete with her gaze. "It's only a matter of time before those other ladies—and your truck—are history anyway, ain't so? When you join the church and get a buggy, I'll sit next to you, Shetler."

When his mouth clapped shut, she knew she'd won this round—and Riley congratulated her by giving her a wet, sloppy kiss on the cheek. Molly wrapped her arm around the big, affectionate golden, chuckling at his excitement.

"It's *gut* to see you, boy," she said in the singsong voice she reserved for Pete's dog. "Marietta and I have really missed having you around, Riley, but it sounds like you'll be back soon—at least while your *dat* does the remodeling work at our place. By the time he's finished, maybe he'll have earned enough brownie points that you can live there all the time! Would you like that?"

Riley woofed loudly, thumping the seat with his tail. He was so excited that the windshield fogged over with his panting.

Pete closed his door and started the engine, shaking his head. "I should've known the dang dog would get more attention than I—"

"*Jah*, you should've!" Molly put in with a laugh. "Riley will always be cuter than you, so you might as well accept that. I only spend time with cute boys who wiggle when they see me—which might explain why I've reached the ripe old age of thirty-five without being married, *jah*?"

"Oh, there are *lots* of reasons you're not married, Moll," Pete shot back. "What man in his right mind would put up with you?"

Molly smiled. He was back to trading insults with her, just like in the earlier days of their friendship. It felt good to know he hadn't given up that part of his personality just because he'd made some serious changes in his life. "So how old are you, Pete? Not that it really matters."

"Oh, it matters. I'm old enough to know better than to take up with the likes of *you*," he replied as he prodded the gas pedal. His truck shot down to the next intersection, fishtailing on an icy patch before he could bring it to a stop. "I'm twenty-eight. A late bloomer, compared to most guys who decide to stay with the Amish faith and—and *maybe* get serious about marriage. Never thought I'd cave in on those two situations, but hey. I've learned never to say never."

Molly nodded, following his conversation with a rising sense of hope. "I'm sure folks are wondering why a prime fellow like you is interested in a stubborn, outspoken *maidel* who's a much later bloomer than you are, Shetler."

"Puh. I feel sorry for you, Moll. It's a mission of mercy, plain and simple." Pete whipped the truck around the corner onto the county highway, focusing on the road rather than on her. "And now that you've told me Detweiler has plans for your sister and that new house of his, I'm *really* feeling bad for you. You'll be alone on the farm, making noodles all by your lonesome in that factory—"

"Why do you think that?" Molly demanded playfully. "Marietta's schedule will change when she hitches up with Glenn, but she and I were making noodles with our *mamm* when we were wee girls. She'll keep working with me, Shetler—it's our family business, after all. And she'll no doubt bring Reuben and Billy Jay along as helpers."

"*Jah*, but then she'll go home to fix supper and see to her new family, and there you'll be, the odd woman out," Pete continued without missing a beat. "Breaks my heart to picture you sitting at the supper table all by yourself, Moll. If you make a pan of noodle pudding, how long will it take you to eat it if no one else is around?"

Molly blinked. In her mind, she pictured the scene Pete had described, and it took her aback. He was teasing . . . but he wasn't.

"Well, don't go sacrificing your young, smart-aleck self for my sake, Shetler," she fired back. "I've lived this long without a husband, and I'll do just fine. I have a thriving business to run. My sister will invite me to her new home several times a week, you know—because we've always done everything together—"

"And no matter what—if you're single or married—that will change when Marietta takes up with the Detweilers. Are you ready for that?"

For a teaser like Pete, that was a question with a lot of perceptive depth. And it smacked her right between the eyes, too.

Molly remained quiet for a few moments. "Okay, so you're right about that part," she conceded softly. "But we Helfings have always found a way to push beyond change and hardship—like when Marietta conquered her cancer. I—I'll be fine, Pete. Really I will."

She blinked. Even to her own ears, her words sounded wistful and plaintive.

Molly hugged Riley harder. She refused to admit it aloud, but maybe Pete *would* be the man to save her from herself after Marietta followed her heart into the Detweiler family.

She pondered this as Pete drove up the street leading to Morning Star's park. The swings were swaying in the wintry breeze, as though invisible children sat in them. The splash pad was deserted, as were the slide and the jungle gym. A snowman with a carrot nose, a cowboy hat, and two sticks for arms showed the earlier presence of children, but at this hour on Sunday afternoon it seemed she and Pete—and Riley—were the only souls present.

Pete killed the engine and opened his door. "Out you go, boy."

The golden sprang eagerly over Pete's lap and hit the

ground. After he ran in a few circles, he stopped to gaze back at them.

Without a word, Pete stepped outside and came around to open Molly's door. As he waited for her to step down from the truck, his brown eyes shone with an intensity she wasn't sure how to interpret.

"Come here, you," he whispered.

Molly blinked. Something told her not to smart back at him this time, because he was a man on a mission—and he was making her a part of that mission. Her feet had barely touched the parking lot when he took her in his arms and kissed her.

Although she'd often dared to wonder what it would be like to kiss cocky, unpredictable Pete Shetler, Molly was caught totally off guard when his lips pressed firmly into hers. She'd heard on the grapevine that he'd dated a number of English girls, while her own social life had been very limited—especially for the last ten years or so, when men had apparently assumed she was destined to remain single.

As the breath left her lungs in a gust of surprise, she heard Pete gasp, as well. He eased away to look into her eyes, but then moved in again, more gently this time. Molly allowed him to take the lead, responding in a way that she hoped was what he wanted—

But as soon as her eyes fluttered shut and her heart took over, her soul took flight and soared effortlessly with his. Molly forgot that they were in the middle of a public park leaning against the side of his truck on a cold day in December. She was bundled in her winter coat and heavy bonnet, and Pete wore a flannel-lined barn coat and stocking cap, yet a different sort of warmth surged through her system. She wrapped her arms around his neck, responding to his every nuance as for several long, lovely moments, his lips led hers in a dance that felt instinctual, perfect.

When Pete eased away this time, his brown eyes were wide, with very dark pupils. Was that *awe* softening his handsome face? Molly wasn't sure of anything anymore, except that their first kiss had been nothing like what she'd expected. It was so much *more*.

"Molly," he whispered.

She swallowed hard, nodding.

"That was . . . incredible."

"It—it was," she agreed.

"Um, about those sketches," Pete began hesitantly. "I should've given you more of a clue about—"

"I shouldn't have shot off my mouth this morning about—"

"—and I shouldn't have assumed you'd *like* it if I remodeled your home," he continued, gazing intently into her eyes. "I just thought you might prefer that to moving into a home where the Detweilers are already set in their patterns and—"

Molly pressed a gloved finger across his lips. "Why are we talking about Glenn?" she murmured. "Kiss me again, Shetler. That's something else you're really, really *gut* at."

His delighted laughter rang out in the cold air. He slipped his arm behind her neck to cushion it before moving in for another mind-boggling meeting of their eager mouths.

Molly got lost in the wonder of Pete's affection. His teasing sense of swagger had melted away, and the man

in her arms seemed as genuinely attracted to her as she
was to him. His kiss wasn't out to *prove* anything. Pete's
lips made her feel feminine and desirable, indescribably
buoyant.

*If he wasn't holding me against his truck, I might float
away.*

A *yip* and an insistent paw on Pete's leg made them
move apart, chuckling. Riley sat in the snow at their feet,
gazing up at them as though he, too, realized something wonderful had just happened—even if it didn't include *him*.

Pete cleared his throat. He held her gaze as though he
couldn't possibly look away. "Wow. We're in trouble now,
Moll."

Her cheeks tingled with the awareness of their close-
ness, both physical and emotional. "*Jah. Gut* thing we
both know how to dish up trouble and then deal with it
when it's flung back at us, ain't so?"

His brown eyes reminded her of fresh-perked coffee.
"How do you come up with these ideas just off the cuff
like that? Maybe that's why I like you, Molly," he added
in a pensive tone. "You're a quick thinker. I need somebody like you in my life, because I tend to act first and
then think about it—usually too late."

"You do need me, Shetler," she agreed, brushing a
windblown lock of blond hair from his face. "High time
you admitted that, ain't so?"

Monday afternoon, Pete was still high on his new-
found love for Molly. He was determined to live up to the
standard she'd set for him and to be the man who'd make

her happy. *Forever* hadn't been a concept he'd pondered in his days of roaming around in his truck with his dog—especially when it came to settling down with a wife.

But Molly's kiss had brought his life into sharper focus. He felt like a man with a purpose now.

As he eased his way higher on Glenn's new roof to replace a shingle that had blown off, Pete realized the light drizzle they'd gotten earlier had frozen into more of a coating than he'd anticipated. But he'd gotten out the ladder, and he was only a couple of feet from completing his quick task. He carefully clambered into place and positioned the shingle, planting his feet firmly on the textured surface of the roof to steady himself.

As he raised his hammer, Molly's beautiful face—those long lashes that brushed her cheeks when she closed her eyes to kiss him—sent a surge of adrenaline through him.

Pete struck the first tack just as his lower foot slipped. When he scrambled for traction, his body went into a slide that he was powerless to stop. As he plummeted past the guttering into a free fall, all he could do was cry out in shock and anger at himself. Only an idiot repaired a roof on a slick winter's day. Glenn had warned him, and had Molly been there, she would've told him in no uncertain terms to stay on the ground.

When he hit the snowdrift and landed—racking his body with the impact—everything went black.

Chapter 20

Tired and cold to the bone, Glenn walked toward the Helfings' home early that evening filled with a lingering sense of dread. When Pete had hollered that morning, he'd looked out the window just in time to see his friend hit the snowdrift. As Glenn and Gabe and their Mennonite friends Howard and Chuck had rushed outside, the unnatural angle of Pete's body had sent a frisson of fear through him.

What was going on with God and His world that Glenn had lost his wife, his mother, and his home in recent months, and now Pete's life might be hanging by a fragile strand, as well?

Howard, the local fire chief, had called nine-one-one on his cell phone, so help had arrived quickly. Glenn had accompanied Pete in the ambulance, and not long after the folks in the emergency room had whisked him away, Bishop Jeremiah had arrived.

"What happened?" Pete's uncle asked, his brow furrowed with worry. "He was on top of the world this morning, happier than I've seen him in years."

Glenn shrugged, exasperated. "Not five minutes after

I warned him not to replace that dumb shingle, I heard him setting the ladder against the house," he replied hoarsely. "Next thing I knew, he was sprawled on the ground, unconscious. Probably doesn't have a bone in his body that's not broken or dislocated. I—I'm sorry I couldn't talk him out of—"

"Don't blame yourself," the bishop had said with a shake of his head. "Pete was on another planet when he came home from driving around with Molly yesterday. After all these years it took us to convince him to join the church and get hitched, *now* he falls off the roof. *Denki* for taking care of him, Glenn—or trying to, anyway."

Lost in his troubling thoughts, Glenn stumbled in the darkness and nearly hit the ground himself before he reached the Helfings' porch steps. It was small comfort that Molly was at the hospital with Pete so he wouldn't wake up terrified and alone, attached to monitors and racked with pain. Just when the new house had been coming along so well—Glenn thought they might move into it after Christmas—the man who'd spearheaded its construction would be out of commission for months. If he survived.

Pete still hadn't regained consciousness when Glenn had left the hospital, nearly two hours after nurses had whisked Shetler's motionless body away on a gurney.

Glenn stepped in out of the cold and shut the mudroom door behind him. It seemed a minor miracle that after all he'd been through during the past hours, the aroma of baking chicken wafted around him. He shrugged out of his coat and entered the kitchen, where the table was set for supper and a pie waited on the counter—such ordinary details, yet he no longer took them for granted.

Voices came from the front room. As often happened at this time of day, Marietta and Billy Jay were working on his recitation for the Christmas Eve program, so Glenn remained in the kitchen. Keeping out of his son's sight, Glenn peered through the door. What he beheld made his breath catch in his throat.

Marietta sat on the sofa, cradling Levi in the crook of her arm as she held a bottle of goat's milk to his lips. Dat sat tipped back in the recliner, probably snoozing. And Billy Jay stood near the end table, in the glow of the battery lamp, facing Marietta.

"'And there were in the same country shepherds abiding in the field, keeping watch over their flock by night,'" he recited in a calm, steady voice. Then the boy's eyes widened, and his face lit up. "'And lo, the angel of the Lord came upon them, and the glory of the Lord shone round about them: and they were sore afraid.'"

Glenn blinked. That was his son in there, his rumple-haired second-grade scholar with a gap where a front tooth was missing, telling this ancient story with a precision— a quiet excitement—that grabbed Glenn by the heartstrings and wouldn't let go.

Marietta was nodding her encouragement, hanging on the child's every word. She looked proud enough to pop.

Billy Jay took in a deep breath and raised his voice. "'And the angel said unto them, *fear not*! For, behold, I bring you good tidings of great joy which shall be to all people,'" he said, quickening his pace with the urgency of the words. "'For unto you is born this day in the city of David a Savior, which is Christ the Lord.'"

Filled with wonder, as though he stood among those long-ago shepherds, Glenn pressed his lips together to keep from blurting out his praise as Billy Jay continued. This kid—*his* kid!—who couldn't sit still and do his homework for ten minutes at a time was recounting the ancient story of Jesus' birth with an amazement that bespoke a deep, trusting faith. And who could've guessed that Billy Jay would have the patience to learn these passages, much less speak them with an obvious understanding of what they meant?

"'Glory to God in the highest, and on earth peace, good will toward men!'"

Billy Jay's voice filled the front room, as though he was playing the part of the entire heavenly host all by himself.

"You did it, Billy Jay! You said your whole passage, and you said it exactly right!" Marietta crowed from the couch.

When she extended her arm, Billy Jay rushed over to land beside her on the couch. As they cuddled, Glenn suddenly envied his son . . . and he knew he was in love. In slightly more than a week, with her gentle, regular assistance, Marietta had taught his little boy an entire passage of the Bible—not just the words, but the feeling behind them.

And meanwhile, she looked utterly comfortable holding Levi, feeding him his bottle as though she'd done it since his birth.

Because of the body trauma her cancer treatment had caused, Marietta Helfing was far too thin—flatter than a pancake—and sometimes she got tired more quickly than she was willing to admit. Her short hair escaped her *kapp* in tousled waves in the front, and it would take years for it to grow long enough to wear in a traditional Amish bun.

Yet in the halo of lamplight, as she gazed at his two sons with such love in her eyes, she took on the tranquil beauty of Mary beholding Jesus in His newborn glory.

It was a holy moment Glenn knew he'd never forget.

When Marietta caught sight of him, the spell was broken—yet the way her slender face lit up filled his heart with hope. "Oh, Glenn, you just missed hearing Billy Jay recite—"

"No, I heard every word," he said, approaching the couch with an accelerating heartbeat. "Billy Jay, you were awesome! And Marietta, I can't thank you enough for helping him learn his piece for the program. Had I been working with him, we'd still be on the first line."

Marietta winked. She winked at *him*! "Ah, but Billy Jay and I, we're special-*gut* friends," she explained, nodding along with his son. "And sometimes friends work together better than parents and kids, *jah*?"

Glenn couldn't answer. He suddenly yearned to be Marietta's special-*gut* friend—

Oh, it goes way, way deeper than that.

As he looked at the small remaining space on the couch beside her, his heart hammered in his chest. Did he dare scoot in to sit with them, or would that blow the moment? Little Levi was dozing so peacefully—

Marietta slid toward Billy Jay, and then her eyes issued the invitation Glenn had secretly yearned for—for longer than he'd realized. Before he lost his nerve, he wedged himself between the arm of the couch and Marietta.

The space was tight enough that the only way to make his position work was to slip his arm around her shoulders. As if he'd plugged in a cord, Marietta's face lit up—and so did Billy Jay's.

"Well, now," Dat said from across the room. "That's a sight for sore eyes. Everybody cozied up on the couch like a family. Best Christmas present ever."

Glenn's pulse raced as he sat against Marietta, with her face mere inches from his. His father sounded groggy from his nap, but his perception was spot-on: when Marietta was with them, they felt like a *family* again.

It was the wrong moment to kiss her for the first time, yet that urge told Glenn how far his feelings for her had come in the past couple of weeks. It was also a poor time to talk about Pete's situation, but maybe the day's tragedy would keep him from blundering ahead too quickly, saying something to Marietta that he wasn't yet ready to express. And perhaps her calming presence was exactly what he needed to help him deal with Pete's accident.

"I suppose you heard what happened at the house this morning," Glenn said softly. He glanced across the room to include his *dat* in the conversation.

"*Jah*, when Chuck stopped by to tell us about Pete's fall, Molly went straight to the hospital with him," Marietta said in a worried voice.

"I bet she shot outta here like a chicken bein' chased by an alligator!" Billy Jay piped up. "Teacher Lydianne read us a story about that today—"

Marietta gently shushed him, but she was smiling at the picture his words had created. "What's the latest on his condition, Glenn? What a horrible thing for Pete— and for you, now that you're so close to being finished with the house."

Glenn's body relaxed. He squeezed Marietta's shoulder, grateful for her support. Between his son's comic relief and Marietta's quiet concern, he was better able to sort out his feelings about the calamity he'd witnessed.

"They weren't telling me a lot at the hospital, except that he's scheduled for some immediate surgery to repair his broken bones and injured muscles," Glenn replied. "Their biggest concern was that he hadn't regained consciousness. All of his systems seemed to be functioning, but they couldn't rouse him."

"Molly must be at wit's end if she can see him but can't speak with him," Marietta murmured. "The way those two shoot words at each other—like kids with toy bows and arrows—she'll be feeling very desperate until she hears his voice again. Let's pray for both of them, shall we? It's the best thing we can do to help them, so God will hear us and work out His will in their lives."

When Marietta bowed her head, Glenn followed her lead.

"Father God, we ask for Your presence with Pete and Molly," she said in simple sincerity. "Heal him and guide his doctors to do the right things to restore his health. Help Molly find ways to help him, as well, and grant her the strength to accept Your will for Pete's life—and for their life together going forward. We ask these things in the name of Your dear and holy son, Jesus, come down from heaven to save us from our sins. Amen."

Glenn exhaled slowly. He felt better knowing that his friend's life was indeed in God's hands—and that Pete had a good woman beside him to help him through the aftermath of his accident.

Life is finer with a gut *woman beside you. And I'm grateful to You for that, too, Lord.*

* * *

Through her tears, Molly gazed at Pete in his hospital bed. As she sat beside him, grasping his hand—one of the few body parts that wasn't covered in a bandage or attached to a monitor—she wondered what must be going on inside his head. Was he aware of his surroundings, aware she was with him? Or was his mind a dark, empty void?

If he doesn't come around, what'll I do? How will I ever get along without Pete, now that we've finally agreed we're meant to be together?

She was listening to his shallow breathing so intently that she didn't notice when someone entered the dim room, which was lit only by the glow of the monitors.

"Still no response from him?"

Molly jumped, letting out a little yelp.

"I'm sorry, dear," Bishop Jeremiah said in a louder voice. "I should've let you know I was here, but I thought—with your head on the mattress that way—you might be taking a nap. You could probably use one, late as it is."

Molly blinked. She glanced up at the wall clock, wondering how it was already after eight o'clock. "I, uh—maybe I did drift off," she admitted. "But no, he hasn't made a peep. Hasn't moved a muscle, either. I—I don't know what to do, or what to think."

Pete's uncle brought a folding chair over and set it beside hers. He placed a lidded plastic container on the bedside table and rolled it over so she could reach it. "I figured you might still be here, so Mamm sent you some dinner. Considering that the surgeon told us they'd sedated Pete pretty heavily before they patched him up, I'm not surprised he's still zonked out."

Molly didn't feel the least bit hungry, but she popped off the container's lid. "What if . . . what if he doesn't come out of it?"

The bishop gently grasped her wrist. "Let's keep the faith and not worry about that yet, all right? Pete took a hard fall, but he's strong and fit and young—and feisty, *jah*?"

Molly nodded doubtfully.

"And now that you two have finally realized you're meant for each other, he has every reason to fight his way back to us," Jeremiah continued with utter conviction. "Have you told him you expect to see him up and around?"

Molly's eyes widened. "I—I haven't said anything. What *gut* would that do?"

The bishop shrugged. "They say the sense of hearing works long after it seems the other senses aren't functioning. Pete will listen to you better than anyone else, Molly—and you don't hold back when it comes to telling him what to do."

Molly laughed despite her desperation. "*Jah*, that's true."

He nodded toward her dinner box, which included a ham sandwich, a container of applesauce, and a couple of cookies. "Eat up, and then why don't we head home? Tomorrow's another day, and everything looks better after a night's rest. Pete's going to be out cold all night, I imagine."

Even though she didn't want to leave Pete alone in this

strange, intimidating place, Jeremiah was right. Molly bit into the sandwich and realized she was famished.

"What about Riley? How's he doing?" she asked. "He was surely at Glenn's house while they were working today, *jah*?"

"He was, and he's wandering from room to room at home now with a bewildered expression on his face, looking for Pete." Jeremiah glanced at the monitors around them, gathering his thoughts. "When Pete comes around, I might ask the doctor if Riley can come for a visit—but we'll take things as they come. The surgeon determined that Pete suffered a concussion, among other things, and he'll need to be kept quiet and perfectly still for a while—without a big, busy dog jumping on the bed or begging him to play ball."

Molly nodded, taking another bite of her sandwich. "Riley's very persuasive that way. He refuses to be ignored."

"He does. I bet if you came over and romped in the snow with him every now and again, he'd be a much happier dog."

It was a good idea, and Molly brightened. "I will—and I'll bring Billy Jay to run him around. Pete'll feel better knowing somebody's playing with Riley."

While she finished her sandwich, Jeremiah walked around the bed for a closer look at his nephew. "Well, at least he didn't land on his face. Pete often counts on his *gut* looks to get him what he wants—but don't tell him I said that!"

Molly laughed, and it made her feel better. "I tease him about that. Truth be told, his shaggy blond hair and daredevil smile suckered me in a long time ago—and I can't wait to see that smile again."

"You will, Molly," the bishop assured her. "Keep praying and believing. Ask and you'll receive—knock and Pete will answer when he's ready. He's still in there behind this motionless face, waiting to come out of his temporary darkness. You'll be the light of his life, you know."

As they left the hospital, Molly hoped the bishop was right. It was a short ride home in his rig, and she was grateful for his uplifting company—just as she was pleased to see her sister, Glenn, and Reuben at the kitchen table playing Monopoly when she arrived. Their faces reflected their concern as they looked up at her.

"How is he?" Glenn asked.

"You stayed at the hospital so long, we were wondering if something had gone wrong," Marietta put in softly. "I left you a plate of supper in the oven."

Molly stepped up behind her sister's chair to embrace her. "*Denki* for thinking of me—and Pete, too. He came through surgery all right, but he's still heavily sedated and—and the doctor's biggest concern is that he has a bad concussion. They couldn't rouse him before they had to sedate him for surgery."

"After a fall like that, rest is the best thing for him," Reuben remarked. He rolled the dice and slid his top hat token down the side of the game board to Marvin Gardens. "I've taken a tumble or two from a roof in my day. Wasn't the most fun I've ever had, recovering from them, but I lived to tell about it. Pete will, too. He's every bit as hardheaded as I am, you know."

Molly smiled in spite of her concerns, fetching her warm plate from the oven. As she sat down at the table, it occurred to her that the scene was a little cozier than usual—that a subtle shift had occurred in her absence. Instead of sitting across from each other in their usual places, Glenn was seated at the head of the table with Marietta close beside him on his left . . . the traditional places for a husband and wife. Reuben sat on Glenn's other side, smiling like the cat that ate the canary. He focused on the piles of colored money neatly tucked under the game board in front of him.

As Molly cut into her chicken breast with her fork, she also realized that the other three people at the table had chosen to play Monopoly because they were waiting up for her, to hear news of Pete. Their concern and dedication touched her. It was the sort of thing she expected of her twin, but she was surprised to find the Detweilers in the kitchen, as well—maybe because she wasn't accustomed to having additional folks around who felt like . . . family.

Marietta reached in front of Glenn to jab the board repeatedly near Reuben's top hat. "Welcome to Marvin Gardens!" she crowed, keeping her voice low so she wouldn't wake the kids. "You owe me five hundred bucks in rent, Reuben!"

"No way! That's highway robbery!" Glenn's *dat* shot back. "Show me where it says that on your property card."

Marietta arched her eyebrow at him. "Maybe you'd rather recount the number of spaces you traveled, then?" she teased, uncovering the dice. "Seems to me you were distracting us with your talk of falling off rooftops and you should've landed one space farther along, *jah*?"

Reuben sighed dramatically. He smacked the Go to Jail square with his token before placing it in the opposite corner, where the jail was. "I can't get anything past you, missy," he muttered playfully. "Glenn, however, is clueless. He's been so busy gawking at you, he hasn't noticed that I've snuck a couple of ten-dollar bills from his stash. Serves him right for piling his money willy-nilly instead of organizing it nice and neat under the edge of the board, the way you and I have."

Reuben blithely returned the bills to his son's disorganized cash stack. "Okay, I've confessed now. The game can go on."

Molly started laughing, and everyone else joined her, grateful for a moment of mirth on this day when such serious things had happened to Pete.

It was also a moment of gratitude to God, as Molly saw it: Glenn's *dat*, bless him, was sharp enough to be cheating at Monopoly. Not long ago, folks had been afraid Reuben's mind was failing him, but now that he was surrounded by folks who were living their lives and loving again, his depression had lifted.

Glenn, too, seemed to realize that he'd turned a corner emotionally. He playfully punched his father's arm before rolling the dice to take his turn. "I suppose we can forgive you for that, Dat," he remarked. He tapped his race car token along the board, passing Marietta's thimble and landing on Park Place.

"Finally, I can buy this property and complete my set!" he said as he pulled the money from his messy pile. "It's late, but let's keep playing so I can clean you two out and *win* this game. It feels *gut* to be having fun again."

Chapter 21

Marietta hummed a carol as she spread pink peppermint frosting on the chocolate cake she'd baked early Tuesday morning. She'd agreed to take lunch to the work site so Molly could visit the hospital to see how Pete was doing, and the whole house shared the tranquil happiness her cooking brought her. Ordinarily, she and her sister would be working in the noodle factory, replenishing what they'd sold at The Marketplace on Saturday, but Pete's accident had changed their day's priorities. With Billy Jay in school, Levi napping in his basket, and Reuben helping Glenn at the Detweiler place, she was savoring some quiet time in the kitchen.

As she snapped the plastic lid on the cake pan, she smiled at the baby. With wisps of dark hair framing his face and long, dark lashes curving on his pink cheeks, he was the image of his handsome *dat*.

This is how it can be every day if you and Glenn get hitched.

Marietta blinked. Ever since she'd received the birthday card declaring the Detweilers' love, thoughts of a possible marriage had flirted with her. But it wasn't her place to pursue that subject. Glenn was still grieving his wife and his mother. She'd thoroughly enjoyed watching his dark eyes sparkle during their Monopoly game, which he'd won around eleven o'clock last night.

But he wasn't out of the emotional woods yet. Pete's accident had only added another layer of worry to the burden Glenn carried. He was a wonderful man and a fine father to his boys, but Marietta knew better than to get her hopes up anytime soon. Life had dealt him a difficult hand over the past months, and his new house didn't guarantee that his dark days of despair were completely behind him.

Marietta glanced at the kitchen clock. If she wanted to reach the construction site with the men's lunch by noon, she needed to leave around eleven thirty. Before that, she had to allow time to hitch up the horse and load the containers of hot food in the buggy—and before those things could happen, she needed to feed and change Levi.

Having a baby in the house had altered her and Molly's routine more than she'd anticipated. Marietta adored Glenn's boys, but each of them required time and attention that she and her sister had previously devoted to their noodle making. It went unsaid between them that their December sales at The Marketplace had been much lower than anticipated because of their youngest guests.

If you marry—and if Molly marries—what will become of your business? Mamm ran it as an integral part of her household schedule for years, but she had the two of us helping her. And who knows whether the church leaders will even allow us to keep our store at The Marketplace after we tie the knot?

As she stirred the big pot of chili on the stove, these

thoughts spiraled in her mind without revealing any answers. Around ten thirty, Marietta eased Levi out of his basket, hoping he would remain in a sleepy state while she changed his diaper—but no. The wee boy let out a wail when she disturbed him, and with all his kicking and crying, it took her twice as long as usual to accomplish that single task. His bottle of goat's milk was awaiting him in a pan of hot water on the stove, but every time she tried to pop the nipple into his open mouth, Levi turned his head and howled even louder.

This is how it can be every day if you and Glenn get hitched.

The words took on a different meaning this time. Deep down, Marietta doubted she would ever adjust to the strident sound of Levi's crying. He would outgrow diapers and inexplicable upsets in time, but did she have the emotional fortitude to weather these daily ordeals? As the baby's wails filled her previously serene kitchen, she quickly made a pacifier of sugar in a handkerchief, as Glenn had shown her, and placed the dampened bulb of it in Levi's mouth.

Instead of trying to feed him, she put him back in his carrier. She packed his warm bottle among the containers of hot food in the cooler, donned her wraps, and brought the hitched buggy to the house. By the time everything was loaded, Marietta was fifteen minutes later than she'd intended to be when she started to the work site.

But we made it, she thought as she glanced at Levi. His carrier rode on the front floor of the buggy, where she could see him, and the rig's rocking motion soothed him into a half-sleepy state again. Marietta hoped he'd remain quiet while she was serving lunch, but who could tell? The whack of a hammer or the whine of a power saw might startle him, and then she'd have to start her settling routine all over again.

There are some advantages to staying single, ain't so?

Though she'd always longed to be a mother, Marietta hated to admit that she might not be cut out to handle the stresses of parenting—which came so naturally to her married friends, for whom having babies and small children underfoot was the rule rather than the exception. She warned herself not to get swept away in a haze of romantic fantasy whenever she thought about Glenn, because he was a package deal. And once she'd said *Yes* and *I do*, there would be no going back to her peaceful *maidel* state.

As the new Detweiler home came into view, Marietta set aside her conflicting thoughts. The structure closely resembled the house that had burned down, except—because the weather had been too cold for painting—white siding covered the outside. The new windows still bore manufacturer's stickers, and the gray roof shingles shone dully in the sunlight.

All around the foundation, dirt had been pressed into place so the rain would drain away from the house, and the remainder of the yard was covered with snow. With the original trees and outbuildings still in place, the Detweiler place didn't look much the worse for wear, although Marietta suspected the lawn would be a muddy mess come spring. No trace of the fire remained, which had to be a big relief to Glenn and Reuben when they came here to work.

Levi's squawk drew Marietta from her woolgathering. When she drove the rig behind the house, where other buggies and a couple of pickups were parked, she was pleased to see Reuben stepping out the back door.

"Hey there, lunch lady!" he called out cheerfully. "What can I help you with?"

Marietta set the buggy's brake. "*Denki* for coming out, Reuben. If you'll take the baby inside and stable the mare, I can handle the food containers."

Glenn's *dat* opened the buggy door and reached for the carrier's handle. "You can handle anything you put your mind to, Marietta," he remarked without missing a beat. "Mighty kind of you to take on all of us Detweilers. The middle two aren't much trouble, but the oldest and this youngest one, we're a handful, ain't so?"

Marietta laughed. "You tend to keep each other occupied, so it all works out, Reuben. How's the work going today?"

He lifted the basket from the floor. "Not as fast, with Pete missing," he replied. "Even so, our Mennonite friends have put in some extra time with us, so we still figure we'll move in a few days after Christmas. Depends on when a couple of appliances we've ordered arrive—and our beds."

As he stepped away with the baby, Marietta slid down from the seat onto the ground. "Bet you'll be really glad to be home again, *jah*?"

Reuben's expression was a mix of emotions she couldn't interpret. "Well, there's a difference between being in a house in the same spot and being *home*," he said softly. "Glenn says the same thing. What with everything being shiny and new, it seems almost too fancy to live in, you know? Or it just feels like somebody else's place rather than ours.

"But I won't complain!" he added, putting on a bright smile. "Thanks to all the help from our friends, we'll have a roof over our heads again real soon."

He glanced at the baby, who was starting to fuss despite the bandanna pacifier in his mouth. "Better get this little guy inside. I'll tell the men to wash up."

As Marietta opened the rig's back compartment, where she'd packed the containers of hot food, she pondered what Reuben had just said. Most women she knew would be ecstatic about having new floors and appliances and fresh walls, but maybe it was different for men. When she entered the kitchen carrying her cooler and a canvas tote full of disposable tableware, she stopped to look around. Men's voices rang in the bedrooms above her, so she had a moment alone to assess the room.

After she took off her coat and bonnet, Marietta walked slowly around the kitchen. From what she recalled of Sunday services in the Detweilers' previous house, it had been about the same size but arranged a bit differently. Reuben had made a valid point: the dark gray countertops, white cabinets, and pale yellow walls were excruciatingly clean and fresh. The holes for a stove and refrigerator gaped like the spaces in Billy Jay's mouth where he'd lost baby teeth.

It looks like nobody lives here.

Marietta set aside her puzzling thought. Many was the time she and Molly had discussed the improvements that would make their careworn old home more efficient, but it wasn't her place to make suggestions for the Detweilers' new place. As she began setting out stacks of plates, napkins, and cups, Levi let out a wail upstairs—which meant it wouldn't be long before the men scattered to escape the baby's earsplitting racket. There weren't any rugs to absorb the sound, so she could imagine how his cries echoed in the empty rooms above her.

Glenn was the first one to enter the kitchen, smiling despite the fussy baby on his shoulder. Before he could say anything, Marietta pulled the bottle of warm goat's milk from between the big pans of chili and corn bread that had kept it warm.

"He was too fussy to take it at home," she explained.

Glenn blinked. "You think of everything! *Denki*, Marietta."

Moments later, a blissful silence filled the kitchen, with only the undertone of Levi's sucking and gurgling. Marietta didn't spend too long looking at father and son, even though the picture they made tugged at her heartstrings. Soon Gabe and the rest of the construction crew were coming in to get their food, so she focused on pouring their water and setting out the butter, jars of jelly, and the pan of corn bread.

"Oh, but this looks wonderful-*gut*!" Gabe said as he ladled chili into a bowl. "We spent the morning installing the toilets and bathroom sinks, so I'm ready to chow down."

Glenn set Levi's empty bottle on the countertop, glancing at Marietta as he spoke to his coworkers. "You fellows go ahead and eat. I'll walk Levi for a bit to settle his stomach—so maybe it's a *gut* time to give you a tour of the place, Marietta?"

Her first thought was that she should stay to serve the meal, but these grown men could surely help themselves, couldn't they? The invitation in Glenn's chocolate brown eyes held a message only for her—something he didn't want to express in front of his friends.

"I'd like to look around, *jah*," she admitted. "Judging from the mudroom and the kitchen, everything's nearly finished."

"Almost," Howard put in as he placed two squares of corn bread on his plate. "Considering that this spot was just a pile of frozen-over ashes a couple of weeks ago, we've made incredible progress."

Marietta nodded at the fire chief's assessment. As she followed Glenn out into the front room, which still had plywood subflooring, she noticed cans of paint sitting in one corner.

"Now that the plumbing's all installed, we'll finish the painting," her tour guide remarked. "What sort of flooring should we choose for this room? Which is easier to keep clean, wood floors or a nice vinyl?"

When Glenn turned to face her, swaying gently with the baby on his shoulder, Marietta wasn't sure what to say. She hadn't missed the way he'd phrased his questions with *we*—and something told her he wasn't alluding to his father.

"I—I've always thought wood floors were homier in the front room and the bedrooms," she replied hesitantly. "And with the newer type of coating they put on hardwoods these days, they're as easy to maintain as vinyl. But it's not my money being spent, and it's not my house, so—"

"But it could be."

Glenn's words were whispered, but to Marietta they sounded so loud and clear that the crew in the kitchen had surely heard them. She glanced back to where the men were eating and hurried toward the far end of the large front room.

"Marietta, please can we talk upstairs?" Glenn pleaded softly as he followed her. "I've got words on my heart that just have to come out."

Her pulse pounded into high gear as she nodded. Her mind was spinning so fast, she barely saw the lustrous oak newel post, banister, and stairway as she hurried up toward the second story.

Still holding the baby against his shoulder, Glenn reached for her hand as they reached the upper landing. "Marietta," he whispered again. "It's a blessing to have a new house, for sure and for certain, but it won't be a home unless you join us here. Please will you marry me?"

Marietta's mouth dropped open, and her cheeks blazed. The first image that popped into her startled mind took her back to the day when they'd buried Elva Detweiler. At the meal after his mamm's funeral, Glenn had shocked the crowd by cornering Lydianne at the dessert table and pleading with her, loudly enough that everyone could hear him.

If I knew you'd be my wife, even if I had to wait awhile, I could make it from one day to the next. I'd have a life again.

Recalling what Glenn had blurted out that day suddenly put everything into perspective for Marietta. Perhaps God had been speaking to her through her uncertain thoughts earlier this morning, and He was probably warning her again now. No matter how much she'd come to care for the man who stood before her with such an earnest expression on his face, she—and Glenn—needed to know if he was speaking out of love for her, or out of desperation.

"I—are you sure about this, Glenn?" she asked gently. "It was only a couple of months ago, in October, that you were saying the same thing to Lydianne. And only a few months before that, in July, you lost your Dorcas."

Glenn's Adam's apple bulged as he swallowed hard. "I was out of my head with grief—didn't know what I was saying—"

"So maybe you should give this matter some more time, *jah*?"

"—but now that I've been with *you*, Marietta, I—"

He pivoted, releasing her hand with a harsh sigh. "I guess my heart and soul haven't been watching the calendar as closely as you have. Time doesn't mean a lot when you've been left alone, except that the days stumble by and the nights feel so desperately endless. I fell head over heels for you last night, when we were all together on the couch, and I thought you felt the same about me."

Marietta clasped her hands in front of her, pondering what she should say next. Over Glenn's shoulder, little Levi was watching her, his face dimpled with recognition that touched her deeply. If Glenn left—if he took his boys with him—her life would have some large empty spots for a while.

But she would still have a life.

"You've had a tough time of it, Glenn," she murmured, praying that her words would say what her heart sincerely meant without sounding cruel. "You and your boys and your *dat* mean the world to me, and it's been such a blessing to get to know you better while you've been staying with us these past couple of weeks. But—"

"*Jah*, there's always a *but*," he muttered.

Marietta paused. She had just turned down his proposal

of marriage, so he had reason to be cross. If she didn't tell him her truth, however, the potential for misunderstanding would always loom between them.

"I can't possibly imagine how devastated you've been these past several months, Glenn—how desperate you must be to have a wife again and to have someone caring for your boys," she said softly.

Glenn showed no sign of refuting her, or of leaving, so she continued carefully.

"But I am *not* desperate," she said. Marietta grasped the upstairs railing to anchor her thoughts, noting how smooth and flawless the woodwork felt in her hand. "Molly and I have made a satisfying life for ourselves, and even if she eventually hitches up with Pete, I will still have a home and a business that supports me. I'm thirty-five, and I'm a cancer survivor. I'm in no hurry to marry—and I *refuse* to marry for any reason other than a love that makes me deliriously happier and more complete than I already am."

Glenn still faced away from her, swaying with his baby boy as though his life depended upon it.

As the silence ticked by with each beat of her heart, Marietta wondered if she should stay or go. She really hadn't given Glenn anything to respond to, she realized. She'd simply stated her side of the story. After a few more excruciating moments, Marietta started down the stairs.

"Wait—please," Glenn murmured. As he looked over the railing at her, his doleful brown eyes resembled those of a forlorn dog begging forgiveness for misbehavior.

Marietta stopped, gazing up at him.

"I guess I never thought of it that way—what you said about already having a satisfying life, not really needing a husband," he continued. "I always assumed that women who didn't marry felt they'd been passed by—felt like outsiders in our Amish society, which is based on couples having families."

She shrugged. "Some women do."

Glenn sighed deeply. "I didn't get the answer I wanted from you today, but you've given me something to think about. And you gave me *gut* insights about the flooring. I guess I'd better leave it at that rather than saying anything more, digging myself into a deeper pit, ain't so?"

Marietta couldn't help smiling. "There's that, *jah*."

He rolled his eyes. "You're not going to help me one little bit, are you?" he asked in a lighter tone. "But remember this, Marietta: Billy Jay may have drawn your birthday card—and that was entirely his idea—but we all signed it. And we all meant what we said."

She nodded. Recalling the love expressed in that hand-drawn card made her throat so tight, she didn't trust her voice.

"So I guess I'll go eat some of that fine chili and corn bread you brought before my cohorts gobble it all down," Glenn continued, sounding somewhat recovered from the intensity of their conversation. "*Denki* for bringing our lunch today, Marietta. If you'll take Levi, Dat and I will bring your pots and dishes back with us this evening."

He'd given her a graceful way out, so she took it. Marietta preceded him into the kitchen and chatted briefly with Gabe and the other fellows while she fetched her wraps. Glenn put the baby back in his carrier and covered him lightly with his blue crocheted blanket before handing him over.

"*Gut* to see you—and thanks again for lunch," he remarked with a smile she couldn't quite interpret.

Marietta nodded, hoping their onlookers weren't speculating about what might've passed between them while she was supposedly touring the rest of the house. As she stepped outside, she inhaled deeply to clear her head with crisp winter air. She was lifting the carrier into the rig when she figured it out: Levi had dirtied his diaper, and pretty badly, by the smell of it.

This is how it would probably be if you and Glenn got hitched. Don't husbands always pass off a stinky baby to their wives as a sign of their devotion?

Marietta laughed out loud. For the time being, she'd sidestepped that issue, hadn't she?

As she drove down the road toward home, she had mixed emotions about turning down the only marriage proposal she'd ever received. "But You were talking to me, Lord, in my doubtful thoughts, and I'm glad I listened," she said aloud. "If we're going to do this, Glenn's got to get it right—for his sake, and for mine, as well."

Chapter 22

Pete floated up to a higher level of awareness, yet he was unsure of whether the disjointed images in his mind were memories or dreams. He had no idea how long he'd been asleep or what had caused the long-running succession of mental movies that seemed to make no sense. Some of the faces that flitted through his mind seemed vaguely familiar, while others appeared grotesquely misshapen and frightening. He was becoming more cognizant of *pain* all over his body—his left leg and arm hurt like the dickens—but he had no idea how to alleviate it. He had a sense that he wasn't in his own bed, but where was he?

He did know, however, that the sounds around him were becoming more distinct—and that one of them was morphing into a voice.

"Hey, Shetler, you really need to wake up now."

Shetler—what was that? Pete was on the verge of calling up a definition, but the voice continued before he could figure it out. There was a metallic jingle and other sounds coming from a lower level, but he couldn't place those, either.

"I won't be able to hold Riley on the floor much longer,

Pete." The speaker sounded closer to his ear now, and more insistent. "If he makes a scene and the nurses find out I sneaked him in, we're in big trouble here."

Woof. And another jingle.

Pete tried desperately to remember what those sounds meant—partly because they weren't making any demands of him, the way the voice was. He couldn't handle demands yet, so he tried to retreat back into the quiet mental void he'd emerged from. But it wasn't working.

"Riley, sit, boy! *Jah*, this is Pete, but he's not ready to see you yet."

Riley . . . Pete . . . Sit, boy! Once again he was aware that those words had meaning, but he couldn't nail them down—

A sudden crunch of moving weight landed on his left side—his bad side—and as a cry escaped him, something wet and rough was bathing his face. The smell was earthy and gamy and—

"Riley, get down! You're hurting him!"

A shrill *beep-beep-beep* made Pete's head throb with a whole new flash of sensation—

"Oh, we're in for it now," the voice said. "The alarm's gone off. Get *down*!"

But the undulating weight on his arm, pressing hard in two places, suddenly became too sharp to tolerate. Pete's eyes flew open, and his loud gasp was greeted by yet another soaking from that rough, wet piece of—

Riley! A furry, golden face swam before Pete's eyes. A cold nose pressed his cheek, and those eager brown eyes sought his gaze—and the pressing of two bony, muscular legs suddenly made sense. Still, the pain was so intense, he was seeing stars, but he couldn't seem to move out from under it or form the words or—

"I see we have a guest," a different voice said, sounding male and stern and authoritarian.

"Pete's coming around!" the first voice said. "Look—his eyes are open and he's trying to talk and—"

"Miss, if you don't get that dog off the bed, I'll have to call security."

Pete frowned. He wasn't yet sure what *security* was, but nobody talked to his dog in such a tone! "No!" he rasped. He wasn't sure why his throat felt as though it were lined with sandpaper, but he tried again. "No! My—my dog!"

A familiar face appeared before his, and its owner was grinning despite her efforts to get Riley's big front legs off of him. "Now you're talking, Shetler! You go, guy. Riley and I will wait right here while your nurse checks you over."

Nurse? Pete again racked his befuddled brain for the concept that went with that word—wasn't it a medical term? Why would a nurse be here, unless he was in—

"Good morning, Pete," the man said, leaning over to study him more closely. "It's good to see you awake. How are you feeling?"

"Hurts!" Pete wheezed.

"Of course it does. Your *dog* was jumping all over the arm you had surgery on. Let's check your monitors here . . ."

Surgery? Monitors? Pete blinked, trying to clarify the conversation that was still whizzing past him much too fast. At least this nurse guy had turned off the alarm, so his nerves weren't quite so a-jangle.

"Okay, Pete, open your eyes wide. Sorry about the bright light."

The air left his lungs in a rush when the nurse flashed a light into each of his eyes. After that ordeal was over, he wanted to complain about the way the nurse was roughing him up, checking the bandages—

Bandages? When he slowly moved his head for a better view, Pete realized that his bad arm was wrapped almost entirely in white—and so was the leg that hurt as if a chainsaw was cutting into it every time the nurse placed his hand on it.

"Ahhh! Stop!" he cried out. "Just leave me alone!"

The nurse cracked a smile. "I'll put in a request to your doctor to increase your pain meds now that you're back to making demands, Mr. Shetler. That's a good sign. We know a patient's on the road to recovery when he starts complaining."

The nurse took a clipboard from the foot of the bed and spent the next several moments scribbling on it. Pete's head was starting to throb so badly that the scratching of the guy's pen on the paper was driving him insane—but finally the nurse replaced the clipboard.

"I'll tell the doctor you've come around," the nurse said in an efficient-sounding voice. "Meanwhile, take it easy while you chat with your girlfriend and your *dog*. Keep it *off* the bed," he added, focusing on the person waiting near the wall.

As the nurse left the room, Pete immediately felt better. But *girlfriend*?

He was trying to process the words that didn't yet make sense when a face appeared several inches above his. Pete realized this face was female—much friendlier and cuter than the nurse's—but he was at a loss for a name. Her green eyes glimmered as she studied him.

"Oh, but it's *gut* to see you awake," she said softly. "Your eyes might be the color of manure, Shetler— probably because you're full of it—but it's so *gut* to see them open again! When you fell off the roof yesterday, you sent all of us into a tizzy, you know. *Sit*, boy!" she added, leaning down to better control Riley.

When she laughed, the musical sound tickled Pete's senses, and he immediately felt better. And when she softly kissed his cheek, his whole body shot into over-drive. His pain was still intense, but her affection made him momentarily forget how badly he hurt all over.

"I'll let you rest now. We'll be back after your pain meds have had a chance to work," she said gently. "Your uncle Jeremiah—and everyone else—will be so glad to hear you're awake, Pete."

She tightened her grip on Riley's leash, convincing his dog they had to leave. Pete turned his head slowly to watch them go. He desperately needed to sleep, yet he was wishing these guests would stay with him.

The woman turned when she reached the door. "I love you, Shetler, but don't let it go to your head," she said in a loud whisper. Then she was gone.

Pete blinked. *That was . . . that was Molly! That was* Molly*!*

He sank back into an exhausted stupor, yet he felt euphorically happy. Now that he was alone again, he could puzzle over the rest of the words he'd heard this morning and piece together what had happened to him— right after he took a nap.

* * *

At the supper table, Molly launched into the story about sneaking Riley into Pete's hospital room, feeling immensely relieved and happy. Billy Jay's eyes lit up— probably because he adored her sense of adventure and he, too, would've broken the rules to make Pete feel better.

Yet by the end of her tale, Molly became aware of a heaviness in Glenn's expression—and of the way her sister was pasting on a smile that didn't reach her eyes. Reuben was the only one of them who seemed to be appreciating the bowl of ham and beans in front of him, and even so, he seemed lackluster.

Molly spread butter and jelly on her corn bread. "So, how'd it go at the house today?" she asked carefully. "Everything all right?"

An awkward silence lasted a beat too long before her twin replied.

"I mixed up a double batch of noodle dough when I got home," Marietta said softly. "How about you and I roll it and cut it this evening, to make up for some of the time we've missed out in the factory this week?"

"*Jah*, you girls are excused as soon as you've finished your dinner," Reuben put in kindly. "We guys can *redd* up the kitchen so you can catch up on your work. This'll be your last Saturday before Christmas, and you'll want to be ready for the crowd at The Marketplace, ain't so?"

"That's very thoughtful of you," Molly murmured.

When Marietta rose from the table moments later, not even glancing at the cherry pie on the counter, Molly realized how upset her sister was. They slipped into their barn coats, and she wasted no time quizzing her twin as they headed outside to their little white factory building.

"All right, spill it, sister," she said as Marietta flipped on their gas ceiling lights.

When Marietta turned to face her, she wore an odd expression. "Glenn asked me to marry him today. I said no."

Molly's jaw dropped. Given time, her sister would elaborate, so Molly stepped over to her workstation and removed the plastic wrap from the big bowl of noodle dough Marietta had made. Judging from the amount of dough they both had, her twin had spent the entire afternoon running the mixer—and she intended to be up half the night cutting noodles.

"It was the most awkward moment of my adult life, I think," Marietta began with a sigh. "Once the other men were digging into their lunch, Glenn offered to show me the house. When he asked whether he should choose hardwood floors or vinyl for the front room, I said that wasn't my decision because it wasn't my home. Then he said it *could* be."

Molly nodded, sensing exactly how hopeful her twin must've felt at that moment. "So you knew what he was working up to, *jah*?" She flipped the power switch for her roller and slowly pressed a block of dough through its wheels to flatten it.

"Oh, there was no mistaking Glenn's intention. He said he had words on his heart that he just had to say," her sister continued in a rush. Her hands were moving with frenetic tension as she, too, pressed dough through her roller. "To keep the guys in the kitchen from listening in on us, I crossed the front room and started up the stairs. My word, but the woodwork in that house is glossy and flawless. That's the most beautiful newel post and railing I've ever seen."

"Of course it is," Molly remarked, carefully guiding the sheet of dough down the length of her table. "That's what Glenn does best, after all."

"Well, he's also had a lot of practice at proposing!"

Molly's eyes widened. Sensing how shaken Marietta was by the day's events, she once again allowed her sister to continue her story at her own pace.

"Don't you remember how he cornered Lydianne by the dessert table at Elva's funeral lunch and declared—in front of God and everybody—that if she'd marry him, he'd have a life again?" Marietta blurted out. "That was only a couple of months ago, *jah*? And he'd been hounding Lydianne before that, too—not all that long after he lost Dorcas."

Molly recalled everything her sister was recounting. She carefully ran her sharp knife along her length of damp dough, cutting strips as she again gave her twin the silence she needed.

"After I—I listened to him bemoaning his desperate days and endless nights, I told him I was *not* desperate," Marietta said resolutely. "I said I have a life I love and a way to support myself, so the only reason I will ever marry is because a man makes me deliriously happier than I already am."

She let out a sigh that filled the noodle factory. "So now, of course, I'm wondering if I'll be sorry for turning him down. It's not like I've got men lining up to—"

"You said exactly the right thing, Marietta, and I'm proud of you."

Molly set aside her knife and went over to Marietta's worktable. The gaps and tears in her sister's rolled-out dough attested to how jittery she was. When Marietta stepped into her arms, Molly wasn't surprised that her twin's slender shoulders were shaking.

"I guess I hadn't thought about the timing on all this stuff with Glenn, but you're right," Molly murmured. "He needs to be absolutely sure what he's doing and who he wants to spend the rest of his life with. I'd hate to see either one of you figure out—after the knot was tied— that you'd made a big, permanent mistake."

Sniffling, Marietta nodded. "Glenn's such a nice man—"

"*Jah*, he is."

"—and I love those little boys to pieces—"

"*Jah*, you do."

"—but . . . well, I want him to marry *me*, Molly," Marietta continued with a hitch in her voice. "For who I am, instead of because he needs someone to take up where Dorcas left off. I could never fill her shoes, and I don't want to!"

"*Gut* for you! You did the right thing for the right reason."

Marietta eased away, wiping her eyes with the back of her hand. "It means a lot, hearing you say that," she whispered. "I knew that of all the people on God's *gut* earth, you'd never tell me something just because I wanted to hear it. *Denki*, sister."

Molly blinked away the tears that sprang to her eyes. "You'd do the same for me, Marietta," she pointed out.

"We've always depended upon each other, and—and if we do happen to get hitched, that won't change."

Her twin studied her face, her green eyes glimmering in the workroom's subdued lighting. "Something tells me you have more news than you've been sharing, Miss Molly," she said with a lift in her voice. "Besides Pete's waking up, what else happened in that hospital room today?"

Molly hugged her twin before returning to her worktable. "It's not so much what happened today—although I did tell him I loved him, and not to let it go to his head. He was still groggy enough that I doubt he'll remember that part."

Marietta's eyes widened. "What else has happened, then? Sneaking Riley into his room was a stroke of genius, but there's more to this story, ain't so?" she demanded playfully. "You haven't said two words about what went on after you left the Hartzler place Sunday in Pete's truck."

Molly shrugged, savoring the deliciousness of her secret a little longer. "Maybe you're not the only one who got a very special birthday card that day," she hinted.

"Pete popped the question, didn't he? In a homemade card?"

"Not quite. He let it slip that he wanted us to get hitched, however—and he presented some plans for remodeling our house," she admitted. "Pete was under the impression that Glenn had been making a play for *me* and that I was falling for it. So he was enticing me with his renovation sketches."

"Plans for remodeling our house?" Marietta switched

off her dough roller, gazing intently at Molly. "What sort of things does our Mr. Shetler have in mind?"

Grinning at the curiosity that burned on her twin's slender face, Molly took Pete's envelope from her apron pocket. She didn't tell Marietta she'd studied the sketches countless times over the past couple of days—or that she'd kept a rare secret from her, either. "When Pete puts his mind to it, he's every bit the carpenter and wood-worker Glenn is—"

"You're right, Molly—but I'd never tell him that to his face," Marietta interrupted with a laugh. "Are you telling me Pete's finally getting serious about something? Actually applying his God-given talent to its fullest potential—because he wants to marry you and live here with us?"

"Oh, you'll be moving into Glenn's new house one of these days," Molly shot back. "You're right to make him wait awhile—and actually court you—though. Meanwhile, here's what the bishop's nephew has in mind for us."

Marietta eagerly unfolded the pages, squinting at the drawings in the meager light from their gas fixtures. "What am I looking at? Is this supposed to be our kitchen? It doesn't look like what we've always had—"

"Because Pete's drawn in some ingenious updates," Molly put in proudly. She stepped over beside her sister to point out the highlights.

"He's put the pantry on the other side of the room and added more counter space—another block of cabinets, too—between the fridge and the sink. And instead of our lazy Susan in this lower corner, he's installing deep shelves that make more efficient use of the space," she said, pointing to each corresponding place on the sketch. "And won't these roll-out shelves in our lower cabinets be fabulous? We won't have to stand on our heads—or lie on our stomachs—anymore to dig out the stuff that's way in the back!"

"Wow," Marietta murmured. "I'm impressed. I don't think Glenn's new kitchen has these features."

Molly shrugged. "Pete thought he had to win me away from Glenn, remember?" She pulled out one of the other sketches. "And look at the new cabinetry along the other side of the kitchen wall, in the front room. That's a built-in corner hutch with a glass front—"

"A perfect place to put Mamm's collection of bone china cups and saucers!"

"That's what I was thinking, too!" Molly agreed excitedly. She flipped to another page. "And look how much more organized the mudroom will be with these shelves on the walls—"

"Instead of those heavy old cabinets that are so hard to move when we need to clean behind them," Marietta put in. She was fighting a grin as she glanced at the other improvements. "Does this mean you've already said yes? I can't imagine any carpenter agreeing to do this much work unless he knows it's an investment in a lifetime relationship. Or unless you're paying him for it."

"Of *course* I haven't accepted yet. We want to keep Pete motivated—give him the incentive to finish all this remodeling, right?" Molly teased. As she accepted the pages her twin returned to her, reality took the place of the dreams they'd been discussing.

"But then, who knows how long it'll be before he's strong enough to work again? He's undergone some serious surgery, and he's probably facing extensive physical therapy to regain full use of his arm and leg," she pointed out. "And there's Glenn's house to finish—not to mention the remodeling that got set aside at Jeremiah's place when the Detweiler house burned down."

Marietta's face brightened. "Minor details. *You* will be the incentive Pete needs to recover, Molly," she said. "I feel so much better now, seeing this proof that's he's serious about you—that you'll be well cared for in this home we've always loved."

"And if you decide not to hitch up with Glenn, you'll still be living here, too," Molly reminded her firmly. "Pete and I have discussed the fact that we twins have always done things together, so—"

"It'll all work out. I have no doubt about that." Marietta flipped the switch on her roller again before flashing Molly a big smile. "What a wonderful birthday we've had—and won't this be our best Christmas ever, too? If we take our time with these fellows and allow these major changes to unfold according to God's plan, I foresee happiness for both of us—even if we won't be living under the same roof forever, *jah*?"

Molly focused on her dough again, fighting a grin. Marietta had just admitted that she would someday be married to Glenn, caring for those boys she adored.

It *would* be their best Christmas ever. They just had to have the faith and patience both of their situations—and their men—required.

Chapter 23

On Saturday, after selling a record number of cookies, breads, and pastries—and running out around two thirty— Jo placed the CLOSED sign on the doorpost of Fussner Bakery. Alice and Adeline would be serving coffee, spiced cider, and the last of the treats in the crowded commons of The Marketplace for a while yet, so Jo was allowing herself some quiet time before she cleaned up her kitchen. As exhausted as she felt, Jo was delighted that the shopkeepers had agreed not to be open on the Saturdays before and after the New Year. They all needed time off following a holiday season that had far exceeded everyone's expectations.

As she dropped into the wooden chair at the back of her kitchen, however, Jo wondered what she'd do with herself—wondered how she'd fill her days now that she wasn't baking to build up inventory for Saturday at the store.

She'd survived this past week by staying too busy to feel sorry for herself. She'd felt Mamm's silent disapproval of all the hours she'd spent in the kitchen, but she hadn't allowed her mother's attitude to stop her. Without any hope of seeing Michael all winter—or maybe ever again, if the Wengerds decided to pull out of The Marketplace—Jo had needed something worthwhile to focus on.

With Christmas only four days away, she should be preparing her heart for the celebration of Jesus' birth. But it was impossible to feel anything resembling *joy* when she was overwhelmed by Mamm's negativity.

Jo sighed, glancing at the stack of pans on the back counter. Her quiet time was backfiring as she picked at the scab of the love Mamm had so cruelly ripped from her life. She stood up. Better to wash dishes than to sit stewing over happiness that would never—

"Psst! Hey there, Jo—can I come in?"

Her heart leaped at the sound of Michael's whispered question. He was standing in the Helfings' store, about a foot away, peering at her between the wall's slats.

His smile was hesitant. "When I saw your CLOSED sign, I thought maybe you'd already left—"

"No, come in—come in!" Jo insisted.

As Michael made his way out of the noodle shop, Jo wondered why she was leaving herself open for more heartache. Whatever he had to say, nothing would come of it. Yet she felt fluttery with the anticipation of seeing him again, even if it was only for a few moments—and even if the Shetler twins would soon be returning with their empty treat trays.

"It's so *gut* to see you, Michael," Jo murmured as he made his way past her empty display cases. She motioned him toward the back, where they could talk without being seen from the commons area. "After the way Mamm treated you and your *dat*, I figured you wouldn't want anything more to do with me—"

"Seriously?" Michael's brow furrowed. "Then you have a lot to learn about me, Jo. Did you think I'd give up on everything you and I shared while you were at our place just because your mother disapproved of it?"

Jo's jaw dropped. His tone sounded firm and absolutely sincere. His gray-blue eyes remained focused on her, as though he never wanted to look at anyone else.

After a moment, he reached for her hand. "Would it be all right to call you every now and again while Dat and I stay in Queen City over the winter?"

It was a wonderful idea—his calls would give her something to look forward to. But they both knew she'd have no guarantee of privacy.

"If you leave me a message on the machine—or set a time when you'll call, so I can be waiting in the phone shanty—Mamm will catch on," Jo pointed out. "Or if she gets to the shanty first to see if we have orders for baked goods, she'll hear your message and delete it, most likely."

Michael nodded. "I thought that's what you'd say. So what if I wrote to you instead?"

Her heart quivered at the thought of receiving—and returning—letters that would help them get better acquainted over the winter, despite being apart. Then she envisioned Mamm's reaction. "I—I would love to hear from you, Michael," she replied softly. "I can't keep you from writing, after all—"

"But sometimes your *mamm* gets the mail, right? And she'll give you no end of grief if she sees my letters."

Jo nodded glumly. "I could be sure to get to the mailbox first and hide your letters in a secret place," she suggested. "But if Mamm found them, there'd be no end to her fussing about how we'd once again defied her wishes."

He sighed, but then his expression became a mixture of determination and affection that stole her breath away.

And suddenly he was kissing her.

Jo was so startled, she didn't have time to worry about whether she was responding the right way with her mouth or had placed her hands in the right spots. Michael had cupped her face with his warm palm—probably so she wouldn't pull away because she feared they'd be caught. As he pressed his lips over hers, she felt overwhelmed by warmth and joy and a dazzling sense of daring. Displays of public affection were frowned upon by the Amish church—

And who could've anticipated a nice, polite guy like Michael Wengerd flinging caution to the wind so he could kiss me this way, right here in the shop?

When he eased away, he held her gaze for several long, delicious moments. Michael's eyes shone with a fervor Jo hadn't seen before. A smile softened his handsome face.

"I couldn't stay away for the next few months without letting you know exactly how I feel—because your mother's response to me has nothing to do with what we share," he whispered.

Jo blinked. "*Jah*, I guess you're right."

"You *know* I'm right," he countered softly. "So think about that while we're apart. I'm not saying *gut*-bye, Jo. I say *keep believing*. Jesus told Thomas that folks who can believe without seeing are blessed—and we will be, too, if we focus on what we know and feel even if we can't see each other for a while."

She let out the breath she'd been holding. "You've given me a lot to think about."

"*Gut!* When you're thinking about me and what I've

said—and thinking about how well suited we are for each other—you're not letting your mother's negativity rule your life, *jah*? No disrespect intended," he added quickly.

As his words sank in, Jo felt better than she had for days. "That's a *gut* way to look at it," she admitted.

At the sound of the Shetler twins' voices, Michael glanced toward the bakery doorway before focusing on Jo again. "Merry, merry Christmas, Jo," he whispered. "We'll be together in our hearts until we're together again in person."

As he made his way out of her shop kitchen, she turned toward the refrigerators to compose herself. While Michael spoke to Alice and Adeline for a few moments, Jo took some deep breaths. She couldn't yet contemplate all she'd just heard—but hadn't Michael given her more than enough food for thought to nourish her soul through the coming months?

She turned quickly. "Merry Christmas, Michael!" she called out as he was leaving. "God bless you—and give my best to your *dat*!"

His slender face glowed like the serene flame of a candle in a window. Michael blew her a kiss, and then he stepped out into the crowded commons.

It was a moment Jo knew she'd remember forever— the moment when hope filled her heart with love, just as the birth of Jesus had brought hope to the world centuries ago. Somehow, peace and joy and the strong promise of Michael's intentions would sustain her until she saw him again.

For no matter what her mother wanted, Jo *would* see Michael again.

Chapter 24

Late Monday morning, as he and Gabe finished sweeping up at the new house, Glenn wished he felt more excited. The cream-colored walls around him glowed, the wood-work was as flawless as he could make it, and the front room still smelled of the stain on the newly installed hard-wood floors. Any other man would surely be ecstatic: his previous home had burned down only three weeks ago, yet with the help of his friends, the Detweilers had a new roof over their heads.

What a blessing it was to live among folks who'd taken such good care of him and his family. What a gift, to be standing in his new, completed home on the twenty-third of December.

Dorcas never said so—never complained—but she would've been deliriously happy to have these fresh walls and the new appliances and flooring. Not to mention windows that closed tight and cabinets that didn't still contain some of her in-laws' belongings after all these years.

Thoughts of his deceased wife made Glenn's throat tighten. During his counseling sessions with the bishop, Jeremiah had warned him that Christmas would be tough this year without his wife and his *mamm*. *Tough* didn't even begin to cover it, however.

Gabe's concerned voice broke through Glenn's darkening thoughts. "You okay, buddy?" he asked kindly. "Can I help you with anything else before I go?"

"Sorry. Just thinking how much Mamm and Dorcas would've loved this place," he murmured. "I'm having one of those moments the bishop warned me about."

"I'm sure you've had more than your share of such moments over the past few months," Gabe remarked with a nod. "I can't imagine how lonely you must feel at times. And I'm sorry, Glenn."

Glenn waved him off. "I know that. Didn't intend to turn this into a pity party, Gabe—and what would I have done without *your* help?" he added emphatically. "You've given my house so much of your time lately, at the expense of your work at the furniture factory. I'll never be able to repay—"

"Oh, never say *never*," Gabe insisted, slipping his arm around Glenn's shoulders. "Every one of us hits some rough patches in this life. You might get your turn helping me out of a bind any time, without warning. I know you'll be there for me, too, Glenn."

Glenn nodded, trying to focus on the positive gifts he'd received recently.

But their footsteps and voices echoed as they gave the upstairs floors a final sweeping. And as he and Gabe walked down the steps, their boots clattering on the freshly stained wood, Glenn felt as empty as the rooms they'd just cleaned. No matter how hard he tried, he couldn't think of this shiny-new place as *home*.

When Gabe pronounced their cleaning finished, he

leaned the broom in the corner of the mudroom. "Planning to work in your wood shop the rest of the day?" he asked as he put on his heavy coat and stocking cap. "From what I saw of your shelves at The Marketplace on Saturday, your inventory's pretty well depleted."

"It is," Glenn agreed. "But since we're not going to be open for the next two Saturdays, I thought I'd go visit Pete. To hear Jeremiah tell it, he's driving his *mammi* crazy with his complaints and demands."

Gabe's laughter echoed in the kitchen. "I'm not surprised. Pete can't sit still for more than five minutes at a time, so he'll be trying everyone's patience during his recuperation at home. I'm sure he—and Margaret—will be glad to see you. Give them my best."

Nodding absently, Glenn watched through the mudroom window as his friend jogged across the backyard to the stable. A few minutes later, Gabe was driving his buggy toward the road—probably in a hurry to share a cozy lunch with Regina in their Craftsman-style bungalow across town.

Glenn stood in the middle of the kitchen, aware of how cavernous it seemed without the table he and his family had eaten at since he was a boy. A swift vision of Marietta standing at the stove made him blink. Her rejection still stung. So many times he'd felt better while he'd imagined her cooking and *redding* up in this room—but that wasn't going to happen anytime soon. If ever.

Why would she want to live here? We don't have any dishes or beds or rugs—no place to sit in the front room, and no towels to use when we step out of the shower.

Glenn grimaced. He and Pete and Gabe hadn't balked for a minute at choosing the new stove, fridge, deep freeze, and washing machine, but he had no idea about buying towels or bed linens—and he certainly couldn't sew curtains for all the windows. This new place needed a woman's touch—

Oh, but I need a woman's touch, too!

Recalling how good he'd felt when he'd slung his arm around Marietta's slender shoulders and sat close to her on the sofa only made Glenn feel more depressed. She'd made it clear she didn't want him. She believed his heart wasn't yet ready to choose a new wife.

Marietta's better off right where she is. She doesn't need a husband—doesn't need me—and she knows it.

A sad, bitter laugh escaped him. The walls rang with the sound, mocking him, so Glenn left the house. It felt good to slam the door loudly behind him, even though that was a juvenile response to his loneliness. As he entered the stable, he told himself he'd better adjust his attitude so he'd be in a better frame of mind when he reached the bishop's place for his visit with Pete.

Glenn bridled Ned and hopped on him bareback for the short trip to Jeremiah's place. He hoped Margaret would invite him to stay for the noon meal so he wouldn't have to eat with Molly, Marietta, and his *dat*. The food at the Helfing place didn't taste nearly as good now that Marietta had said she wasn't going to marry him.

"There goes Glenn, just like Jeremiah planned," Molly said gleefully. From behind the windbreak of evergreens along Howard Gibbs's lane, where she and Marietta sat in their loaded rig, they watched the dark-haired carpenter canter past, completely unaware of their presence. "Pete did us a big favor by coming home from the hospital when he did."

"And aren't we glad that Reuben agreed to watch the baby while we, um, ran a few holiday errands?" Marietta put in with a chuckle. "Let's get over to Glenn's and unload our stuff quickly, in case he takes a notion to eat a late lunch at our house after visiting at the bishop's place. We don't want him to suspect that anything's going on."

"I'd like to be a fly on the wall when Glenn discovers a houseful of furniture that wasn't there when he left!" Molly said, urging Opal toward the road.

It wasn't long before they saw other members of their congregation driving their rigs and wagons toward the new Detweiler house. Gabe, who'd ridden to the Hartzler place to signal everyone who'd been waiting there, arrived just ahead of his *dat*, who was driving the Flaud Furniture delivery wagon. Saul Hartzler pulled into the lane ahead of Molly, hauling a trailer loaded with more furniture. Within minutes, the yard behind the new white house was abuzz with excited friends, all of them bringing household items for Glenn and his family.

"Come on in!" Bishop Jeremiah called out as he propped the back door open. "If we follow the plan we discussed when I visited with each of you this past week, it shouldn't take long to put everything in place. And *denki* ahead of time for your kindness and generosity."

"If anyone's due for a big favor, it's Glenn," Martha Maude said as she flung open the back panels of the Hartlzers' rig.

She looked toward her son, who'd pulled in behind her. "How about if you men carry the bedroom furniture upstairs first?" Martha Maude suggested. "Then we women can make the beds and hang the towels up there while you work downstairs."

Saul laughed good-naturedly at his mother's directive. "Your wish is our command, Mamm," he teased. "I've got Glenn's bedroom set in my trailer. Let's start with that one, as it's the heaviest."

Matthias Wagler, Tim Nissley, Preacher Clarence Miller, and Jude Shetler made a beeline toward Saul's trailer. Soon they were carrying the bedsprings and frame into the house, while Gabe and Jeremiah hefted the matching dresser between them. Molly and Marietta carried the boxes of bedding they'd accumulated over the past few weeks. Rose Wagler, Julia Nissley, Regina, and Cora Miller entered the house with rag rugs, curtain panels, towels, and other linens. Martha Maude and Anne toted bins loaded with nonperishable groceries, while Delores Flaud and Jo were providing dishes, pots, and cooking utensils.

"This is so much fun!" Molly said as she and her sister went up the stairs with some of the other women. As they paused in the hallway, waiting for the men to finish setting up Glenn's bed, she leaned closer to Marietta.

"Say the word to Glenn, and you could be living here," she whispered. "Not every bride has a house that's brand-spanking-new."

Marietta's eyebrows shot up. "Puh! By the time Pete finishes remodeling our place, I'm thinking it'll be *better* than new," she said without missing a beat. "But *jah*, this is an amazing house—especially considering how quickly it came together."

A few moments later the men went downstairs for more furniture, and the women entered Glenn's bedroom.

The Hartzlers hung the crisp white curtains they'd sewn, along with panels of deep blue at the sides of each window. Rose arranged an oval rag rug on either side of the bed, in shades of blue and green. Other women went into the big upstairs bathroom to put away towels and arrange rugs and curtains in there. Because each neighbor had agreed ahead of time to provide specific items, they worked together seamlessly.

In just a couple of hours, the new Detweiler home was put together—including food in the pantry, the fridge, and the deep freeze. Jo had even hung a greenery wreath on the front door, and she'd placed a deep red poinsettia on the kitchen table.

"These are from the Wengerds," she explained. "When Nelson and Michael heard about our surprise for Glenn, they wanted to be part of it."

"And here's a Christmas card to go with it," Molly put in as she pulled a sealed red envelope from her pocket. "Marietta and I thought he should know we're all wishing him well in his new place."

Bishop Jeremiah had been making a final pass through the rooms, and when he joined everyone else in the kitchen, his face was alight with joy. "Friends, while we're gathered here, let's bless this house, shall we?" he suggested.

Molly and everyone around her bowed their heads eagerly. It was a rare privilege to provide a new home and its contents for a friend in need, and because Christmas was only two days away, the occasion felt even more special.

"Dear Lord, we thank You for the opportunity to help

the Detweilers, and we ask Your blessings on them as they take up residence here," the bishop intoned in a resonant voice. "Be in every board and bedspread, every item we've placed here for their use, so that Glenn, Reuben, Billy Jay, and little Levi will know how much we love them—and how much You love them—every moment they're in this home. We ask it in Your name, in the spirit of that most perfect gift You gave us in Your Son. Amen."

Amens echoed around the room.

"I'll see you all tomorrow evening for the Christmas Eve program at the schoolhouse," Bishop Jeremiah said as folks prepared to leave. "Lydianne tells me the scholars have been working hard on their recitations, so it's sure to be a wonderful-*gut* way to welcome the Christ Child into our hearts again."

As Molly and her sister headed toward the buggies with everyone else, she nudged her sister with her elbow. "How long do you think it'll be before Glenn finds his surprise? Are you going to give any hints about it at supper?"

"I'm keeping a straight face," Marietta replied. "If we make the least suggestion that something has happened here today, we'll spill the whole bag of beans. It's been a challenge to keep this secret from Billy Jay, you know."

Molly couldn't miss the fondness in her twin's voice as she spoke of the boy. She'd said enough for one day about Marietta possibly joining the Detweiler family, however, so she focused on untying Opal from the hitching rail.

"For all we know, Pete will let the cat out of the bag," she said as she joined her sister in the buggy. "But we can hope he and Glenn are having a *gut* time and lifting each other's spirits."

"That's what friends are for," Marietta agreed.

"You can't possibly ruin your chances with Marietta, Glenn," Pete insisted. Even though it made pains shoot up his left leg, he sat up straighter on the couch, hoping to convince his friend once and for all. "Okay, so maybe you played your hand a little too soon—but you're still holding all the aces, buddy! Once you leave the Helfing place—and take your boys with you—I guarantee you she'll show up on your doorstep in a day or two, because she'll miss them."

"But what about missing *me*?" Glenn protested. "*I'm* the one who'll be providing for her and giving her a new home and—"

Detweiler speared his hand through his dark hair in frustration. "Of course, all I could think when I left that place today was that no woman in her right mind would want to live there. Every time Gabe and I took a step, it echoed like a tomb without any rugs or curtains or furniture to absorb the sound."

"But if you'll check back over there, I bet you'll find—" Pete caught himself just in time to keep from ruining the surprise Uncle Jeremiah and the others were working on. He glanced at the wall clock. "It—it's only a matter of time before your new home will come together, Glenn. You've just got to *believe*."

"*Believe*," the man seated beside him muttered. "You remind me of one of those English posters that picture Santa and his sleigh and just that one word, *Believe*. Billy

Jay's still of an age to hang his hopes on Christmas magic, but I'm way beyond that."

As Pete's *mammi* came into the front room with their lunch, she winked subtly at Pete, and he returned her gesture. "Oh, but all of us have an inner child, Glenn, no matter how old we get," she said kindly. "And we should let that child out to play every now and again, even when it feels silly or impossible."

She handed Glenn and Pete each a plate that held an open-faced, hot roast beef sandwich, mashed potatoes smothered in gravy, and green beans. "We Amish might not celebrate Christmas with Santa, but the Man in Red has it right when it comes to his spirit of generosity and his unconditional love for children—we are all God's children, ain't so?" she pointed out. "I believe in the basic *gutness* of people. And I believe that when they give with their whole hearts, miracles happen. Just you wait and see, Glenn."

"*Denki* for this fine lunch, Margaret," Glenn mumbled, focusing on his meal. While she returned to the kitchen, he savored a bite of gravy-covered beef so tender he could cut it with his fork.

"I really didn't come over to talk about Marietta, you know," he informed Pete. "I came to tell you that I intend to finish up your remodeling project here as a way to return the huge favor you've done for me and my family."

Pete's forkful of mashed potatoes stopped short of his mouth. "No need to do that, Glenn! Before you know it, I'll be up and around, so I can take up where I left off—"

His companion's raised eyebrows, and his meaningful gaze at Pete's leg cast and bandaged arm, cut Pete's protest short. "How do you figure to heft kitchen cabinets into place with your wing in a sling?" Glenn demanded. "And how long do you think you'll be able to stand on that bum leg while you work?"

"Uncle Jeremiah said he'd help me now that I'm home from the hospital," Pete replied. "He's a pretty fair carpenter—"

"So am I," Detweiler pointed out. "And I'm not going to take *no* for an answer. The Marketplace won't be open for the next two Saturdays, so I'm putting my efforts toward getting your projects finished—if only because Margaret deserves to have her house in order again."

Pete couldn't suppress a grin or miss a chance to lead Glenn astray a little. "It would be perfectly understandable if you chose to work on projects for your own place," he pointed out. "*You're* the one saying Marietta won't want to live there until you can offer her some furniture and the other comforts of a home. Do you figure to build her a special bedroom set, or will you buy one from the Flauds?"

Glenn stuffed a big forkful of mashed potatoes into his mouth. When he'd chewed and swallowed, he glared at Pete. "Will you *lay off* the subject of Marietta? She's declared her intentions, and she says she doesn't need a husband—doesn't need *me*."

Pete had known his friend long enough to hear a different issue between the lines of Glenn's protest. "You came over here to avoid being at her place for lunch today, didn't you?"

"Puh! Dat's there, along with Levi and Molly," Glenn shot back. "It's not as though Marietta and I would be sitting at the table by ourselves trying to figure out what to say to each other."

"Maybe you *should* have a talk with her. Are you going to let *her* have the last word?"

Exasperated, Glenn set his plate on the coffee table with a loud *thunk*. "What'd they do to you in the hospital, Shetler?" he demanded. "Are you on a bunch of drugs? I didn't think it was possible, but you seem even more hardheaded now than you were before you fell off my roof! And I *told* you not to go up there last Monday morning because it was icy, ain't so?"

Pete laughed out loud—but he had to stop, because laughing made his whole upper body hurt. "*Now* you sound like the Detweiler I know," he said. "After all that's happened to you these past several months, it's *gut* to know your spirit—your inner kid—is still in there, trying to shine through."

Before Glenn could shrug him off, Pete added, "I hope that along with celebrating Jesus' birthday, you'll soon be celebrating *you* again, Glenn. With Marietta," he insisted gently. "Because she's *right* for you. And because, hey— it's the season for miracles, *jah*?"

Chapter 25

As Glenn parked his double rig alongside the other buggies lined up on the schoolhouse grounds for the Christmas Eve program, he allowed himself a few moments to adjust his attitude. Billy Jay had been fidgety, insisting he needed to join the other scholars and Teacher Lydianne downstairs for their final instructions, so he'd hopped out at the front steps. Dat and Marietta had gotten out there, too. Molly had driven the Helfings' rig so she could visit Pete when the program was over.

With a steady snow falling, Glenn fastened Nick's fitted blanket over his back before he led the gelding to the corral and pole barn where the other horses were. He gazed up into the clouded night sky, allowing the flakes to tickle his cheeks in the hush of this special evening. When he'd been a scholar, the school program had been exciting yet nerve-racking: he'd been eager to muddle through his recitation so he could enjoy the refreshments and the days of Christmas vacation that followed.

This year, however, Glenn couldn't muster the sense of wonder and joy he usually felt at Christmas. He realized that this was because of his bereavement, yet he longed for a sign that his life would take a turn for the better. He'd worked at Jeremiah's place all day—and with Pete's armchair assistance, he and the bishop had installed the kitchen cabinets and made a lot of progress. He'd been happy to spend the day there rather than at his empty new house or at the Helfing place . . . because Pete had nailed it.

Glenn couldn't muster the courage to speak with Marietta, to change her mind about becoming his wife. Supper had been sheer torture, sitting at the table as she and Molly and Dat chatted with Billy Jay about the Christmas Eve programs of their days as scholars. The girls had carried on an animated conversation—almost as though they shared a secret, as twins often did. Yet when Marietta had glanced his way, it felt as though she'd closed the shutters of her soul to him.

Marietta had been very quiet during the buggy ride to the school, as well. It didn't take a genius to realize that she was uncomfortable in Glenn's presence—and probably deeply disappointed in him. She was undoubtedly ready for him to be at the new place instead of hanging around hers, where she was constantly reminded that he'd proposed to her mere weeks after he'd publicly pursued Lydianne Christner—without bothering to take Marietta on a date or asking to court her first.

But he couldn't take the boys and Dat to stay at the new house, because where would they sleep? And how would they prepare meals without dishes and utensils? Most folks would simply go to a store and buy the items they needed, but in his grief, Glenn felt frozen in place—and totally inept.

He didn't know what it took to restock a home, because

he'd relied upon his wife to do that. And when it came to replacing the curtains Dorcas had sewn and the everyday items she'd created without a second thought, Glenn couldn't seem to make any decisions. He felt he'd be dishonoring his late wife's memory if he chose household items, because the store-bought replacements would never measure up to what she would've created.

So it was easier to stay with the Helfing twins, even though Marietta was giving him the ultimate cold shoulder.

Truth be told, his father and his boys *loved* being in the twins' home. Spending Christmas with the Helfings, where they would enjoy festive food and the comforts they'd grown used to, was a powerful incentive for staying put until the holiday was behind them.

"What am I supposed to do?" Glenn prayed aloud. He gazed into the cloudy heavens, wishing for the appearance of a sign—a bright, unmistakable star to follow.

But he was no wise man. He didn't even qualify as much of a shepherd, because he had no idea how to keep his little flock fed and cared for—and there would be no host of angels coming to proclaim any sort of good news to him. That only happened in Bible stories, after all. Centuries had gone by since anyone had reported such a spectacular angelic happening.

The muffled clip-clopping of hooves in the snow pulled Glenn from his musings. In spite of his misgivings, he greeted Tim Nissley and Matthias Wagler as they approached the corral. "*Gut* evening," he called out. "I bet you've had excited girls at your houses today."

"Oh my," Tim said with a laugh. "Ella is so excited, she spent all day playing with our Nativity figures—"

"*Jah*, Gracie's memorized everyone else's part for the

program as well as her own," Matthias put in jovially. "I've lost count of how many times I've heard the entire program over the past couple of days."

Glenn managed a smile. "I suspect girls catch onto their parts easier than boys—although Billy Jay's been a real trooper. He's learned his lines better than I ever did."

Waving at the two men, he set off toward the school-house. The light spilling from the windows made golden patches on the snow and gave the white building a wel-coming glow. As Glenn stepped inside, he saw that nearly everyone had arrived—and from across the crowd, Dat was waving his arm exuberantly to get his attention.

For this annual occasion, the scholars' desks had been moved downstairs so folding chairs could be set up in the center of the classroom. The chairs were intended for older folks who couldn't stand up through the whole program, so lots of the scholars' parents stood on the two sides and in the back of the room.

Glenn sighed. Dat was seated on the end of the second row, with Marietta beside him, holding Levi on her shoul-der. The only logical place for Glenn to stand was beside her, wasn't it?

And indeed, as Glenn headed toward the woman who'd so bluntly rejected him, folks in the crowd made way for him as though they assumed he and Marietta would soon be a couple. Keeping a pleasant expression on his face, Glenn greeted the Hartzlers and the Slabaughs, Jude Shetler and his family, the Millers, and the Flauds. As he approached his father, he spotted Molly leaning against the schoolroom's side wall—and she seemed to be watch-ing him with a secretive smile.

Did Molly know something he didn't? Or was she

thinking ahead to a visit with Pete? The incapacitated carpenter would be spending the evening at home alone— which sounded like a fine idea to Glenn as he took his place slightly behind Marietta. He playfully tapped Levi's upturned nose, making the boy giggle.

Teacher Lydianne came up from the lower level. She took her place in the center of a specially built dais about two feet high that spanned the front of the room and began to speak.

"Welcome to this program on the holiest of nights," she said happily. "Our scholars have worked very diligently these past weeks, and I'd like to thank you all for practicing with them at home and for supporting them with your presence here. Please join us when we sing the carols that are interspersed between recitations of the Scripture and the other narratives! We'll begin the evening with 'The First Noel.'"

Lydianne led the singing in a clear, resonant voice, and soon the students were filing up the stairs to take their places on the dais. Even though there were only eight scholars, the room was packed, because everyone in the congregation attended the yearly program. As the folks behind him shifted to get a better view, Glenn found himself standing smack against Marietta's shoulder and hip. Levi flashed him a toothless grin, as though he were enjoying his *dat*'s predicament.

Was it his imagination, or had the schoolroom become much warmer? The rise in temperature surely had to be the reason Marietta's dewy cheek was turning pink, because she wasn't paying Glenn a speck of attention. She was focused solely on Billy Jay, who stood in the front row along with Stevie, Ella, and Gracie. Billy Jay was looking right back at her, too, his eyes alight with childlike joy.

Glenn blinked. His boy's black hair was freshly cut—rounded like a bowl, with the bangs straight across. Billy Jay was wearing a new deep green shirt Glenn had never seen—and his black pants were new, too; they reached the tops of his shiny black shoes instead of stopping a few inches short like his old pair. As he sang, flashing the empty gap where a new front tooth was growing in, he appeared happy and well cared for.

And I have Marietta to thank for that. I didn't lift a finger, yet Billy Jay no longer wears that forlorn, hangdog look of a boy who's lost his mother.

At Teacher Lydianne's cue, the crowd began to sing "O Come, All Ye Faithful." Dat's bass voice sounded firm and steady, and around the room other men sang the lower parts while most of the women carried the melody. Beside him, Marietta's alto notes were firm and unwavering—and Glenn found himself blending his voice with hers as he harmonized on the tenor line.

When the carol ended, Lorena Flaud stepped forward to recite the familiar passage from Luke about Caesar Augustus's tax decree. Glenn realized he was breathing in sync with Marietta, who was so close that he could recognize the faint aroma of the ham she'd fried for their supper.

Maybe it wasn't so bad to be pressed against her. She couldn't fault him for taking undue advantage of his positioning in the crowded schoolroom, after all.

Maybe he should savor these moments while they stood together as a family, because when the program was over, Marietta would keep her distance again, and his loneliness would return fourfold to haunt him.

Glenn got so caught up in his thoughts about her, wondering what to do and say so Marietta would want him, that he lost track of the scholars' recitations for several heavenly minutes.

"'. . . and lo, the angel of the Lord came upon them, and the glory of the Lord shone round about them: and they were *sore afraid*!'"

Billy Jay's earnest voice made Glenn refocus on the program, as though he'd never heard the angel's ancient announcement to the shepherds.

"'And the angel said unto them *fear not*!'" his son continued boldly. "'For, behold, I bring you good tidings of great joy which shall be to all people. For—for unto you is born this day in the city of David a—a *Savior*, which is Christ the Lord.'"

Aware that he'd stumbled a bit, Billy Jay took a breath and stood taller. "'And this shall be a sign unto you; Ye shall find the babe wrapped in swaddling clothes, lying in a manger,'" he continued confidently. He was looking straight at Marietta, and she was returning his trusting gaze as she held her breath.

"'And suddenly there was with the angel a multitude of the heavenly host praising God, and saying, Glory to God in the highest, and on earth peace, good will toward men!'"

Marietta let out a delighted sigh, her face aglow with pride—the same sense of accomplishment Glenn acknowledged as he, too, beamed at his boy. Teacher Lydianne began "Angels We Have Heard on High," and everyone in the crowded room joined in with gusto—especially on the "Gloria in excelsis Deo" chorus.

Glenn, however, was so overwhelmed with emotion that he couldn't get the words out. He was having another one of those moments Bishop Jeremiah had warned him about—a sneaky grief attack, just when he'd thought he'd put his sorrow behind him for the evening.

Fear not! The angel—and Billy Jay—have said this so many times lately. Maybe I should listen. Maybe God's speaking to ME, through His word.

Glenn inhaled abruptly, hoping he wasn't being presumptuous.

He realized then, as he tried to identify the many emotions filling his heart, that it was *gratitude* welling up inside him. Marietta, in her quiet and unassuming way, had held his family together during the darkness that had nearly swallowed him whole. She hadn't become caretaker of the Detweiler tribe expecting any repayment— and she clearly hadn't assumed responsibility for his sons to gain favor with Glenn, as some women would've done.

Marietta was simply living out a life of love as Christ had modeled it in the Bible. She was doing what needed to be done, willingly, because she had such a tremendous reservoir of love to share. He and his family were the lucky recipients of her love . . . and God had arranged it all.

Glenn blinked back sudden tears, relieved that Marietta remained unaware of the emotional roller coaster he was riding. He'd made some serious mistakes and some very self-centered assumptions during his time in the Helfing household. He needed to make amends so Marietta would know how much he appreciated all she and her sister had done for him and his family . . . without expecting anything from her in return.

Fear not! For behold, I bring you tidings of great joy . . .

Joy. It had been so long since Glenn had experienced joy, he'd forgotten how it felt. As the crowd around him began a rousing rendition of "Joy to the World," he felt encased in a bubble, separated from their exuberance. He needed to pop that bubble and emerge into a fresh new existence—no, a whole new *life*, with a new attitude— before Marietta would give him another chance.

If she was to become his wife, it would be because she fell in love with him.

Glenn understood that now. As she stood so close to him, holding little Levi, Marietta reminded him of Mary with the baby Jesus. She had a soft glow about her, a wholesome purity and strength that he admired more than he could say.

The realization stirred something within him. Just as Mary had gained favor with God when He'd chosen her as the mother of His Son, Marietta stood far above other women Glenn knew—and she'd not consciously sought such a position. She was just an innately *good woman*.

Glenn sighed. How could he possibly become good enough to deserve her? If he was to find the happiness with Marietta that he so deeply desired, he needed to pay a lot more attention to her—needed to show her exactly how special she was . . .

Fear not! For unto you is born a Savior—Christ the Lord!

And hadn't he seen evidence of Jesus and His love at every turn lately? Gabe and Pete and Howard and all the men who'd built his family a new home . . . Bishop

Jeremiah, with his wise, patient counsel . . . the ladies who'd unfailingly provided lunch at the construction site . . . the friends in this schoolroom who'd never given up on him. And of course Marietta and Molly, who'd housed and fed and cared for him and his family without complaining about how it had cut into their shop's Christmas profits.

What wondrous love was this? And why had he been so oblivious to it?

Applause filled the schoolroom. Glenn blinked. Somehow, the remainder of the program and the carol singing had gone on around him, but he'd been too immersed in his thoughts to pay any attention. He clapped loudly so no one would realize that he'd gotten lost in his own little world.

As the applause faded, Bishop Jeremiah stepped up on the dais. "You scholars have gotten our Christmas celebration off to a wonderful-*gut* start," he said as he smiled at each of them. "We all want to thank you and Teacher Lydianne for the heartfelt way you've shared your faith with us on this most blessed night of our Christian year."

Jeremiah gazed out over the crowd, his face alight with Christmas spirit. "I wish each and every one of you a meaningful day tomorrow, pondering our Lord's birth. And I'll see you all at The Marketplace for our Second Christmas celebration on the twenty-sixth! It'll be a day of food and festivities, with lots of games and singing. Merry Christmas!" he exclaimed. "And now for the best part—the refreshments downstairs!"

"Be careful going home, too," Deacon Saul chimed in. "The snow's coming down fast and furious now."

As the folks around Glenn started for the stairway, chatting excitedly about upcoming events and the weather, his thoughts returned to a more practical level. It was his responsibility to get everyone home safely, no matter what condition the roads were in. "I'll go fetch the horse, Dat, while you folks have some quick punch and—"

"Glenn, are you all right? You got very quiet for a while." Marietta's green eyes, mere inches from his, reflected the concern in her whispered observation.

He held his breath. Oh, but he wanted to pull her close and thank her for—no, he really wanted to *kiss* her and ask if he could start again—

"Dat! Marietta! Dawdi!" Billy Jay called out as he broke through the people around them. "I did it! We *all* did it! It was a wonderful-*gut* Christmas program, and—"

When his son reached for him, Glenn realized once again that his priorities needed shifting. Nothing was more important—or a more direct display of love come down from heaven—than the amazing, resilient bundle of energy God had entrusted to his care.

"Billy Jay!" Glenn crowed as he grabbed his boy up in a hug. "You did a fine job, son! And you clean up pretty *gut*, too—are these clothes new?"

"*Jah*, Marietta made 'em this week!"

Glenn hugged his son again and then let the squirming boy hurry downstairs with his friends. As he looked at Marietta, he prayed he wouldn't say anything clueless. "*Denki* for all you've done for Billy Jay, and for Levi and Dat—and for me, Marietta," he said beneath the noise of the crowd. "And *jah*, I'm all right now. Better than I've been for a long while. *Denki* for asking—and for caring."

Her shy smile ignited a tiny spark of hope in his heart. "You're welcome, Glenn. Merry Christmas to you."

He swallowed hard. It was such a commonplace sentiment at this time of year, yet her words seemed to ring with a deeper meaning. Or was he hearing more than she was saying?

Fear not!

Glenn chose to believe the angel's message this time—for wasn't he gazing at a real-life angel? "And Merry Christmas to you, dear Marietta," he whispered.

Chapter 26

Clutching the harness lines, Molly urged Opal along the two-lane county highway. The snow on the curving road was drifting in places, which made it impossible to drive on the shoulder, as she preferred. Because the English had a penchant for last-minute Christmas Eve shopping, the traffic was trickier than she'd hoped. For a few minutes her rig would be the only vehicle on the road, and then suddenly she'd have four or five cars behind her. Headlights flickered from side to side in her rearview mirrors as impatient drivers pulled out to pass her and then swerved back into the lane.

Molly couldn't let her concentration waver. Her windshield wipers were going full-tilt, barely keeping up with the snowfall. Even with her safety lights flashing, she felt vulnerable on the blacktop's unlit, hilly stretches. If a speeding driver popped over a rise and hit her rig before he saw it, her holiday plans would take a deadly detour.

As Molly turned off the highway and spotted the bishop's tall, white house on the next rise, she relaxed. Someone—a Mennonite neighbor, most likely—had plowed the road and people's lanes, so the rig rolled along more smoothly.

When she'd left the schoolhouse, Jeremiah and his *mamm* had still been chatting over refreshments, so she was hoping for some time alone with Pete. After she'd turned onto the Shetlers' lane, the mare stopped near the house, but Molly clucked to keep her going.

"Go to the barn, Opal," she called out. "Something tells me we'll be spending the night here. And that's not such a *bad* thing, ain't so?" she added with a chuckle.

After she'd parked her rig and situated the mare in a stall, Molly grabbed the tote bag she'd brought along. She jogged across the bishop's yard and entered the house through the mudroom. Not wanting Pete to quiz her about the contents of her bag, she hung it on a wall peg and put her coat and bonnet beside it. She took off her boots and placed them on the old rug beneath her coat.

"Shetler, you slacker!" she called out, pausing to smooth her apron and dress. "I saved you a spot at the Christmas Eve program, and you never showed up!"

This was a fib, of course, but why should she let him off the hook just because it was a holy night? By the light of Margaret's kitchen lamp, Molly saw that the new cabinets were in place and that their contents had been put back into them. She knew Glenn and Jeremiah had accomplished this, but she intended to tease Pete about being able to do carpentry work yet not come to the school program—

But he was asleep on the sofa.

Pete's arm had drifted down to rest on Riley's back— which explained why the dog hadn't barked or greeted her at the door. The golden lifted his head, giving her a doggy grin as his tail beat a quick rhythm on the floor.

"What a friend we have in Riley," Molly murmured as she took in the scene from the kitchen doorway.

Should she wake Pete or let him rest? There'd been a time when she wouldn't have considered keeping quiet, yet something—maybe Christmas Eve generosity—told Molly to wait him out in the recliner.

Pete's face, bathed in soft lamplight, made her pause. His pale features appeared pinched, as though he might be in pain—or exhausted from the discomfort his injuries had caused him all day.

She'd never seen him looking so vulnerable. With his leg in a cast, propped on the arm of the sofa to keep it elevated, and his left arm bound against his body in a black sling, Pete Shetler wasn't the swaggering, cocksure daredevil she'd come to love. And she was sure he'd never intended for her to see him this way—defenseless against her scrutiny.

Molly smiled. She could razz him about this scene later, when Pete would be able to fire back insult for insult.

As she leaned back in the recliner to keep watch, Riley resettled himself against the bottom of the sofa as though he, too, was content to let Pete sleep.

About ten minutes later, the back door opened. Molly heard the bishop and his *mamm* in the mudroom, taking off their coats. They'd known she was coming for a visit—and they would've seen Opal in the barn—so she slipped out of the chair to greet them.

"Pete's zonked out," she said softly.

Margaret nodded as she hung her heavy black coat and bonnet on a peg. "I suspect he overdid it today, supervising

Glenn and Jeremiah while they put the kitchen back together," she remarked.

"I'm glad you put your mare up for the night, Molly," the bishop said as he stepped out of his unbuckled galoshes. "I couldn't in *gut* conscience let you drive back home. It's nasty out there—bet we've already gotten four inches, and the snow shows no sign of letting up."

Molly tried not to appear too delighted by Bishop Jeremiah's declaration. Even if she was thirty-five, it made the situation seem more respectable than if *she* had invited herself to sleep over.

"It'll be nice to have a guest for Christmas—and you'll surely improve Pete's mood," Margaret put in. "Your sister knows you were coming here, *jah*?"

Molly nodded. "She rode to the school with Glenn's bunch so I could leave when I was ready. I, um, brought something along as a surprise for Pete," she added, nodding toward her tote bag. "It's not quite Christmas Day, so would it be all right if I whipped it up in your kitchen? I ran short of time today and—"

Margaret squeezed her shoulder. "Matter of fact, I have a few last details to finish for tomorrow's dinner myself," she remarked. "We can do our cooking now—so the bishop won't chastise us for working on a sacred day, you know."

The two of them chuckled as Jeremiah playfully raised his eyebrows. "You ladies have a couple of hours," he said, glancing at the wall clock. "Meanwhile, why don't I rouse Pete and get him to bed? He'll have *quite* a surprise tomorrow when he sees you at the breakfast table, Molly."

"Sounds like a plan—and *denki* ahead of time for putting up with me," Molly added.

She couldn't help grinning as she grabbed her tote bag. Her visit with Pete was working out even better than she'd planned.

"While the roads are still passable, I'm going to fetch more horse feed and hay from our barn and bring Ned back with me," Glenn said as he pulled the double rig up close to the Helfings' house. "I suspect we'll be snowed in tomorrow, and it's not right for you girls to be feeding my horses as well as your own."

"The roads are none too *gut* even now," Marietta said from the back seat. "Don't feel you're putting us out, Glenn. You can certainly wait a day or two to get that feed, and if you ask, a neighbor will look in on Ned, *jah*?"

"Snowed in?" Billy Jay echoed hopefully. He wiggled on the seat beside Glenn. "You better let me help you get that hay and stuff, Dat. It's not like I have to get to bed, coz there's no school tomorrow—or for a long time—coz it's Christmas!"

Glenn rumpled his son's hair, laughing. He recalled being just as excited about the holidays when he'd been Billy Jay's age.

"I'll help, too, if you need me," his father put in from the seat behind Glenn. "But I can tell you that the metal folding chair I sat in all evening didn't do my hips any favors—even if it was the best Christmas program *ever*, Billy Jay."

"How about if you help me set the table for breakfast, Reuben?" Marietta suggested kindly. "Some hot cocoa and aspirin will help those hips, I bet."

"Cocoa?" Billy Jay whispered hopefully. "And cookies, maybe?"

"You had a handful of cookies after the program," Marietta reminded him as she lifted Levi's carrier into her lap. "Maybe more sugar right before bed isn't such a fine idea."

"But it *is* Christmas Eve," Glenn put in indulgently. "And if you'd rather keep your *dawdi* and Marietta company while I'm gone, Billy Jay, I'm fine with that. Won't take me long to load that feed and get back—and if you're still up, I'll join you at the table."

"*Jah!* Let's do that," Billy Jay said. "I'll get the door!"

As the boy clambered over Glenn's lap, popped the rig door open, and dashed through the snow toward the house, Marietta chuckled. "I don't think I've ever seen him this wound up," she remarked softly. "It's been quite a night for him."

Glenn sensed she was in a receptive mood, and he wanted to make the most of it. "You made his success possible, Marietta," he murmured. "I can't thank you enough for sprucing him up and helping him learn his recitation, and—"

She reached over the back of the seat to grasp his shoulder. "I was happy to do it for him, Glenn. It's *gut* to see him smiling again. And maybe after you've loaded your feed," she added, "you might want to see that your furnace is set the way you want it, in case you don't get back to the house for a few days."

"*Gut* idea," Dat put in. "And be sure the doors are shut tight. Remember how the door blew open once while we were at Sadie's place, and we had a drift in the front room when we got home?"

Glenn nodded as his father stepped out of the rig and took Levi's carrier so Marietta could get out more easily. He was confident that the doors on their new house were shut firmly—but what would it hurt to check, if it would make his *dat* feel better?

A few minutes later he was rolling down the road, paying special attention as he approached the inter- sections. He was grateful that in the moonlight, the accu- mulating snow made the edges of the unlit pavement easier to distinguish—and he was glad he could reach their place on lesser-traveled roads. Someone had plowed recently—Howard, most likely—so the going was easier than Glenn had anticipated.

As he pulled into the home place several minutes later, Glenn mentally thanked the fire chief for clearing the lane there, as well. At the sight of the dark house, he sighed. He and Dat—or Dorcas—had always left a lamp burning when they went someplace in the evening. But he focused on the task at hand. No sense in ruining Christmas Eve by getting lost in memories that would only make him miss his wife and his *mamm*.

He pulled up close to the barn door. After he put a tarp on the back floor of the rig to keep it cleaner, Glenn stacked several bales of hay between the back seats, which faced each other. Then he tossed in a bag of oats.

"Come on, Ned, we're taking you with us this time," he said as he led his other gelding outside to tether him to the rear of the rig.

As Glenn hopped back in to drive closer to the house, he was tempted to just head back to the Helfing place— it was obvious that the doors were shut tight. He clearly recalled setting the thermostat at sixty—warm enough to keep the pipes from freezing, in case he couldn't convince himself to return to the empty house anytime soon.

Something told him to peek inside, however, so he wouldn't have to fib to Dat and Marietta. Glenn told himself he needed to get past his aversion to this vacant place and *do* something about it. Maybe he could ask Marietta's opinions about where to get the bedding and curtains and rugs . . .

I'll have plenty of time to think about that tomorrow. Christmas Day's going to be even quieter than usual if we get as much snow as I think we will.

Glenn opened the mudroom door and flipped the switch of the gas light fixture. As he leaned down to unbuckle his galoshes, he paused, frowning. A white curtain as well as a panel of blue fabric pulled to the side—just like the ones Dorcas had made years ago—hung at the window.

Glenn straightened slowly, his mind spinning. As he looked toward the unlit kitchen, the shadows suggested other objects he *knew* had not been there when he and Gabe had finished their sweeping the day before.

When he flipped the kitchen light switch, his jaw dropped. A new table with six chairs filled the empty space that had bothered him so much the last time he'd been here, and a huge poinsettia sat in the center of it. A fresh towel hung on the handle of the oven, and a cheerful blue canister set was lined up in one corner of the countertop, near the stove. The kitchen windows had fresh curtains, as well, and when he eased one of the top drawers open, he found a silverware organizer filled with eating utensils and new knives.

Glenn's hands began to shake, and his throat tightened. Who had done all this—and when?

On impulse he rushed into the front room, gaping at a sofa and chairs and tables with lamps. His feet couldn't seem to stop, and when he'd raced up the stairs he found room after room filled with new furniture. The beds were made up with colorful quilts, and coordinating rugs covered the bedroom floors. There was a bassinet for Levi and a twin bed with a kid-sized table and chairs in Billy Jay's room, along with a bookshelf. The bathroom had fresh towels hanging on the racks.

Questions buzzed like bees in Glenn's mind as he returned to the bedroom at the top of the stairs . . . the room he'd shared with Dorcas. The beautiful maple bed, dresser, and chest had surely come from the Flauds' furniture factory—and as he fell facedown on its fresh blue and green quilt, he suspected that Martha Maude and Anne Hartzler had made it.

Glenn began to weep uncontrollably. His friends from church had sprung the biggest surprise of his life on him— and they'd known by his expression, at the school program, that he hadn't yet discovered it. Molly and Marietta had surely been a part of orchestrating this household refurbishing, yet they hadn't dropped a single hint . . . until Marietta had suggested that he should check the thermostat. Even then, she'd kept a straight face.

And what a dear face it was—still too thin and hollowed out, framed by short brown waves that were just long enough to lie flat under her *kapp*. She was flat-chested, and he'd heard she would never bear children. But wasn't

Marietta the most beautiful woman in the world, from the inside out?

"Get your act together, Detweiler," he muttered as he sat up. He mopped his face with his shirtsleeve as he looked around the simple, beautiful room. "You've got no excuses now."

Never in his life had he owned such fine, matching furniture that wasn't handed down or salvaged from somebody's attic. As he went back down the hallway, stopping briefly in each of the bedrooms again, Glenn was still agog with the wonder of what he saw. To his way of thinking, the house looked as fine as a catalog advertising the kind of top-dollar furniture that usually graced the homes of English folks. It wasn't as fancy as Saul Hartzler's place, but it was a far cry from what his parents and his wife had lived with.

Glenn knew he had a whopping bill at Martin and Gabe's shop—and it might take him years to pay it off—yet the money didn't matter. His friends knew he'd needed help, and they'd come through for him. They'd made his echoing, empty house look like a *home*.

Well, almost. This place still needs a woman's touch—and so do I. And now I can provide everything Marietta could possibly want . . . if I can convince her to want me, too.

Glenn headed downstairs to check the thermostat. Sixty, just as he'd left it. He bumped it up a few degrees so it wouldn't be quite so chilly when he brought Marietta, Dat, and the boys over to see the place—although she knew exactly how wonderful everything looked, because she'd had a hand in making it that way.

In the kitchen, Glenn checked the soil in the poinsettia's pot to see if it needed watering. It was undoubtedly one of the Wengerds' plants, large and full of beautiful red blooms—because despite his misgivings about his life, his friends seemed to believe he deserved the very best.

He spotted an envelope propped against the pot then. After all he'd seen while touring the rooms, he suspected it might contain the bills for the furniture, rugs, and quilts.

Glenn would pay every dime, too. It was one thing to accept a new house funded by the church district's aid fund, because every family paid into it—and every family received help when they needed it. But the furnishings and linens and accessories had been provided by Amish crafters like himself—folks who depended upon the income from their wares to support their families. It was just *wrong* to assume he didn't owe them the full price they would charge for these items in their stores.

And it would be a small price to pay for the overwhelming *joy* they'd given him. Glenn couldn't possibly put a dollar amount on how loved and accepted his friends had made him feel with their surprise.

His fingers shook a little as he eased a Christmas card out of the envelope. The front featured the usual *Merry Christmas*, with a picture of a red cardinal perched on a greenery wreath. As he opened it, his eyes skipped over the printed message to read the handwriting he thought was Molly's:

> *Glenn, as you and your family begin life in your*
> *new home, we in your church family hope you'll*

accept these gifts, along with the love that comes
with them. May our Lord bless you this Christmas
and always!

His mouth dropped open. He couldn't believe what
he'd read, so he read it again.

"I need to have a talk with you people," Glenn murmured, shaking his head. Then he noticed a little arrow
pointing to the back of the card.

He turned it over and read, *P.S. Don't give up on my*
sister!

"Hah! This *is* your handwriting, Molly!" Glenn crowed.
He laughed until tears streamed into his beard again—
but this time he felt full of joy rather than overwhelmed
by the weight of the losses he'd suffered. It was as though
Billy Jay's Scripture passage had foretold Glenn's recovery: *Glory to God in the highest and on earth peace,*
goodwill toward all men.

Bishop Jeremiah sometimes talked about a peace that
passed all understanding, and Glenn understood that
concept now. The goodwill of his friends had blessed him
beyond anything he'd known before. The joy and serenity
in his heart convinced him that someday soon, his life
would be back on track—happy again. He'd heard the
term "Christmas miracle" often enough, usually referring
to Christ's birth, but he felt that a miraculous power had
filled his spirit and granted him the chance to re-create
himself and his life.

And for that, Glenn was extremely grateful to God and
his friends.

He left the house whistling "I Heard the Bells on

Christmas Day," hearing the carol in his mind as it sounded when the men harmonized during their Friday night singing sessions. Within minutes he was rolling down the road in his loaded rig, with Ned following behind it. The trip back to the Helfing place didn't take very long, because car traffic was light. In the twins' barn he unloaded the horse feed and tended his geldings. As he approached the house, a lamp was burning in the kitchen, and he hoped it meant Marietta was still up . . . maybe waiting for him.

When Glenn stepped inside, however, the house was quiet. He sensed that once Billy Jay had finally wound down, Dat and Marietta had gone to bed, as well. They'd had a long, busy day.

His mind was buzzing, however, and it would be a while before he got to sleep. Marietta had left him a note about warming the cocoa she'd left on the stove if he wanted it. Glenn turned the burner on and got a mug from the cupboard. Across the kitchen, he found the twins' box of Christmas cards and a pen. He selected a card with a picture of a red candle burning in a window.

After a moment's thought, he began to write inside it.

Thank you for helping with the wonderful surprise
I found at the house. Thank you for all you do for
me—and please don't give up on me, okay? I love
you with all my heart, Marietta, and I'll do
whatever it takes to prove that. Merry Christmas!

Love, Glenn

He put the card in the envelope, wrote Marietta's name on it, and propped it against the lidded pan of coffee cake she'd baked for their Christmas breakfast.

Warmed by the cocoa and his hopes for the future, Glenn went to bed a happy man.

Chapter 27

When Pete jerked awake, his arm and leg were throbbing with intense pain. As he maneuvered himself into a sitting position with his legs over the side of his bed, his head swam, and he had to take a deep breath to make it stop spinning. He felt disoriented until he remembered that Mammi had moved out of her main-level *dawdi haus*, which was down the hall from the front room, so he could sleep there instead of climbing the stairs to his bedroom.

"Merry Christmas, Mr. Shetler," he muttered hoarsely. "Now tell me again why you just *had* to replace that shingle on Detweiler's—"

He'd hoped his chatter would alert Mammi or his uncle that he needed his meds, but the woman in the doorway was *not* his grandmother.

"It *is* a merry Christmas, Mr. Shetler," she repeated way too cheerfully. "Your uncle, your *mammi*, and your dog are out shoveling a path to the barn to tend the horses, so you're stuck with me. What can I do for you?"

"Seriously?" he snapped. His guest sprouted a second head and then went back to having just one. "Go home. Your smart remarks are the *last* thing I need right now."

Molly—or he *thought* she was Molly—shrugged. "Sorry, Pete. We got a foot of snow last night, so I'm going nowhere," she replied breezily. "I made you a surprise, but you'll have to talk a whole lot nicer to me before I let you have any of it."

"Get my uncle. I have to use the bathroom."

As he'd hoped, her eyes widened with alarm—but she hurried off. Pete took a few deep breaths, reconciling himself to what Molly had said about a foot of snow and the fact that she was here for the duration. Why didn't he recall that she'd come to see him last night?

Pete heard her calling outside for his uncle. He waited for an eternity until heavier footsteps approached his temporary quarters. Riley reached him first, however, leaping onto the bed to lick Pete's face. The sudden shifting of the mattress made the dog fall against his bad arm, and Pete cried out.

"Riley, get off the bed. *Sit*," Uncle Jeremiah said softly. He pointed toward the floor.

As always, the golden obeyed his uncle immediately. Jeremiah's technique had never worked for Pete, and his lack of control over his big, excitable dog only added to his list of complaints.

Uncle Jeremiah stopped beside the bed, one eyebrow raised. "Molly tells me Prince Charming greeted her a little while ago," he said as he carefully put a hand beneath Pete's sling to steady him. "Are you not happy to see her, or—"

"Everything *hurts*," Pete muttered. "And I'm not in the mood for her mouth."

His uncle laughed. "Last I knew, your mouth could keep right up with Molly's, and you two rather enjoyed seeing who could have the last word," he said as he helped Pete into his wheelchair. "For your *mammi*'s sake, I hope you'll be polite to our guest rather than ruining everyone's Christmas, Pete. Yes, you're in pain, but you don't have to *be* a pain."

Pete bit back a retort, scowling when his uncle tried to push him toward the bathroom. There were things a man just had to do for himself. But Uncle Jeremiah was right: he'd been awfully testy since his return home from the hospital.

"Fine," he muttered. When he reached the bathroom doorway, he was already worn out from the effort of wheeling himself with one hand. "I'll be nicer after I've had some coffee and my pain meds have kicked in."

"Holler when you're done in here. I'll get your pills ready."

It made Pete feel old and decrepit, depending upon a toilet contraption that gave him metal arms to steady himself as he sat down—and helped him boost himself up one-handed when he'd finished. Over the top of his flannel pajamas, the sling was rubbing him the wrong way. It was a chore to pull up his baggy pajama pants with just one hand, too, but he refused to call for help.

"Pajamas—*me*, wearing old fogy pajamas," he muttered as he finally got the pants positioned correctly. He preferred to sleep in worn-out sweat pants and a ratty T-shirt, but Mammi had told him it was time for an upgrade.

When he steadied himself against the vanity to brush his teeth, Pete got another unpleasant surprise. The pale man in the mirror looked like he'd seen a ghost or stuck his finger in an electrical socket. His blond hair stuck out in several directions, and he needed a shower—but that wasn't going to happen this morning.

Molly might decide to go home pretty quick. And maybe that'll keep me from biting her head off.

As he finished in the bathroom, it occurred to Pete that not so long ago, he couldn't get enough of Molly's company—but that was before he'd gotten hurt. As Dr. Douthit had outlined a plan for physical therapy after the holidays, Pete saw himself being laid up for way too long. If he couldn't take larger doses of the pain relievers Douthit had prescribed, Pete wouldn't be able to endure his therapy or function at even half capacity anytime soon.

And that ticked him off. He was already sick of being an invalid.

Uncle Jeremiah returned to get him into some clean clothes, but it was a slow, painful process. "I'll be back in for breakfast after I shovel some more snow," his uncle said when Pete was sitting on the side of the bed. "I hope you feel better by then—"

"Make sure Molly can get out and go home," Pete interrupted. "She won't want to stay long."

His uncle shot him a warning look. As he was leaving, Mammi came in with some buttered toast, coffee, and his pills. She was wearing a deep red dress, and the plate she carried was from the hand-painted holly-and-ivy set she only used at Christmastime. She set a big mug of coffee on the bedside table.

"Eat this toast before you torture your empty stomach with your medications. You can have the rest of your breakfast when you've made your way to the couch," she said gently. She studied him, cocking her head. "Did you purposely not comb your hair, Pete, or is this your new look? Molly will be impressed."

"That's the whole point," he retorted. "She might as well see what a mess I've become, ain't so?"

"So you're inviting her to your pity party?" Mammi shot back. "You seemed fine when Glenn was here working on the kitchen Monday—perfectly able to advise him on his love life, too."

"That was then, this is Wednesday." He shrugged and sent a new shock wave of pain through his left arm. "Detweiler's a man with a plan—and a brand-new house full of brand-new stuff. I'm glad *somebody's* happy."

With a shake of her head, Mammi placed his comb on the nightstand and left.

Pete jammed the first piece of toast into his mouth before washing his pills down with coffee. Riley whimpered, but Pete devoured the second piece of toast without offering him even a scrap.

He wouldn't sleep, but he was tempted to lie down again. Pete wanted nothing more than to hibernate in his cave for the rest of the day rather than deal with people . . . especially Molly.

What had possessed her to drive through the snow last night? She usually had more sense than to risk bad weather and getting stuck someplace other than home. Surely she wasn't descending to the level of females who didn't pay attention to such things—or who depended upon men to do their thinking for them.

But if she is, that's all the more reason for her to go home, ain't so? Why would I give up my happy bachelorhood to deal with her dependency for the rest of my life?

Then again, she'd mentioned a surprise. Something edible . . .

Pete propped his pillow against the headboard and stretched out, settling into a semicomfortable position. Riley curled up on the floor beside the bed, his joints thumping against the hardwood floor. As Pete slurped his coffee, resting the mug against his chest, he waited for the caffeine to clear his fogged head. He was just feeling the first hint of the medication's relief—just allowing his eyelids to flutter shut—when a voice very close to his head startled him awake.

"Shetler! You look like something the cat dragged in. *Here*."

Coffee sloshed onto his shirt. With a groan, Pete opened one eye. Molly relieved him of his mug and held out the comb with a determined expression on her face.

"I'm blind," he muttered. "Can't see combing my hair just because it's Christmas."

"So I'll comb it for you. Sit up," she insisted. "If you think for one minute I'm going to let you sleep through my visit, you've got another think coming."

He let out a sigh and complied. It was easier than arguing with her.

Once he'd struggled to sit up again, Molly placed a hand on his shoulder to steady him. "I'm sorry you don't feel *gut*, Pete," she said, managing to sound sincere about it. "From what your *mammi* tells me, you've got a long row to hoe, what with therapy and a lengthy recovery time. I bet you hate it that you're so weak you can't even swat the comb out of my hand."

He almost took her bait—but as Molly gently ran the comb through his hair, he felt better. "You don't have to stay," he said. "I'm an invalid with a bad attitude. Not very *gut* company today, Christmas or not."

"Puh! You *always* have a bad attitude, Shetler. Why should Christmas be any different?"

When she cupped the side of his face with her warm hand to put his head in a better position, Pete didn't fight her. Her attention—or maybe it was the pain pills—seemed to be mellowing his sharp edges.

"I see you shaved for me, too," she remarked softly. "Or are you getting a head start for when you're married, growing your beard because you're so eager to—"

"Don't push it, Moll," Pete retorted, but he was chuckling. "By the time you've spent the morning with me and my attitude, you'll forget any thoughts you might've had about me marrying you and living at your place after your remodeling's done. Because—as you can see—it'll be *years* before I can work again. If ever."

Molly stepped back to look at his hair, seemingly satisfied with it. "Okay, let's get you into your wheel-chair," she said, oblivious to what he'd just said. "You'll feel better once you get out of this sickroom and onto the sofa."

His eyes widened. "If you think you can boss me around and make me go—"

"Shetler," she cut in, "I can whip your sorry butt any day of the week. We're going out to the couch so I can sit someplace besides your bed—because that's improper on Christmas, you know," she added with a winsome smile. "There'll be none of that hanky-panky stuff like you pulled when we went driving in your truck."

The memory of kissing Molly shot through Pete's system

like a triple dose of his meds. She was gently guiding him toward the wheelchair, so he eased himself onto its seat. Before she could start pushing him out of the room, Pete felt he should tell her the obvious truth.

"Don't get your hopes up, Molly," he stated. "I might never fully recover from that fall—might not be the man you want anymore, when I'm unable to climb a ladder or build stuff or—"

Molly leaned closer until her nose nearly touched his.

"Pete," she murmured, "you're mad at yourself for going up onto that slippery roof. And you're ticked off because being laid up wasn't in your plans, and because you're a lousy patient. You're suffering debilitating pain, and nobody else seems to know how bad you've got it. And on top of that," she added, widening her eyes at him, "Detweiler's recovering, ready to move into his new house—and he came here on Monday to do your work. And you didn't want his help. Am I right?"

Pete blinked. Molly had nailed it—but he didn't want to admit that. She'd read his thoughts and distilled them into a challenge—because wasn't she always after him to step up and do *better*?

"*So?*" he blurted.

Her green, green eyes weren't letting him off the hook. "*So*," she replied, "take a message from the angels you missed out on at the Christmas Eve program. Billy Jay's not here to say it, so I will—*fear not*, Shetler. You'll get through this, and you *will* be climbing ladders and building stuff again. I'm sticking with you. It'll work out, I promise."

Pete blinked. How could Molly promise such a thing when nobody knew how long—

Hasn't Molly always been right? Hasn't she always seen through my bluster to the core issues? I could do worse than trust this woman. She seems to believe in me.

It was more than he could comprehend. He was worn out from haggling, so he gave in. For the moment.

"Okay, let's go to the sofa. Then I want my surprise—for breakfast, even if it's a dessert," he added firmly. "After that, we'll see whether this conversation's worth continuing."

"Oh, I'll keep you talking, Shetler," she said as she pushed his chair forward. "And I won't listen to any more of your pouting, because that's behind you now—and because I'm too bossy and insensitive to put up with it."

Well, she had that part right, didn't she?

When they got to the front room, Molly patiently guided him out of the wheelchair and onto the sofa. She was a strong woman, in many ways, but nobody—not even Dr. Douthit—could predict how well he would come out of his physical ordeal. Because he wanted her surprise, however, he behaved himself.

"Okay, I'm dressed and groomed and the meds are working," he said as he carefully sat down. "What'd you bring me?"

Molly's smile teased at something deep inside him. Back in the day, when he'd worked at the pet food factory and spent his time mostly among English, her looks wouldn't have turned his head. Now, however, Pete couldn't resist her down-to-earth appeal—and the way she returned his gaze rather than turning away.

"You'll have to wait and see," she replied as she started toward the kitchen. "Don't go away, now!"

Pete wanted to spring up from the couch and make her pay for that remark—and wasn't that thought an improvement over his morning's whining? And where had that negative attitude come from? When had he sunk so low that he could only predict the most dire of circumstances for himself?

Molly might be the best pain medication yet. But I can't tell her that.

Riley pushed his head under Pete's hand, refusing to be ignored. As Pete savored the thick silkiness of the animal's coat, he realized he'd even been shortchanging his poor dog lately. In his book, only the most despicable man would do that.

"I've been a big meanie, Riley," he murmured, looking into his dog's adoring eyes. "Someday we'll get back to horsing around again and having fun, okay? But meanwhile, will you stick with me?"

Riley let out a conversational moan, blessing Pete with a tongue-lolling grin.

"Yeah, you're just saying that because Molly's coming with a pan of something," Pete teased the retriever. "When she's got food, you like her best, ain't so?"

The dog's immediate *woof* made Molly laugh out loud as she approached the sofa. "Riley always likes me best," she countered. She sat down at Pete's left, careful not to bump his sling. "Here—a spoon for you, and a spoon for me."

Pete inhaled the vaguely sweet aroma that had preceded her to the couch, feeling as happy as a kid at Christmas.

"Noodle pudding! You made me a pan of noodle pudding. Wow, Moll, this is the best surprise—"

"No, I made *everyone* a pan of noodle pudding," she corrected him. "Do you really think I'd let you eat it all just because it's Christmas and you're crippled, Shetler?"

He gaped at her, his spoon poised above the glass pan she held between them on a red and green pot holder.

"Let's eat out of this corner," Molly continued, tapping the noodle concoction with her spoon. "Then I'll cut around it before your uncle and *mammi* take some—so they don't catch your cooties."

Spurred on by her teasing, Pete dug deep into the pudding, right in the middle of the pan. He closed his eyes to better enjoy the unbeatable combination of soft noodles and buttery-sweet cottage cheese filling with raisins and a hint of orange. He could do much worse than marry a woman who surprised him with food he loved and who could haul him up out of his well of self-pity . . .

So be nice to her. Make her happy. Why should she expect anything less? And what can I give Molly Helfing that she is not expecting?

When he opened his eyes, she was sticking a big spoonful of the dessert into her mouth. It was a rare opportunity to say something when she couldn't make a comeback.

"I'm sorry I was such a crank this morning—and acting so pathetic," Pete said softly.

"You *are* pathetic," she retorted around her mouthful of pudding. "I only came here last night and made your favorite dessert because I felt sorry for you."

"High time," he shot back. Maybe it was the meds, but Pete felt buoyant and light. "I'm going to suffer the life of a henpecked, browbeaten husband if I fall for your sweet talk, Moll."

"Too late. You already have."

He sighed to himself. She was right, of course. And he was feeling so good about it that he couldn't resist upping the game a bit. "You'd be kind of cute if you had some hair, Helfing."

When she blinked, Pete realized his over-the-top remark might've hurt her feelings. She'd shaved her head when Marietta's hair had fallen out during her chemo treatments—how many Amish women would've sacrificed their mane of thick, brown hair and defied the no-haircutting rule to support a suffering sister?

Molly swallowed her pudding, her gaze unwavering. "You'd be kind of cute if you'd *cut* yours once in a while, Shetler," she stated. "You look like a girl. Maybe I should lend you one of my *kapps*."

Maybe she was reading his mind—knew exactly what he intended to do when he let his spoon drop—and she *would* get her revenge. But Pete's longtime curiosity got the better of him anyway. Her *kapp* strings were dangling down her back, loose and free; when would he ever have a better opportunity?

He reached over and slipped his fingers beneath her crisp, white head covering to rumple her hair . . . the short, feathery-soft, exquisitely thick, warm, brown hair that he'd never dared to touch before.

Molly's mouth dropped open. She was speechless! And while she was holding the pan of pudding and her spoon, she couldn't strike back, could she?

Driven by his need to demonstrate how he felt without letting chatter get in the way, Pete made his move.

With his hand still beneath her *kapp*, he cupped her head. Despite the prickle of pain that shot through his bad arm, he leaned close to kiss her.

When their mouths met, he forgot about his injuries. Molly kissed him briefly and then broke away—but only so she could set aside the pan of noodle pudding and her spoon. Turning carefully so she wouldn't jostle him, she resumed their kissing the way he'd often imagined she would in his sweetest dreams. With her arm lightly slung across him and her hand at his jaw, she met his lips with hers to begin the age-old courtship ritual that felt so vibrant and exciting.

Pete lost track of everything except the way their lips and tongues moved together so effortlessly, so perfectly. He was vaguely aware of Riley's collar tags jingling against glass, but what did that matter when he finally had Molly right where he wanted her? She tasted sweet and responsive, and he made the kiss last as long as possible.

When he finally eased away, he whispered, "I love you, Molly. When I've gotten rid of this cast and sling, can we—can we get married?"

Molly's eyes resembled green plates. "I, um, well—*jah*, Pete! *Jah*, I love you, too," she blurted. "I was just too stubborn to say so until you said it first."

Pete suddenly felt twenty feet tall and invincible. He hadn't planned to propose, but the words had slipped out—and she'd said yes! If this unconventional, strong-willed woman had so quickly agreed to be his wife, his life had just taken a huge leap forward, hadn't it?

"Of course, that means you *will* be taking your physical therapy and getting back to work," she reminded him gently.

"Can't have you thinking I'm weak and whiny like—like some *girl*, can I?"

Molly laughed, tugging on the hair over his ear. "I wouldn't be kissing you—or marrying you—if you were anything like a girl, Shetler. But I have some bad news for you," she added, her expression sobering suddenly.

Pete's heart stopped. What could possibly interfere with the happiness they'd just promised each other? Just when his life had taken such a dramatic turn for the better, why would Molly want to drag him down again?

"What's that?" he whispered doubtfully.

With her head, she gestured behind her. "Riley ate the rest of the noodle pudding," she replied with a sigh. "I shouldn't have set it on the couch, but I didn't want to stop kissing you to grab the pan away from him."

Pete exhaled, reminding himself that such a disappointment was at least fixable. When he looked at the golden retriever watching him and Molly with adoring brown eyes, he saw a few crumbles of cottage cheese filling clinging to Riley's muzzle. The dog let out a *woof*, thumping his tail on the floor as though he thought the whole episode was pretty funny.

"Well, my dog's happier than he's been for days, and I've just gotten engaged—and we're headed down the right road if you'd rather kiss me than fuss at Riley," he said lightly. "It's all *gut*, Moll—and we're going to have ourselves a merry little Christmas today—and even more of one tomorrow, *jah*?"

Her giggle made his heart dance. "*Jah*, we are, Pete."

Chapter 28

As she prepared their simple Christmas morning breakfast, Marietta felt twitchy. Glenn's card was burning a hole in her apron pocket. She'd only read it once, very quickly, because she'd heard him, Reuben, and Billy Jay coming down the stairs shortly after she'd found it propped against the pan of coffee cake.

But his words were emblazoned upon her anxious heart.

> . . . *please don't give up on me, okay? I love you with all my heart, Marietta, and I'll do whatever it takes to prove that.*

When the three fellows had greeted her as they passed through the kitchen on their way outside to shovel a path to the stable and tend the horses, she'd flashed them a fast smile. Then she'd focused on stirring the bowl of ruby-red cranberry, orange, and apple salad she'd made the day before, avoiding Glenn's gaze as he and his family headed outside in their coats and stocking caps.

But she couldn't avoid him forever. Glenn's heartfelt

message deserved a response . . . even if she wondered how she could possibly deliver it without breaking his poor, fragile heart. Again.

Because the Christmas Eve blizzard had blanketed the yard with several inches of fresh snow, Marietta figured she had about an hour to compose her thoughts and settle her nerves so she could respond to Glenn. After doing so much shoveling, the two men and Billy Jay would be hungry for more than coffee cake, so she opened the deep freeze. A ham steak would be a nice addition to their morning meal, and she also pulled out a package of cinnamon rolls. Her hands were trembling so badly that half a dozen other packages of food tumbled onto the mudroom floor.

Molly would be laughing at me and my nerves, telling me to believe in Glenn's love instead of doubting my ability to meet his needs. It's so odd not to have her here. For the first time in our lives, we're not together on Christmas Day.

Marietta blinked back sudden tears. She chided herself for missing Molly, knowing that her sister and Pete would be laughing together and making the most of their day. Her twin would not be hanging back, reluctant to dive into the love she and the handsome blond carpenter had discovered—nor would Molly have any regrets about being separated from her sister on Christmas.

But Molly is fully a woman, with everything to offer a husband.

Levi's laughter brought Marietta out of her wool-gathering. She quickly put the fallen packages of food back into the deep freeze and returned to find the baby wiggling and shaking his rattle—maybe because a ray of morning sunshine had just beamed through the window, bathing him in its glow. What a blessing that he was such a happy child and so easily entertained by the simple pleasures of God's world.

Marietta picked him up, calmed by his gurgling and the warm weight of him in her arms. She loved this wee boy fiercely, and her heart would ache for him when the Detweilers moved into their new home tomorrow. Yet the baby was a blatant reminder of why Glenn really shouldn't marry her.

She sighed as she set Levi back in his basket so she could continue preparing their breakfast. She turned on the burner under the percolator so the coffee would be ready when the men came inside. When the ham steak was in a skillet to thaw and cook, she arranged the frozen cinnamon rolls on a pan, covered them with foil, and placed them in the warming oven.

As Marietta prepared Levi's next bottle of goat's milk, she spotted Billy Jay through the window, lobbing a snowball at his father. Glenn's laughter—and the way he pitched a snowball back at his son—was a sure sign he was recovering from his grief and living in the moment again. It struck her how handsome he was when he laughed.

And that only makes it more difficult to turn him down. But it really is for the best.

Smiling wistfully at Levi, Marietta poured milk for Billy Jay and got out mugs for the adults' coffee. In only three weeks, it had become a normal part of her day to include these extra efforts for the Detweilers—and she suspected it would take months to forget how easily that family had filled her heart with unexpected love. Already she ached with the idea that Glenn would surely write her off and search for someone else after he'd settled into his beautiful new home.

When she heard the two men and Billy Jay enter the mudroom to remove their wraps and boots, Marietta braced herself. She was hoping for a private moment with Glenn, yet those were rare—and a seven-year-old's Christmas excitement might make her intentions even more difficult to carry out.

"Marietta! Marietta!" the boy called out as he ran up and threw his arms around her waist. "Dat says our new house is full of *stuff* now. Is that true?"

Her eyebrows rose as she looked from the boy to his father. Glenn's subtle nod encouraged her to continue. "*Jah*, it is," she replied, chuckling despite her inner tension. "What did he tell you about that?"

"Did Santa Claus bring it?"

At that, Marietta's mouth dropped open. She placed her hands gently on his shoulders. "No, the families in our church put everything in place as a surprise for you and Levi and your *dat* and your *dawdi*," she replied. "Santa's an English tradition we Plain folks don't believe in—because he's only make-believe. Today we celebrate Jesus' birthday, *jah*?"

Undaunted, Billy Jay grinned up at her. The gap in the front of his mouth made him even more adorable, and she couldn't resist brushing his dark, straight-cut bangs with her fingers. She tried not to remind herself that her chances of doing that would soon be very limited.

"English folks can believe in Jesus and Santa both," he pointed out hopefully. "And Santa brings lots of presents to *gut* girls and boys—the Christmas songs *those* folks sing are all about decorated trees and Santa in his sleigh up on the housetops."

Marietta thought for a moment, wondering how to nip Billy Jay's fascination with Santa in the bud without being needlessly harsh. "When you came downstairs this morning, did you see a Christmas tree with presents underneath it, or stockings full of gifts hanging at the fireplace? Or did you hear anyone tromping around on the roof last night before he came down the chimney?"

"No, but there's presents out in the front room!"

"And those are from me and your *dat* and Marietta and Molly," Reuben put in as he sat at the table to put on his slippers. "If Santa had intended to come, he would've already been here—but he didn't. And besides," he added with a gentle smile, "do you think a fat man could really get down a chimney or drive reindeer across the sky?"

"Santa's fun to think about, but he's only a story," Glenn put in firmly. "What *we* should focus on is telling every one of our friends *denki* for all the wonderful-*gut* gifts they brought to our new house. With friends like we have, who needs Santa? And with a Lord and Savior like Jesus caring for us every day of the year—all through our lives and beyond them—who needs to believe in anyone else?"

A wave of sheer admiration went through Marietta's soul. Fine father that he was, Glenn had set his son straight about where his allegiance should lie without chastising him for his little-boy fantasies.

"Your *dat* got it exactly right," she murmured as she gazed into Billy Jay's big brown eyes. "How about if you fellows wash up and we'll have our breakfast? Then it'll be time to open the gift I picked out for you."

* * *

All during the meal Glenn was on pins and needles. Marietta had found his card, but she wasn't giving him a clue about her reaction to his declaration of love. Such a private topic wasn't meant to be discussed at the breakfast table, however, so he tried to be patient as they ate their ham, coffee cake, sweet rolls, and cranberry salad. When he offered to help her clean up the kitchen, hoping for time alone with her, his *dat* and Billy Jay both jumped in on that offer, as well.

"So what's my present?" the boy asked eagerly as they were hanging up the damp dish towels. "Can I open it *now*?"

Bless her, Marietta smiled at him patiently, so Glenn didn't chide his boy for being so insistent upon opening his gifts on a day reserved for quiet reflection.

"Right this way," she said, gesturing toward the front room. She glanced back at Glenn. "Levi's next bottle will be ready if you'll warm it, please."

Just like that, Marietta had assigned him a task that would keep him away from her—and her expression remained unreadable. As Glenn turned on the burner beneath the warming pan, he wondered if she was preparing him for another letdown. It was Christmas Day, and he'd told Marietta exactly how he felt about her, so why wasn't she acting more excited? She'd hardly said ten words during their meal.

"What's your take on this, Levi?" he murmured, watching his baby boy squirm in his padded basket. "When we move our clothes to the new house tomorrow, do you think it'll be just us guys, the way it was before the fire?"

Levi swatted the air with his tiny hand, unconcerned about the subtle drama playing out between his father and the woman they'd both become so attached to.

When the milk had reached the right temperature, he scooped his boy out of the carrier basket and took the bottle out to where the rest of the family was gathered. He noticed that his *dat* had claimed the recliner, probably hoping Glenn would sit on the sofa with Marietta and Billy Jay—reenacting their earlier cozy scene.

Glenn thought better of interrupting the story she was about to read, however. Instead he sat in the padded rocking chair and let the sound of Marietta's calming voice cast its serene spell.

"This is a book my *mamm* and *dat* gave Molly and me when we were about your age," she was saying as Billy Jay cast aside the last of the simple wrapping paper. "It's our favorite version of the Nativity story because even now we love the pictures and the pretty colors so much."

Billy Jay appeared a bit disappointed, but he studied the book's worn cover. "There's Mary and Joseph and Baby Jesus," he said, pointing at each figure. "And the cow and the sheep and the donkey are watchin' from the back of the stable—and here's a chicken on a nest!"

Marietta chuckled. "We always thought it was funny to have a hen in the picture, because the Bible doesn't mention one," she remarked. "But all manner of animals might have been there that night, sharing their stable with the Holy Family. You can read most of the words in this book, Billy Jay, so maybe *you* can tell *me* the story this time, *jah*?"

"I can't wait to hear it," Dat chimed in. "Do you suppose that hen will play a whole new part in the story?"

Billy Jay's eyes lit up with interest as he opened the book. "Here they are, with Mary ridin' the donkey and Joseph walkin' along," he said—and then he turned the book so his *dawdi* and Glenn could see the picture before he began to read. "'A long, long time ago, a ruler named Cay . . .'"

"Caesar," Marietta murmured.

"Oh, that guy! 'A long, long time ago, a ruler named Caesar Augustus told all the people they had to pay a tax,'" Billy Jay began earnestly. "'So Joseph and Mary set out for Bethlehem. It was a long trip from Naz . . . *Nazareth*! It was a long trip from Nazareth. Mary was going to have a baby, so she rode the donkey most of the way.'"

As his son turned the page, Glenn was glad the children's book didn't get into the details about Mary and Joseph not yet being married. As he shifted Levi so the baby could drink more of his milk, Glenn couldn't help putting Marietta into the role of Mary in his mind, even though he suspected her cancer had rendered her unable to have children. Molly—and the other women around town—probably knew those details, but childbearing wasn't a topic he and his men friends usually discussed.

Billy Jay began to read again, impressing Glenn with his ability to sound out words because he'd heard the names and places as he and the other scholars had prepared for the Christmas Eve program. He also realized that Marietta's patient help had settled his son—given him a firm foundation for learning again—despite all the turmoil they'd gone through the past few months.

I owe her so much, Lord. She fills the empty spots in our lives with her gentle love, even though she seems

*determined not to declare her feelings. You've got to
help me get it right when I talk to her about joining our
family—because thanks to her, I realize that despite our
losses, Christmas has come anyway. There's no greater
gift than being in Marietta's presence.*

Glenn blinked. Somehow, after all the depression and
heartache and times when he'd felt too low to see anything higher than the scuffed toes of his boots, *Christmas
had come anyway.*

As Billy Jay kept reading, Glenn was reminded that
the world had been wallowing in sin and chaos when God
had sent His son to save humanity, His greatest creation.
Wasn't it just like God, who held the world in the palm of
His hand, to once again reach out during troubled times
to save His all-too-human son Glenn Detweiler from the
turmoil that had overwhelmed him? It was too wonderful—too amazing—that the Lord of all had known exactly what he'd needed in his hour of darkest desperation.
Yet Jesus' *dat* had reached out and offered hope and the
possibility of a whole new life when he'd prompted Glenn
to accept Marietta's hospitality.

Glenn blinked, suddenly overcome with emotion. As
he listened to Billy Jay reading the simplified version of
the Christmas story, leaning against Marietta because he
loved her so much, Glenn knew he couldn't take no for
her answer. The baby he held, who'd become dependent
upon Marietta's devotion, and the seven-year-old who
looked to her for guidance, would be even more devastated than he would if she refused his offer of marriage.

"Look! The nest has little chicks in it!" Billy Jay exclaimed as he came to the end of the story. "Mary had a
baby, and the hen hatched three!"

"She did," Marietta agreed, turning the book's final page. "And what's this final Scripture? Teacher Lydianne has probably written it on the board for you—or she will, sometime this school year."

Billy Jay's face lit up as he recognized the words. "*Jah*, we learn a verse every day, and we had this one a while back. If I stumble over the big words, help me out, okay?"

He closed his eyes, squinting a bit to remember. "'For God so loved the world—'"

"'—that He gave His only-begotten Son,'" Marietta joined him softly.

"'—that whosoever believeth in Him,'" Dat recited with them, his voice low and serene.

"'—should not perish but have eternal life,'" Glenn put in. He sighed with the rightness of the moment, at the way his little child had led them into sharing a verse that stated the very essence of love come down at Christmas—and sharing it as a *family*.

Billy Jay's smile lit up the entire front room. "We sound really *gut* together, ain't so? Almost as *gut* as when the men's group sings their songs, except we were just talkin'."

"*Jah*, there's a harmony to it when folks share the Gut News together," Glenn's father agreed. With a knowing glance at Glenn, Dat rose from the recliner. "After listening to you read that fine Christmas story, Billy Jay, I feel like taking a walk to enjoy the sunshine and the fresh snow. How about if you come with me? You never know—we might find the makings for a snowman out there."

"I'm on it!" Billy Jay crowed as he sprang from the sofa. "I'll grab a carrot for his nose, and we can find some sticks for his arms—"

As the boy raced out to the mudroom ahead of his *dawdi*, Glenn knew exactly what Dat was up to—and he knew better than to waste this rare time alone with Marietta. Before she could find another excuse to avoid him, he headed over to the sofa and handed Levi to her. As he'd hoped, she accepted the baby without thinking about it—which allowed Glenn to sit down beside her.

"Please hear me out, honey," he pleaded softly. "You've been so quiet this morning, as though my card must've—"

"Glenn, you need a wife who can give you more children. A wife who's not flat and—and *deformed*," Marietta blurted. And then she burst into tears.

He hadn't anticipated such an emotional outburst—and he'd never been good at consoling Dorcas or his mother when they'd gotten upset enough to cry. Glenn had no response to the way Marietta felt about her body, yet he sensed this was his last chance to make things right with her.

"We've known each other for years, Marietta—since before you had your cancer and before I lost my wife and *mamm* and home. I *love* you. I know that now," he countered gently, slipping his arm around her slender, trembling shoulders. "I love *you*—and *jah*, I *need* you—just the way you are, Marietta."

Glenn inhaled deeply, gathering his fortitude to go on—although he had no idea what to say. "Your body went through some tough stuff fighting off your cancer, but you came through your ordeal with your spirit intact," he offered. "My body is just fine, but my spirit has taken a beating these past months. Maybe our weaknesses can balance out and we can be whole again if we're together, *jah*?"

Marietta's lip was trembling as she wiped her eyes with the back of her hand. She didn't say anything, but she was listening to him, so Glenn dared to continue.

"Without your help and kindness, I might not have been celebrating Christmas today," he insisted. "After I lost Mamm and Dorcas, I seemed to alternate between trying too hard for some woman's attention—as you pointed out earlier—and feeling so low I could hardly talk at all. If we hadn't come here a few weeks ago, there would've been no telling of the Christmas story for our family. I probably would've rolled myself into a ball and stayed in bed this morning, waiting to die."

He had no idea where the words had come from, but they caught Marietta's attention. Her green eyes, alight with protective fire, held his gaze. "But you did come. And I would *never* have allowed you to stay in bed on Christmas morning—"

"See there?" Glenn pointed out. "You care about me— I can *feel* it—but you've let your worries about your body get in the way of your happiness. I can't allow *that* to happen—and why would I?" he asked as he leaned closer to her. "You're the most beautiful woman I know, Marietta—beautiful from the inside out. And I'm not just saying that to win you over."

Her mouth opened but then shut again. She sniffled loudly, so Glenn pulled his handkerchief from his pocket and offered it to her.

Marietta gazed at his bandanna as though no one had ever offered her a finer gift. "I don't know, Glenn," she murmured. "I've been single so long, maybe I won't adjust well to being a wife and a—a *mamm* to your boys."

"But you're already their *mamm*," he whispered. "You slipped into that role the moment you took us into your home, and you're a natural at it. Far as I'm concerned, you made Billy Jay a happy, sociable boy again—and you've been so *gut* about including Dat, giving him useful things to do. And look at Levi," he added softly, nodding toward the baby dozing in her arms. "You hold him just right. You fix his goat's milk the way he likes it, and he's getting bigger and stronger by the day."

Glenn paused. Overkill was the last thing he wanted, but he needed Marietta to know that he'd noticed all of the ways she'd helped the Detweiler family during a trying time. "You've made a *difference* to everyone in our family, Marietta," he said. "When you're ready, we'd all love for you to join us, honey."

Her eyes shone with unshed tears and their rims were red from her crying spell, yet Glenn couldn't resist her. He gently brushed his lips against hers and eased away, for fear he'd scare her off for the final time.

Marietta sighed softly, exhaling until the tension left her shoulders. When a stray tear slipped down her cheek, he thumbed it away, marveling at the softness of her skin and the solid emotional strength that resided beneath her apparent fragility.

"Take your time giving me your answer, honey," he murmured. "Meanwhile, I hope you'll allow me to back up my words with actions that will prove my intentions are only the best. Will that be all right?"

After a slight hesitation that left him hanging, Marietta nodded.

Relief surged through him. She hadn't shut him down! Glenn sensed he still had to proceed carefully, however.

"Can I hold you while we sit here?" he whispered. "Once Billy Jay and Dat get back, there won't be much chance for private conversation—but I'll find ways for us to have time together, if you'll let me."

A hesitant smile, like the sun peeking out from behind winter's gray clouds, brightened Marietta's dear face.

As he held her close and felt the warmth of her body settling against his, Glenn dared to hope that something wonderful—and permanent—might come from their Christmas Day conversation.

Chapter 29

As Molly stepped into the mudroom at her home place on Second Christmas morning, she was met by the aromas of frying hamburger and something cinnamon-sweet in the oven—and utter silence. The Detweilers' buggy hadn't been in the stable when she'd arrived, but Molly had expected to hear a baby chattering and see Levi's carrier in the kitchen with her sister—

But Marietta sat at the kitchen table alone, with her head down on her arms. How could this be, on the most joyous of Amish holidays?

"Did you miss me, Marietta?" Molly called out cautiously as she hung up her coat and bonnet.

Her twin quickly sat up, as though she didn't want to be caught napping—or crying. "I *did* miss you," she replied. "It felt so odd not having you around on Christmas Day, Molly. I—I hope that never happens again."

Red flags fluttered in the back of Molly's mind. This was not the response she'd been expecting after Marietta had spent the past day and a half with the Detweilers. Or had something gone wrong? Had Glenn and his tribe left—or had Marietta sent them home?

Molly slid into the chair beside her sister, choosing her words carefully. She'd been ready to burst with the exciting news of her engagement, but it didn't feel like the right time to share so much happiness. "What happened? Did Glenn finally find his big surprise? Have the guys gone to their new house—without *you*?"

When Marietta focused on her, Molly saw the telltale shine of unshed tears in her sister's eyes. "*Jah*, Glenn saw all the stuff the congregation took to the house when he went last night," she replied. "They took their clothes over there this morning, now that the roads are passable."

She looked away, lowering her voice. "Glenn asked me to marry him again this morning, Molly. At first I refused—I had a *gut*bye speech all planned out after I found a Christmas card from him that said . . . he loves me."

Molly's eyes widened. "But? We already knew how he felt about you, after you got his family's birthday card."

Her sister laughed softly, shaking her head. "When I told him that I couldn't give him children and that I'm damaged goods—not a whole woman—he was having none of that. He said I was *beautiful*, from the inside out—"

"And he has that right, Marietta."

"—and that he'd give me time to be sure of my answer, but he really wants me to be a part of their family," she continued in a rush. "Molly, if I'd had you here to reassure me, maybe I would've been more positive about his proposal. And I don't want to leave you here at the farm all alone—"

"*Fear not*, sister," Molly put in firmly. "Follow your heart where Glenn's concerned, and don't worry about me, because Pete and I are getting hitched as soon as he's completed his physical therapy and he's working again. I told him I wasn't letting him out of the remodeling job he's promised us just because he's laid up for a while."

Her sister gasped and threw her arms around Molly's neck. "Oh, that's such *gut* news!" she exclaimed. "I'm so happy for you—and I wish I weren't such a worrywart when it comes to the future. I wish I had more of your grit, sister."

"Oh, Pete accused me of being plenty gritty, because I yanked the rug out from under his pity party," Molly put in with a chuckle. "But getting married is the right thing for us, and we both know that now."

Molly paused, grasping her sister's hand. "You'll always have a place here after Pete and I marry, if that's what you really want, Marietta. But how will you feel, watching our happiness and missing out on your own? If you ask me, it doesn't sound like much of a life."

Marietta blinked, as if a light bulb had just come on in her mind. "When you put it that way . . . I would feel like a third wheel, ain't so?"

"And you'd be putting up with Riley for constant company instead of having two cute little boys to cuddle with," Molly reminded her. "Then there's the deep disappointment you'd see on all four of those Detweilers' faces at church and around town—because you *would* see them. Meanwhile, Pete and I would be enduring the same sort of hangdog sadness on *your* face all the time, *jah*?"

When Molly emphasized her point by pulling the corners of her mouth into an exaggerated frown, Marietta finally laughed.

"You're right about that part," she admitted.

"Of course I'm right! Just ask Pete."

Marietta smiled, looking more like her usual confident self. "*Denki* for talking some sense into me, sister," she said softly. "What would I do if I didn't have you?"

"We'll always have each other," Molly insisted, wrapping her arms around her sister's slender shoulders. "Even after we're married and taking charge of our separate families, we'll be twins—and we'll have noodles to make, and we won't live very far away from each other. It's all *gut*, Marietta."

Her sister raised an eyebrow. "Are you sure about the noodle-making part? After we marry, our husbands—or Bishop Jeremiah—might lay down the law and declare that we're not to work at that anymore."

"Maybe," Molly agreed. "But we'd be working at home, after all, and lots of wives bolster their family's income with home businesses—just like our *mamm* did for all those years."

She thumbed a stray tear from Marietta's cheek, happy to see her sister looking brighter. "How about if we cross that noodle-making bridge when we get there? It's Second Christmas, and it's time to have some fun!" she exclaimed. "After I shower and put on some clean clothes, I'll help you with the food we're taking to The Marketplace party, all right?"

"More than all right," Marietta said with a smile. "You're the best Christmas present ever, Molly."

"No, *you* are," she fired back. "And who knows? Maybe next year at this time, we'll have different perspectives about what—or who—is really the best Christmas gift."

* * *

As Marietta sang "O Come, All Ye Faithful," surrounded by her *maidel* friends and the rest of their congregation, the music that soared into the high ceiling of The Marketplace commons area made her heart swell. Seated on either side of her at a long table where they'd eaten their potluck lunch, Molly and Jo sang harmony on the chorus, while across from them, Lydianne's voice rose on the soprano melody. Regina sat with them, too, because her Gabe was up front on the dais with the other men, who led everyone in singing all the familiar, favorite Christmas carols. It was just like the best Sunday morning church services, when Marietta was always filled with such love for her closest friends.

Was it her imagination, or was Glenn smiling especially brightly at her as he sang with the men's group? He looked several years younger than he had for the past few months, as though a great burden had been lifted from his heart. The kids were playing games together behind the crowd, and Bishop Jeremiah's *mamm* had latched onto baby Levi, so Marietta was sitting as a single woman would, without little boys to tend.

She felt different, however. She'd become so accustomed to having Billy Jay alongside her, like a bubbly, curious shadow, that she instinctively glanced back at the children now and then to keep track of him. It was a delight to watch him and Stevie Shetler challenging each other, tossing beanbags into boxes about fifteen feet away from them. Gracie Wagler and Ella Nissley cheered them on until it was their turn to pitch the bags.

Maybe Glenn has it right. If I become Billy Jay's and Levi's mamm, I can also be more involved with their friends—and before long, I'll have Molly's wee ones to love, and Regina and Lydianne will be having babies, too. The new year can bring me a chance at a whole new life!

Marietta's heart swelled. When "O Come, All Ye Faithful" ended, Gabe sang the first few words of "Joy to the World," and everyone joined in with gusto. Even Drusilla Fussner, seated among the Hartzler women, Cora Miller, and Delores Flaud at the next table, appeared caught up in the happiness of the moment. She and her daughter had gone through a rough patch over the Wengerd men, yet the smile on Jo's face suggested that she wasn't nearly ready to give up on the romance she'd found with Michael.

Love has indeed come down at Christmas, for so many of us. I'd be a fool to turn my back on Glenn when he might well be the precious gift God is giving me this year.

Marietta blinked. Hadn't the past few weeks of hosting the Detweiler family given her a clear picture of how happy all of them could be together? She would never accuse God of causing the fire at Glenn's house to bring about this revelation, but He had certainly given her every opportunity to experience the roles of wife and *mamm* before she committed to them permanently. Not many women got that chance.

"Time for dessert!" Billy Jay called out when the carol ended.

"*Jah*, bring on the cakes and pies and cookies!" Stevie chimed in.

The adults laughed, several of them nodding in agreement. As the women rose to remove the lids from their pans of goodies, which filled an entire table at the side of the room, Molly leaned close to Marietta.

"I'll load up a plate with desserts and head over to

see Pete now," she said. "It's time he and Riley had some company, don't you think?"

"Give him my best," Marietta replied. "Hope he's feeling better today."

"Oh, that'll happen the minute I walk through the door," her sister assured her with a grin. "Think about what we discussed before we came, okay? I suspect Glenn won't waste any time coming over now that the men have finished leading the carols."

Marietta laughed and rose to follow her sister to the dessert table. Without even glancing at Glenn, she sensed that his attention was focused on her—and wasn't that a sign that she was becoming attuned to his ways? She'd just removed the cover from her chocolate layer cake when his warm hand gently clasped her shoulder.

"What if you and I went for a ride, Marietta?" Glenn murmured. He was standing behind her, so close that his breath tickled her neck. "Dat and the others will keep track of the boys so we can have the sleigh all to ourselves on this sunny winter's afternoon."

Marietta's heart stilled. "You—you have a sleigh out there?"

"*Jah.* It's been stashed in our stable for a long while, so I cleaned it up this morning and put in some of those quilts the ladies brought over. Sounds cozy, ain't so?"

"Just you and me?" She turned to face him, oblivious to the other folks around them. "Are you asking me for a date, Glenn Detweiler?"

His expression softened into an endearing smile. "High time, I'd say."

Marietta's pulse pounded, and for a moment she was too nervous to speak. The shine in his deep brown eyes refused to let her go, however. How could she turn him down? Glenn was making every effort to win her rather than expecting her to step into the void Dorcas had created with her passing. He'd promised to give her all the time she needed to make her decision, and this would be the perfect opportunity to be alone with him. She suddenly hoped she could look forward to *many* such cozy occasions with Glenn.

"It's been years since I rode in a sleigh," she whispered. "Let's go!"

Within minutes they'd put on their wraps and left the crowd behind. As Marietta waited eagerly outside the entry to The Marketplace while Glenn hitched the horse to the sleigh, she lifted her face to the bright sunshine. Folks inside were probably speculating about her and Glenn—maybe even peering out the windows at them—but it didn't matter. Most of them already seemed to know where this relationship was headed.

I've been dragging my feet, Lord, so point me in the right direction. Help me set aside my worries and live into the love You would have me accept—just the way Glenn has accepted me for exactly who I am.

As Glenn pulled the sleigh up, Marietta felt like a young girl going on a long-awaited date with a fellow she'd always hoped would notice her. When she'd positioned herself on the padded seat beside him, he unfolded a multicolored quilt and tucked it around her before covering his legs and midsection with it.

"Ready?" he whispered.

Marietta nodded, sheer joy making her entire being tingle. Had she ever known such a handsome, caring man with a heart big enough to love his family and make room for her, as well? Glenn was gazing at her as though he, too, was finding new things to like—and to love—about her, even after all the years he'd known her.

"Ready," she replied. "I—I haven't felt this excited in a long, long time, Glenn."

He smiled as he urged Ned into a trot. "I intend to keep you feeling that way for years to come, if you'll have me."

As the sleigh went gliding down the plowed path toward the road, the sunshine sparkled like countless tiny diamonds on the new snow. Exhilaration thrummed through her veins as the breeze made her cheeks tingle, and Marietta believed she was at long last heading toward a dream she'd never dared to believe would come true.

"I *will* have you, Glenn," she said as she scooted against him. "I—I want to be your wife and become part of your family."

"Seriously?" He put the lines into one hand so he could wrap his arm around her shoulders. "You're sure now? I don't want to rush your decision or—"

She held his gaze, nodding happily. "I love you, Glenn. I know that now—but I like the idea of not rushing. This'll be my first wedding, and I'd like to plan it and do it up right."

Glenn's head fell back against the sleigh. "Woo-*hoo*!" he yelled, so loud that it startled Ned—and made Marietta jump, as well. He flashed her a grin before he hollered again. "Woo-*hoo*! I feel like a million bucks, and I don't care who knows it!"

Right before they reached the gate and the county highway, he stopped the horse, his eyes alight with love and joy. "Marietta, you've made me happier than—well, I was happy when I married Dorcas and overjoyed when our boys were born, but you've just wrapped me like a Christmas present and tied me up with a big red bow!"

When Glenn kissed her, he was laughing, and so was she—but then a more soulful, quiet sort of joy filled her heart as his lips continued to express his love for her. Did Molly feel all this crazy elation when Pete kissed her?

It didn't matter, did it? Glenn was offering Marietta a new life on her own terms as the woman she was without her twin—beside the man he could be because he was with *her* now. His kisses left no doubt that she was the one he loved, and the one he wanted to spend the rest of his life with.

"Wow," he murmured when they paused for a breath. "Wow."

Marietta giggled. "Let's keep riding, Glenn. I feel like my Christmas fairy tale has just begun, and I don't ever want it to end."

Connect with

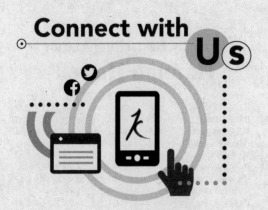

Us

Visit us online at
KensingtonBooks.com
to read more from your favorite authors, see books
by series, view reading group guides, and more.

Join us on social media

for sneak peeks, chances to win books and prize packs,
and to share your thoughts with other readers.

facebook.com/kensingtonpublishing
twitter.com/kensingtonbooks

Tell us what you think!

To share your thoughts, submit a review,
or sign up for our eNewsletters, please visit:
KensingtonBooks.com/TellUs.

More by Bestselling Author
Hannah Howell

__Highland Angel	978-1-4201-0864-4	$6.99US/$8.99CAN
__If He's Sinful	978-1-4201-0461-5	$6.99US/$8.99CAN
__Wild Conquest	978-1-4201-0464-6	$6.99US/$8.99CAN
__If He's Wicked	978-1-4201-0460-8	$6.99US/$8.49CAN
__My Lady Captor	978-0-8217-7430-4	$6.99US/$8.49CAN
__Highland Sinner	978-0-8217-8001-5	$6.99US/$8.49CAN
__Highland Captive	978-0-8217-8003-9	$6.99US/$8.49CAN
__Nature of the Beast	978-1-4201-0435-6	$6.99US/$8.49CAN
__Highland Fire	978-0-8217-7429-8	$6.99US/$8.49CAN
__Silver Flame	978-1-4201-0107-2	$6.99US/$8.49CAN
__Highland Wolf	978-0-8217-8000-8	$6.99US/$9.99CAN
__Highland Wedding	978-0-8217-8002-2	$4.99US/$6.99CAN
__Highland Destiny	978-1-4201-0259-8	$4.99US/$6.99CAN
__Only for You	978-0-8217-8151-7	$6.99US/$8.99CAN
__Highland Promise	978-1-4201-0261-1	$4.99US/$6.99CAN
__Highland Vow	978-1-4201-0260-4	$4.99US/$6.99CAN
__Highland Savage	978-0-8217-7999-6	$6.99US/$9.99CAN
__Beauty and the Beast	978-0-8217-8004-6	$4.99US/$6.99CAN
__Unconquered	978-0-8217-8088-6	$4.99US/$6.99CAN
__Highland Barbarian	978-0-8217-7998-9	$6.99US/$9.99CAN
__Highland Conqueror	978-0-8217-8148-7	$6.99US/$9.99CAN
__Conqueror's Kiss	978-0-8217-8005-3	$4.99US/$6.99CAN
__A Stockingful of Joy	978-1-4201-0018-1	$4.99US/$6.99CAN
__Highland Bride	978-0-8217-7995-8	$4.99US/$6.99CAN
__Highland Lover	978-0-8217-7759-6	$6.99US/$9.99CAN

Available Wherever Books Are Sold!

Check out our website at
http://www.kensingtonbooks.com

Books by Bestselling Author

Fern Michaels

___ The Jury	0-8217-7878-1	$6.99US/$9.99CAN
___ Sweet Revenge	0-8217-7879-X	$6.99US/$9.99CAN
___ Lethal Justice	0-8217-7880-3	$6.99US/$9.99CAN
___ Free Fall	0-8217-7881-1	$6.99US/$9.99CAN
___ Fool Me Once	0-8217-8071-9	$7.99US/$10.99CAN
___ Vegas Rich	0-8217-8112-X	$7.99US/$10.99CAN
___ Hide and Seek	1-4201-0184-6	$6.99US/$9.99CAN
___ Hokus Pokus	1-4201-0185-4	$6.99US/$9.99CAN
___ Fast Track	1-4201-0186-2	$6.99US/$9.99CAN
___ Collateral Damage	1-4201-0187-0	$6.99US/$9.99CAN
___ Final Justice	1-4201-0188-9	$6.99US/$9.99CAN
___ Up Close and Personal	0-8217-7956-7	$7.99US/$9.99CAN
___ Under the Radar	1-4201-0683-X	$6.99US/$9.99CAN
___ Razor Sharp	1-4201-0684-8	$7.99US/$10.99CAN
___ Yesterday	1-4201-1494-8	$5.99US/$6.99CAN
___ Vanishing Act	1-4201-0685-6	$7.99US/$10.99CAN
___ Sara's Song	1-4201-1493-X	$5.99US/$6.99CAN
___ Deadly Deals	1-4201-0686-4	$7.99US/$10.99CAN
___ Game Over	1-4201-0687-2	$7.99US/$10.99CAN
___ Sins of Omission	1-4201-1153-1	$7.99US/$10.99CAN
___ Sins of the Flesh	1-4201-1154-X	$7.99US/$10.99CAN
___ Cross Roads	1-4201-1192-2	$7.99US/$10.99CAN

Available Wherever Books Are Sold!
Check out our website at **www.kensingtonbooks.com**

Romantic Suspense from
Lisa Jackson

Absolute Fear	0-8217-7936-2	$7.99US/$9.99CAN
Afraid to Die	1-4201-1850-1	$7.99US/$9.99CAN
Almost Dead	0-8217-7579-0	$7.99US/$10.99CAN
Born to Die	1-4201-0278-8	$7.99US/$9.99CAN
Chosen to Die	1-4201-0277-X	$7.99US/$10.99CAN
Cold Blooded	1-4201-2581-8	$7.99US/$8.99CAN
Deep Freeze	0-8217-7296-1	$7.99US/$10.99CAN
Devious	1-4201-0275-3	$7.99US/$9.99CAN
Fatal Burn	0-8217-7577-4	$7.99US/$10.99CAN
Final Scream	0-8217-7712-2	$7.99US/$10.99CAN
Hot Blooded	1-4201-0678-3	$7.99US/$9.49CAN
If She Only Knew	1-4201-3241-5	$7.99US/$9.99CAN
Left to Die	1-4201-0276-1	$7.99US/$10.99CAN
Lost Souls	0-8217-7938-9	$7.99US/$10.99CAN
Malice	0-8217-7940-0	$7.99US/$10.99CAN
The Morning After	1-4201-3370-5	$7.99US/$9.99CAN
The Night Before	1-4201-3371-3	$7.99US/$9.99CAN
Ready to Die	1-4201-1851-X	$7.99US/$9.99CAN
Running Scared	1-4201-0182-X	$7.99US/$10.99CAN
See How She Dies	1-4201-2584-2	$7.99US/$8.99CAN
Shiver	0-8217-7578-2	$7.99US/$10.99CAN
Tell Me	1-4201-1854-4	$7.99US/$9.99CAN
Twice Kissed	0-8217-7944-3	$7.99US/$9.99CAN
Unspoken	1-4201-0093-9	$7.99US/$9.99CAN
Whispers	1-4201-5158-4	$7.99US/$9.99CAN
Wicked Game	1-4201-0338-5	$7.99US/$9.99CAN
Wicked Lies	1-4201-0339-3	$7.99US/$9.99CAN
Without Mercy	1-4201-0274-5	$7.99US/$10.99CAN
You Don't Want to Know	1-4201-1853-6	$7.99US/$9.99CAN

Available Wherever Books Are Sold!
Visit our website at **www.kensingtonbooks.com**